FACE OFF

BY DAVID HAGBERG

Twister
The Capsule
Last Come the Children
Heartland
Heroes
Without Honor*
Countdown*
Crossfire*
Critical Mass*
Desert Fire
High Flight*
Assassin*
White House*
Joshua's Hammer*
Eden's Gate
The Kill Zone*
By Dawn's Early Light
Soldier of God*
Allah's Scorpion*
Dance with the Dragon*
The Expediter*
The Cabal*
Abyss*
Castro's Daughter*
Burned
Blood Pact*
Retribution*
The Fourth Horseman*
End Game*

Tower Down*
Flash Points*
The Shadowmen*+
24 Hours*+
Face Off*

WRITING AS
SEAN FLANNERY

The Kremlin Conspiracy
Eagles Fly
The Trinity Factor
The Hollow Men
Broken Idols
Gulag
Moscow Crossing
The Zebra Network
Crossed Swords
Moving Targets
Winner Take All
Kilo Option
Achilles' Heel

WITH BYRON L. DORGAN

Blowout
Gridlock

NONFICTION WITH
BORIS GINDEN

Mutiny!

*Kirk McGarvey adventures
*+Kirk McGarvey Ebook original novellas

FACE OFF

DAVID HAGBERG

A TOM DOHERTY ASSOCIATES BOOK
NEW YORK

This is a work of fiction. All of the characters, organizations, and events portrayed in this novel are either products of the author's imagination or are used fictitiously.

FACE OFF

A Forge Book
Published by Tom Doherty Associates
175 Fifth Avenue
New York, NY 10010

www.tor-forge.com

Forge® is a registered trademark of Macmillan Publishing Group, LLC.

The Library of Congress Cataloging-in-Publication Data is available upon request.

ISBN 978-0-7653-8491-1 (hardcover)
ISBN 978-0-7653-8600-7 (ebook)

Our books may be purchased in bulk for promotional, educational, or business use. Please contact your local bookseller or the Macmillan Corporate and Premium Sales Department at 1-800-221-7945, extension 5442, or by email at MacmillanSpecialMarkets@macmillan.com.

First Edition: October 2018

Printed in the United States of America

0 9 8 7 6 5 4 3 2 1

FOR LORREL AS ALWAYS

PART
ONE

Paris

ONE

Karim Najjir, a former midlevel Saudi intelligence officer, easily made the circle around the Arc de Triomphe exactly on schedule at eleven in the morning, the Peugeot 308 anonymous in the heavy July traffic. Next month most of the country would all but shut down, because August was when the French took their vacations. But for now the City of Light, arguably the most famous metro area in the world, was brimming with tourists from just about everywhere.

It was exactly the condition that the tall, slender man with narrow pinched features and wide, dark, interesting eyes, who traveled under the work name Giles Worley, had trained his people for, over the past six months.

An old Chinese curse hurled at your enemies said, "May you live in interesting times."

These past several years, ISIS attacks against Western cities from here in Paris to London, New York, Munich, Berlin, and even Toronto and Mexico City, had steadily brought the message that these indeed were interesting times.

Today would be the most spectacular of them all.

New York had its twin trade towers—a symbol of American decadence. London had its Eye on the Thames. Berlin its new house of parliament. Toronto its needle into the sky. And Munich its Hofbräuhaus. Not to mention the downed airliners, the attacks on places such as train stations, gay nightclubs, marathons, football stadiums, and even magazines that published cartoons and articles about the Prophet.

And this morning the Eiffel Tower, at the height of a tourist season that no one would ever forget.

Miriam Halabi, a girl whose record showed that she was from Jeddah—though she was actually Russian—and whose parents had immigrated to Britain when she was very young, had supposedly been radicalized at a madrassa in London's East End. She had come to Najjir's attention almost from the moment he'd begun recruiting soldiers for this mission. She was of medium height and slender, with wide dark eyes, thick black hair, and a beautiful face—good looks that were spoiled whenever she spoke in a thick cockney accent that most people took for a sign of stupidity, which couldn't be further from the truth.

"I'm not strapping on a fucking bomb vest for you or any other martyr to the fucking cause," she'd told him after they'd gone to bed with each other for the first time and he'd explained a little of what he was planning. "No matter how good a lay you are."

"You'll be my misdirection," he'd told her.

"You're going to bomb the shit out of something. Means you're recruiting grist for the fucking mill. Cannon fodder."

"That's right."

"And what's my role?"

"You'll be my well-dressed, well-jeweled mistress who in the middle of everything will suddenly get angry with me and start such a public row that the tourists will appreciate the circus and flics will have to escort us off the premises."

Her smile had been avaricious. "What happens then, love?"

"You keep the wardrobe and enough money to get you back to London first class, plus what's already been put in the bank account I set up for you. You won't be wealthy, but you'll be well off."

"And the ice?"

"You keep the jewelry."

"London's expensive. I'll hock the fuckin' bling."

"Fine. But just don't open your mouth in public until we start our row."

She had batted her eyes at him. "Pull a Lisa Doolittle, that it?"

Najjir, whose formal education had mostly been in Switzerland, his final year at Harvard for his MBA, caught the reference. "Transformation, indeed," he'd said. Not unlike his own, from a minor royal cousin to an off-the-books—but nevertheless paid—special ops arranger for Saudi intel, the GIP.

His own transformation had come during the second major oil crisis, which had been going on now for nearly five years. Saudi Arabia's economy, which had always been more than generous for its people, had gone to hell. Even muscling the OPEC signatories into restricting output in an effort to drive up prices had not really worked in the long run.

The country had been sliding into its own desert nomad past the entire time. Its voice at the UN was mostly ignored. Oil was cheap—compounded by the US role as an exporter—and the Chinese had taken over as the heavy hitters at the casinos in Monaco, Singapore, Sun City in South Africa, and the Kurhaus in Baden-Baden.

Only a very few of the still wealthy Saudi royal princes showed up at the gaming tables—and then their stakes tended to be a shadow of their former glory.

And so the pressure was on to bring Saudi Arabia back into the champion's circle by identifying the ISIS leaders and planners and eliminating them.

It was a delicate plan, and Paris was only the first, and smallest, step.

They crossed the river at the Place de la Concorde and started along the Quai d'Orsay, the Eiffel Tower coming into view.

"Jesus, Mary, and Joseph," Miriam said, suddenly getting it. "You guys are totally bug shit, do you know that?"

"I'll drop you off at the next corner and you can get a cab back to the hotel," Najjir lied to her.

"But at least I get to keep the bling?"

"What do you think?"

She looked away and after a moment she shook her head. "I'm not going back. So I'm in."

They'd bought her designer slacks, strappy high heels, and a couple of expensive silk blouses at Givenchy, and her rings, bracelets, earrings, and necklace at Chez Nana on the rue d'Hauteville in the tenth. The transformation from a cockney broad to what she looked like now was nothing short of stunning.

In the end, of course, none of it would matter. She could keep the clothes and the jewelry all the way to her grave here in Paris.

Najjir pulled in to the Parking Pullman ramp on the avenue de Suffren, just down the block from the Eiffel Tower. He had bought a twenty-four-hour pass online last night. It was just past eleven in the morning, so the rental car would not be noticed until tomorrow, by which time the three martyrs, plus Miriam, would be dead and he would be well on his way back to Riyadh via his twenty-four-hour layover in Cairo.

He parked on the third level, and down on the street Miriam linked her arm in his and they sauntered to the Quai Branly, where they descended to the river walk to join the other lovers strolling arm in arm.

Their reservation at the restaurant Le Jules Verne on the third level in the tower was for noon. Najjir wanted to be exactly on time, because at one o'clock precisely, powerful explosives would detonate at the south pillar at that level. If their German engineers had done their CAD modeling correctly, the Eiffel Tower would collapse and fall across the length of the Parc du Champ de Mars, with hundreds in the tower and perhaps as many as one thousand or more tourists on the ground.

"It's pretty here," Miriam said.

"Each time I come here it gets better."

She looked at him. "Seems a shame."

"Depends on how you think about the outcome and the reasons."

"Just following orders, is that it?"

More than that, he wanted to tell her, but he didn't think that she would understand. He didn't know if he did.

Politics? He spouted the GIP line he'd been fed since the academy. Saudi Arabia stands alone with Allah. But of course that was nonsense. In the forties Germany and Japan had been the enemies of all of Europe, Great

Britain, and the US. Now they were the West's major trading partners. And even Tel Aviv had made peace with Berlin.

So then why? What was the answer to her question?

He didn't honestly know, because he'd never asked himself at a deep enough level to reveal his own truth.

I am what I am, he wanted to tell her.

But she wouldn't understand that answer any better than he did himself.

TWO

Kirk McGarvey handed Pete Boylan into the backseat of the taxi in front of the boutique hotel Le Pavillon de la Reine in the Marais district of Paris a little before 11:30, the morning stunningly beautiful.

The doorman closed the door after Mac got in. "La Tour Eiffel," the man told the driver.

"I've been to Paris a half dozen times but never to the Eiffel Tower," Pete said, a huge smile on her pretty round face, which was framed with fairly short-cropped red hair.

Before he'd taken on the role of what was being called at Langley a "special circumstances troubleshooter," McGarvey—Mac to his friends—had worked as a field officer for the CIA, briefly rising to head the Company's Clandestine Service Directorate, and even for a very short time serving as the director of the entire agency. All that before he'd turned fifty.

He was a well-built man, a little under six feet, with an athlete's physique and gray eyes that in times of trouble took on a green hue.

A couple of years ago his wife and only daughter had been killed in a car explosion meant for him, and until very recently he'd held back from any sort of a romantic relationship.

Pete, who was almost ten years younger than him and never married, had worked as a special agent/interrogator for the Company, and she'd been pulled in to the tail end of an assignment with McGarvey and had gotten wounded. Wasn't long after that she had begun to fall in love with him. It had taken him much longer to feel the same for her.

"A honeymoon without benefit of the clergy," she said, as the cab headed away from the hotel.

"Do you mind?"

"Not terribly. I got ninety-nine percent of what I wanted."

And that's what bothered McGarvey. Every woman who'd ever gotten close to him had been murdered because of who he was, what he had done. A Swiss undercover cop who'd fallen in love with him had been assassinated here in Paris. Another had been killed in an explosion at a restaurant in Georgetown. And then his wife and daughter. He was afraid now for Pete, because despite himself he'd fallen in love with her. And almost from the moment they'd began working together she had come under fire— nearly losing her life on more than one occasion.

Sooner or later the odds would swing against her, and he didn't know what he would do in the aftermath to keep from taking out every single person who had even the slightest connection with her assassin. He was afraid of himself.

"I'm working on it," he told her, keeping that part of his feelings from showing. He absently rubbed his left knee where his prosthesis was attached.

"Sore?" Pete asked.

"My foot itches. Damnedest thing."

Two months ago a kilo of Semtex had been placed in his '59 Porsche Super cabriolet parked in one of the lots at New College in Sarasota. He taught Voltaire there to some seriously bright kids. And on a Friday afternoon after class he'd gotten behind the wheel, but something had felt wrong, and he'd bailed out moments before the powerful explosion sent pieces of sheet metal fifty feet into the air. His back had been so badly burned he'd needed skin grafts, and his left leg had been taken off just below the knee.

His past had caught up with him again, and as soon as he was ambulatory he had been thrown into one of the most bizarre operations of his career, which had pitted him against the newly elected president of the United States.

Pete had been at his side throughout the entire ordeal, and this trip to Paris was a much-needed vacation for both of them.

The only problem so far was that neither of them was carrying, and McGarvey felt vulnerable walking around unarmed. But he had a history with the French intelligence service, not all of it especially good. And it had taken a phone call from Marty Bambridge, the current deputy director of the CIA, to the number two at the DGSE, promising that McGarvey and Ms. Boylan would behave themselves inside France, and that under no circumstances would they bring firearms into the country.

They had been sitting in Marty's office on the seventh floor of the Original Headquarters Building as he made the call.

"I'm counting on both of you to stay out of trouble," he'd warned them. He looked more like a banker than the number two chief spy, but that morning he'd taken off his jacket and loosened his tie. It was something he'd once admitted that he did when he was telling a lie.

"Disinformation," McGarvey had said, and they'd laughed about it.

This morning, riding toward the Eiffel Tower, Mac's radar was up and humming. As he talked with Pete and rubbed at the phantom itch, he was watching the traffic ahead of them on the rue de Rivoli.

It seemed like every time he'd come to France, and especially to this city, he'd wound up in the middle of trouble.

Pete picked up on it. "Penny."

He gave her a smile. "Nothing."

"It's me you're talking to, Kirk. What's on your mind?"

"An itchy foot."

"That why all of a sudden your interest in traffic?"

"Old habits, I guess. But there's been a lot of stuff happening in this country over the past few years. Saint-Denis, Nice, Charlie Hebdo."

"But none lately, and that's what's worrying you?"

"Like I said, old habits."

"Give Otto a call."

It was 6:30 in the morning when Otto Rencke's number rolled over to his office on the third floor of the OHB in Langley.

"Oh, wow, Mac," he answered on the first ring. "What's up?"

Rencke, who was the CIA's ranking odd duck computer genius and McGarvey's closest friend for more years than either of them wanted to count, was considered by just about everyone anywhere in the world in the know to be unequaled in the business. No one had a neutral opinion about him: everyone was either grateful for his expertise or frightened out of their wits, or both.

He'd designed most of the computer programs for the CIA as well as the Defense Intelligence Agency, the office of the National Director of Intelligence, and even the FBI and Pentagon. The one notable exception was the State Department, whose system had always leaked like a sieve.

His encryption systems, including the backscatter method that could scramble both sides of a telephone conversation even if one of the phones was not protected, was so state of the art that even Russian, Chinese, and Japanese engineers had been unable to duplicate them.

"Anything looming on your threat board?" McGarvey asked.

"You got a case of the premos?"

McGarvey's premos were his premonitions, which had almost always been right on the mark or close to it. Willies, he called them. The feeling at the base of his neck. Something just slightly out of kilter for him. A man in the blue sweater who didn't seem to belong. The odd glint of light from a pair of binoculars or the lens of a sniper rifle's scope on the roof of a building. The miscellaneous car or windowless van here or there with an odd-looking antenna. An SUV with tinted windows that seemed heavy on its shocks and was probably carrying armor. But its license tags were civilian, not government or military.

"Nothing specific."

"An explosion last night at a construction site in Aleppo. A sixty-five percent probability that Iran is reactivating one of its nuclear enrichment centrifuges. A possible theft of a tactical nuclear warhead from a depot outside of Saratov."

"What's your confidence level on the Russian thing?"

"Fifty-fifty. I sent it upstairs last night."

"Anything brewing here in Paris?"

"Nothing my darlings have picked up," Rencke said. His darlings were a set of sophisticated computer programs that searched and analyzed inputs from every electronic source on the planet that he was able to hack into. They found possible connections, from which they made predictions with varying degrees of confidence.

"Dig deeper, just for the hell of it," McGarvey said.

"Already on it. Shit starts to go lavender and you'll be the first to know."

Lavender on his monitors meant trouble.

THREE

☐

Najjir, dressed in a dove-gray Armani suit, white silk shirt unbuttoned at the neck, no tie, led Miriam directly across to the stairs up to the Jules Verne's private elevator.

The lines for one of the public elevators to take them into the tower snaked back almost half the length of the park, nearly to the rue Saint-Dominique. A waiting time of one hour forty-five minutes was displayed on a couple of electronic signs, and more people were joining the queue.

There was no line for the Jules Verne.

"Worley, for two," Najjir told the maître d', who checked his notepad.

"Welcome to the Jules Verne, monsieur et madam."

"Mademoiselle," Miriam corrected him, her French accent perfect.

"Pardon, mademoiselle."

"And thank God we don't have to stand in some miserable line just for a bite to eat," she told Najjir, not bothering to keep her voice or bitchy attitude in check.

He'd explained the general scenario to her several times over the past two months, but she was improvising.

"Act natural."

"You mean my shitty self, luv?" she'd laughed. "Won't be a problem. Always wanted to be a stage actor."

In the past week or so he'd begun to think that it would almost be a shame to kill her in the end. But he was going to have to go deep, anywhere other than the home outside Riyadh he'd made for himself three years ago. And depending on how thorough or just lucky the French authorities might be, it was possible he'd be on the run until the furor died down. Possibly as long as a year, depending what his next assignment would be.

"Something very big" was all he'd been told by his control officer.

He'd wanted to ask: Bigger than taking down the Eiffel Tower? But he'd held that and a dozen other questions to himself. A trick he'd learned as a young boy in school in Belfast a million years ago.

"Keep your mouth shut and maybe your balls will stay attached," an older friend had told him. He'd been a ten-year-old, wise beyond his years, who'd been hit by a stray Catholic bullet and had bled out on the street corner before the fighting stopped and an ambulance could get to him.

Najjir—who'd gone by the name of Patrick O'Brian—had been sent by a Saudi crown prince highly connected with the GIP to be raised as Irish, to learn to keep his wits when he was under fire, and in the end, when he received his training at the new SVR's School 1 outside of Moscow, and afterward disappeared in the US, he was finally contacted by a series of Saudi control officers, most of them working out of the United Nations.

He was fluent in a half dozen languages, with as many different accents, but he had no home country—not even Saudi Arabia, where he'd been born thirty-two years ago. And nowhere, not in Ireland, the US, or England, and especially Russia, did he feel comfortable. All of his life he had been a person under stress who had no place to go where he would feel a sense of belonging, feel truly safe.

He told himself practically every day that he didn't care. But it was a lie.

The restaurant was nearly full when they got up to the third level, and the only two tables available were one by the hidden entry to the kitchen doors and the other in the middle of the room. Both of them were as far away as possible from the windows that gave a panoramic view of the city, and of the south pillar.

Najjir opted for the table by the kitchen.

"This is absolutely shit," Miriam said, not bothering to keep her voice low.

"If madam would like the center table," the headwaiter who had escorted them from his stand at the elevator suggested.

"It's 'mademoiselle,'" she screeched. "And maybe you could suggest seats in the loo, where we could take a piss between courses."

The waiter was nonplussed, but Najjir smiled. "This table will be fine, thank you," he said.

He held the chair for Miriam, who sat down after a hesitation.

The waiter gave them menus and departed. Servers came with water, a bread basket, several types of butter, small plates of herbs, and a cruet of olive oil. Another came with the wine list in a thickly padded leather-bound book.

"May I recommend a white or red wine for monsieur and mademoiselle?"

"Tanqueray martini straight up, one olive, stirred, not shaken, just like Double-O Seven," Miriam said.

"I'll have a glass of Krug," Najjir said.

As soon as the sommelier was out of earshot Najjir gave Miriam a harsh look. "Good job," he said.

"Piece of cake. I'm a natural bitch," she said. "What's next?"

"I'll let you know when."

A refrigerated Mercedes transit van bearing the logo for Produit Fourquette, with the stylized painting of a field of flowers, mountains in dark blues in the distance, pulled up at the service elevator for the restaurant. Three husky men, one of them very young, in spotless white coveralls, their heads and faces closely shaved, got out, took three large plastic bins from the back of the truck, and made for the elevator.

A police officer stopped them. "May I see your delivery order?" he asked. Things like this type of inspection had become routine over the past several years.

The lead delivery man pulled the manifest from his vest pocket and handed it over. It showed an order for nine kilos of dressed rabbits, seven of pheasants, six of quail, and three of sweetbreads.

"They always eat well up there," the cop said.

"Not today if these get warm and spoil. *Ca te defrise?*" *Any objection?*

"*Ouvrir, s'il vous plais.*"

The men lowered the boxes to the pavement and opened the lids, cold air rising as steam. Inside were individually wrapped and marked plastic packages of the birds, rabbits, and beef.

The cop handed the delivery order back and stepped away. "*Allez.*"

"*D'ac,*" Omar Haddad told the cop. *Okay.* He was the strike leader, only by virtue of the fact that his French was passable. Until recently he'd been an ISIS infiltrator for the GIP and a liaison officer for operations inside France. This was to be his last mission before he would be allowed to return home and take a desk job for the interior ministry.

If all went well he would be long gone before the C-4 vests his two martyrs were wearing were detonated. First to a safe house in Saint-Ouen, then by stages back to Saudi Arabia.

Haddad called the elevator with the key he'd been provided in training six weeks ago, and when the door opened the three of them piled inside and started up.

Shamz Naser, a nineteen-year-old kid from a small town outside of Jeddah, started to say something, but Haddad overrode him.

"We'll take our lunch break when we've made this delivery."

Naser wanted to say something, but Haddad glanced up at the security camera and the kid got the idea that he was to keep his mouth shut.

The elevator opened at the end of a short pantry corridor that led to the kitchen. The cold storage locker was on the left. A man dressed in a cutaway, who Haddad guessed was the sommelier or assistant, came through the big door to the right, with a bottle of champagne in hand.

He stopped. "We're not expecting you," he said.

Haddad pulled out his silenced Glock 29SF and was on the man in three steps, pushing him back into the climate-controlled wine storage room, where he fired one 10mm round into the man's forehead. He caught the bottle of champagne before it hit the floor.

He stood lookout while Naser dragged the body to the back of the wine room and concealed it behind the racks. No blood had gotten on the floor, and it would take a thorough search of the dimly lit room to find the dead man.

It was noon, and the countdown clock had started.

FOUR

☐

McGarvey and Pete had reservations at the Jules Verne under Mac's name. They went up in the private elevator to the third level, where they were shown to their table by a window looking out at the south pillar and the city spread out toward Montmartre in the haze.

The restaurant was filled with mostly tourists, McGarvey guessed by their casual dress. Only a few other couples, including a man and woman seated near the kitchen, wore jackets and decent dresses. But he had been brought up old-school by his strict, by-the-book parents, where even on their ranch out on the western Kansas plains he and his older sister, Joanne, had been taught manners.

"Good breeding will take you far," their mother had told them.

Their parents had inherited and worked the family cattle ranch, but they also worked as theoretical physicists for the government at Los Alamos, until their deaths in an automobile accident. The FBI had speculated, but had never been able to prove, that John and Lilly McGarvey had been assassinated by Russian agents.

When Mac had joined the CIA and had the opportunity, he'd searched the agency's records for anything about the accident, but he'd found nothing. Nor had Otto found much, except that the driver of the car that had forced them off the road had never been found. Nor had the Bureau ever found any forensics evidence in the car. No DNA, no fingerprints, nothing. The car had been wiped clean by experts.

The family's assets, other than the ranch which McGarvey inherited, had been left to Joanne, who'd married and moved to Salt Lake City. A few years later, after Mac had gotten out of the air force and went to work for the Company, he had sold the ranch and turned over the money to an investment broker—vetted by the CIA—who had done very well by him. Although he wasn't wealthy, he'd always been comfortable.

"The place has been in the family for three generations and you're simply going to sell it to the highest bidder?" Joanne had berated him. "You bastard."

"I'm not a rancher and never will be," McGarvey had told her. "I'll give you the ranch, if you want it. You and Stan can move back and run it."

"I won't trade my inheritance with you for the place."

"Not interested. You want the ranch, it's yours. I'll sell it to you."

"We don't have the money."

"One dollar."

She'd given her brother an odd look, almost as if he were a stranger, but finally shook her head and walked away. That'd been more than twenty years ago, and they'd never been close since.

Waiters came with their menus and bread, and McGarvey asked to have the sommelier, who had not yet appeared, to pick a nice Dom Pérignon.

"Of course, monsieur."

The sun was high in the cloudless sky, but it reflected and re-reflected off the windows and even the glassware on the tables, framing Pete's face and shoulders almost as if she were wearing a halo. McGarvey was nervous, and it was so obvious all of a sudden that Pete could see it.

"What is it?" she asked.

"Nice view from here."

"Champagne? Top-shelf digs?" she asked. She glanced at the other diners. "What gives? Camouflage? Another one of your premos?"

"Nothing like that. We're good here."

"What, then?"

So much had happened in twenty-plus years. He'd been down so many bitter paths, had been backed into so many dark corners—situations and places where he'd sometimes not been able to tell a friend, or at least an ally, from an enemy. So many difficult choices, very often with no definite outcomes or even happy endings. His actions so many times totally against the wishes and even orders of reasonable men and women who knew what their duty was all about. Contrary to logic, to good thinking, to what was right and just under the law. Unnatural, even deeply immoral.

"I am what I am," he'd told a deputy director of operations years ago.

Even then it had been too late for him to get off the path that he had stumbled onto ever since his parents' murders—he'd believed from the beginning that their deaths had not been accidental. They'd been the lead theorists on a new type of defense weapon that the Russians wanted to delay until their own scientists could catch up.

It had been the end of the Cold War and the beginning of a new, more personal war of individual acts of terrorism—some as simple as the assassination of a political leader, others as far-reaching and complicated as 9/11.

"Kirk?" Pete prompted.

A man in white coveralls appeared briefly on the catwalk outside the window to the left, and then disappeared. Almost certainly a maintenance man, McGarvey figured, though it seemed odd to him that a work order or even an inspection would be scheduled during the lunch hour, when the restaurant was full.

Unless something was wrong.

No one else had noticed the workman outside except for the couple seated by the kitchen. The man had looked up, but the woman, her back to the window, was talking to him.

Pete turned in the same direction he was looking. "Okay, now I'm nervous. What's going on?"

"I don't know," McGarvey said. "Nothing."

"It's something, for Christ's sake."

He forced a smile. "You're right. It's the real reason we came to Paris and I booked us a table here."

Pete's eyes were suddenly very bright.

Mac felt like a kid. It was stupid.

"Spit it out, unless you're all of a sudden a coward."

"Marry me?"

"Say again?"

"I'm not getting down on one knee," McGarvey said. "If that's what you want."

"No, but after everything that's happened over the past couple of years I'm going to stretch it out for as long as I can."

The man seated with the woman by the kitchen entrance got to his feet. McGarvey caught the motion out of the corner of his eye and he glanced over.

The woman, medium height, slender, and very well put together—though in Mac's mind there was something not quite right about her appearance or her manner—jumped up, tipping her chair over backwards.

"You son of a bitch," she brayed at the top of her lungs.

The soft murmurs in the restaurant stopped as the other diners turned toward the couple.

The man said something to the woman, but his words didn't calm her down.

"Fuck you," she screamed. "If I had a fucking gun right now I'd shoot you in your fucking head, you miserable cocksucker."

"Not only lunch and champers, but you arranged the entertainment package," Pete said. "Nice."

The man came around the table and tried to take the woman's arm, but she pulled away.

McGarvey thought that the guy was holding something in his left hand. Down at his side. Like a gun.

The woman screeched something unintelligible and snatched a butter knife from the table.

A pair of uniformed cops came from the stairway next to the elevators, and the maître d' from the ground level stood aside.

"I'm pregnant, you motherfucker," the woman screeched.

The man glanced toward the oncoming cops, then raised what looked like a cell phone, said something, and then quickly pocketed it.

"Fuck you, bitch," he shouted, and the cops were on them, hustling them out of the restaurant.

FIVE

☐

The cops took Najjir and Miriam around the corner from the restaurant entrance, away from the still growing crowds. But they'd not pulled out their handcuffs or drawn their pistols. If anything, they looked amused and just a little vexed.

It was exactly what Najjir had wanted to happen. He'd sent the electronic signal to the military grade explosives his three operatives had strapped to their bodies beneath their coveralls, and from this point nothing could alter the upcoming course of events. In twenty minutes the nearly ninety kilos of C-4 would explode and the Eiffel Tower would come twisting and crashing to the ground.

"Passports, please," the lead cop, whose name tag identified him as Guyot, said.

Najjir took his out of his jacket pocket and handed it over. It took a moment for Miriam to find hers in her purse.

The cop studied them, comparing their faces to the photos. "What are you two doing here?"

"A few days' holiday," Najjir said.

"I meant upstairs, disturbing the people trying to enjoy their meals?"

"I'm sorry," Miriam said. "But I'm preggers and the son of a bitch won't do a thing about it."

"Take your troubles elsewhere," the other, younger cop, whose name tag identified him as Lemaire, said.

"I wanted to embarrass him."

Guyot smiled. "It didn't seem to work."

"Then what the fuck am I supposed to do?" Miriam demanded, her voice rising.

"In the first place, calm yourself, mademoiselle, or we will take you into custody for disturbing the public order and you can spend the night in jail waiting for a judge to listen to your story."

"Fine, as long as he's locked up as well."

"Just you, mademoiselle."

Miriam started to protest, but Najjir took her by the elbow. "Let's go for a walk, darling, and I promise we'll work it out."

"In a pig's eye."

"Trust me."

"All men are bastards," she said, raising her voice.

"*A la noix*," Lemaire said. *Useless.*

"I'll marry you," Najjir said.

Miriam looked up, her eyes wide. "No shit?"

"*Bonne chance*," Lemaire said half under his breath.

"I promise," Najjir said. It was going to be too bad to kill her. She was such a superb actress, he could think of a lot of scenarios where she would come in handy as a misdirection, a smoke screen, like upstairs in the dining room, and right here, right now. "Anyway, I didn't know that you were pregnant."

Najjir turned to the cops and shrugged. "My apologies to you, the restaurant staff, and the other diners."

"Settle your difference elsewhere, in private," Guyot said. "Preferably out of France."

He and the other cop stepped back.

Najjir took Miriam's arm and they headed back toward the parking ramp where they'd left the car. When they were lost in the crowd and out of earshot of the cops, Najjir put his arm around her waist.

"You were nothing short of perfect," he said.

"I thought I was pretty good," she agreed. She looked up at him. "So now what?"

"We go home."

"Back to London?"

"Sure," Najjir said.

Miriam looked over her shoulder at the tower. "It's coming down, no shit?"

"No shit," Najjir assured her. "In about fifteen minutes."

"Then let's get the fuck out of here, okay?"

Haddad joined the others in the equipment room between the kitchen and the delivery and storage corridor. The restaurant had its own air-conditioning, heating plant, and emergency generator equipment, the control panels for which were all located in this space.

"The situation is as we have studied," he told his people, the kids, as he thought of them.

At twenty-two, he was the oldest of the three soldiers for Allah, and the best trained. His father, two uncles, and his older brother had all worked the Saudi oil fields outside of Ras Az Zawr on the Persian Gulf, and at sixteen he'd joined them.

But he had been radicalized in school and at the mosque in Jeddah and firmly believed in his heart of hearts that the West was Satan's domain and that he had no other recourse than to give his all in the war for the survival of all Islam. Especially Wahhabism as practiced by his countrymen.

The imam at the mosque in Ras had come to him with another man, whose name was Zishan and who had promised to put action to Omar's hate for the West.

His first training camp where he had learned about weapons—everything from pistols to compact submachine guns and even the Russian Grail and American Stinger ground-to-air man-portable missiles—had been on the desert near Ash Sha'ra, nearly three hundred kilometers west of Riyadh.

From there he'd been sent on a training mission to northern Iraq, where, working under cover, he joined an ISIS brigade that was reinforcing Mosul, where an attack by the Americans was expected at any time.

During his two months in the field he'd learned about several impending attacks against the Saudi ground forces along the border with Syria.

One night he'd killed two fellow guards watching over fifty Iraqi women who'd been captured and were being used as sexual slaves, then made his way to Jordan in the southeast and from there across the border back into Saudi Arabia at Turaif, where there was a small airport.

He'd come to the attention of the GIP's special operations division and was sent to another desert training camp, this one south of Bi'r Fardān, just within the boundaries of the vast Rub' al Khali, one of the most inhospitable deserts in the entire world.

He was trained as an operational commander, which meant he became an expert with weapons, explosives of all types, leading men in the field by motivation, how to survive, and especially how to blend in. Groups like his were called chameleon squads.

But on the way he'd also picked up survival tips. Operations for the cause was one thing, but martyrdom was not his bag.

He looked at his watch. The signal their front man had sent would cause the explosive vests to go off in just under ten minutes.

But after he'd checked the south pillar girders, he had disconnected the trigger from his vest.

He wasn't going to die here, but if he were cornered trying to make his escape, he would not be captured alive. Under no circumstances was he ever to allow such a thing to happen, his control officer—a man he only knew as "Uncle"—had drummed into his head.

The kids were looking at him, their eyes round.

"Are your weapons ready?" he asked. Each of them carried a Heckler & Koch personal defense weapon—a compact submachine gun called the "room broom" in the West.

They nodded.

Their orders were clear. They were to place their bodies up against the south pillar and no matter what happened they were not to move from the spot until detonation. If anyone tried to clear them away, they were to fight back.

Haddad checked his watch again.

"You are Allah's chosen. Blessed be your lives and the paradise that awaits you."

SIX

☐

From where they were seated they could see the couple the police had escorted out of the restaurant crossing the park, the man's arm around the woman's waist. They were lovers now, and it made absolutely no sense to McGarvey.

"There goes the entertainment," Pete said. "Too bad."

The man looked over his shoulder, back at the tower, his face raised as if he was looking in the restaurant's windows. At Mac.

Pete was suddenly serious. "What gives?"

"Nothing, probably," McGarvey said absently. But his inner warning siren was coming alive, almost as if he were heading into battle.

A waiter came over with a pair of flutes, and the maître d' himself brought an ice bucket on a silver stand with a bottle of champagne.

"May I do the honors, monsieur?"

"You're not the sommelier."

"No, monsieur. That would be Monsieur Gaston. But he is temporarily indisposed."

McGarvey glanced again at the people down in the park. The couple had stopped and were still looking back toward the tower, as if they thought something was about to happen.

"Stay put," he told Pete and got to his feet. "Take me to your wine room."

"Monsieur?"

"Now."

The maître d' was flustered, which in itself struck McGarvey as odd. French waiters lost their tempers, but never their poise.

Other diners were looking their way now, curious about the latest disturbance in what was supposed to be an oasis of calm.

McGarvey headed toward the kitchen, the maître d' catching up with him.

"Is there trouble?"

"I don't know."

"Are you a policeman?"

"No."

The maître d' led him through the compact and busy kitchen and through a swinging door into a short corridor that went past the storage lockers to the service elevator.

"The wine room," McGarvey prompted.

The maître d' went to the wine room and opened the heavy door.

McGarvey brushed past him and stopped just inside the door. The room was about the size of a walk-in closet, but with a high ceiling. The temperature was cool, and along the left wall a floor-to-ceiling temperature-controlled space behind tall glass doors was filled with bottles of champagne and other wines that needed to be kept at a lower and more constant temperature.

Nothing was wrong here. Yet McGarvey's innards were singing.

Something about the couple who'd created such a disturbance that they had to be escorted out by the police was bothersome. The man had called someone on his cell phone, but he couldn't have said more than a word or two. A code word. A signal.

McGarvey went to the back of the room. The wine racks reached the ceiling, twelve feet up, and a ladder on tracks—like the ones in the libraries of mansions—was positioned near the middle.

The racks stopped a couple of feet from the rear wall. The body of a man, lying on his back, was stuffed into the space. Even though the light was dim, Mac could see that he had been shot in the middle of the forehead.

"Call the bomb squad, and get everyone out of here—your staff as well as the customers."

The maître d' was frozen.

"*Plus vite, salopard*," McGarvey shouted, brushing past the man. *Fast, you son of a bitch.*

Pete had come through the kitchen and was standing in the doorway.

"I think they put a bomb in here somewhere," McGarvey shouted. "Get everyone out now!"

Pete nodded, her expression tight. "There're at least two guys in white coveralls out on the catwalk," she said in a rush. She turned and started shouting at the kitchen staff to leave.

Haddad was aware of a commotion in the restaurant. Naser had already taken up a position on the south pillar, his arms hugging the girders as if he were a lover of the steel.

Hanni Safar, at fifteen the youngest of them, was rooted to his spot, his eyes closed, his lips moving. He was praying.

People inside were getting up and heading toward the elevator. A woman with short red hair seemed to be directing the evacuation.

She looked over her shoulder and their eyes locked for just an instant, but then she went back to her business of getting people out.

She knew!

Naser had promised that would be impossible. "No one knows the complete operation except for us," he'd warned repeatedly from the beginning, months ago. And he'd said it again at the apartment.

But somehow the bitch knew!

Haddad shoved Safar toward the empty spot on the girder. "Go, now, Safar," he said. "For Allah."

"For Allah," the young man mumbled.

Haddad pulled out his room broom with his right hand and his cell phone with the other and speed dialed Najjir's number as he backed against the wall just to the left of the service door in the kitchen.

It rang three times before Najjir picked up. "Yes."

"They know."

"In four minutes it won't matter."

The connection was ended, and Haddad tossed the phone aside. He raised his weapon as he turned toward the window, when someone was suddenly beside him, shoving him aside, and the submachine gun fired a short burst into the air.

McGarvey could feel the bricks of what almost certainly were explosives attached to the young man's torso beneath the white coveralls.

The terrorist was momentarily off balance. McGarvey snatched the Heckler & Koch from his hands and smashed the butt of the weapon into the kid's jaw, sending him sprawling to his knees.

Haddad recovered almost instantly and sprang to his feet.

McGarvey raised the weapon and fired two shots into the kid's face.

The other two were shouting something in Arabic, spittle flying from their mouths.

Without a doubt the explosives were on some sort of a timer that the bastard watching from below in the park had activated by cell phone.

Sirens were incoming from a distance, in all directions.

But it was too late to let it work itself out.

The explosives, if they were powerful enough and if there were enough of them, could possibly take out the south pillar. The entire tower could come crashing down. It was something no less likely than the downing of the twin trade towers in New York.

All that went through his head at the speed of light.

But there was no time to try to disarm the vests.

He opened fire at the terrorists, the bullets ripping through their necks and heads. They lost their holds on the girders and, almost as if in slow motion, their bodies pitched over the edge.

There would be casualties below when the vests exploded. But the Eiffel Tower would not come down.

SEVEN

☐

McGarvey laid the room broom on the deck and ripped open the front of the terrorist's white coveralls. The man was carrying what had to be more than thirty kilos of C-4, but the detonator wired to the cell phone receiver had been disconnected. All it would take to set off the charge was to reconnect the wire.

The kid had decided that he wasn't going to die here, but he had the weapon and the explosive vest. He had planned on trying to make his escape in the confusion after the blast. Only if he'd been cornered, with no other way out, was he going to set off the explosives.

McGarvey looked over the rail. The bodies of the two terrorists were splayed out on the concrete apron about thirty feet to the left of the entrance to the Jules Verne's elevator.

But people were crowding in toward them, trying to get a better look.

"Get away," McGarvey shouted. He waved his arms, but no one seemed to pay any attention.

The same police officers who'd escorted the couple out of the restaurant were there, pushing their way through the growing crowd.

Sirens converging from all directions were getting closer.

McGarvey snatched up the Heckler & Koch and fired two short bursts into the air.

People below screamed in terror and started to scatter.

The officers started to draw their weapons. Pete came into view. She looked up, spotted Mac, then headed in a dead run for the cops, waving her arms and screaming.

"Get away! Get away! They have vest bombs!"

McGarvey snatched two magazines of ammunition from the downed terrorist's pocket, and as he raced through the kitchen and out into the short back corridor, he ejected the nearly spent magazine from the submachine gun and reloaded the weapon.

The man and woman had stopped at the edge of the crowd and had watched everything. There was no mistaking the high probability that they were involved in the attempted attack. His only question was what the hell they had been doing so close to the action. Something could have gone wrong at the last minute and they could have been killed, or arrested.

Not bothering with the elevator, Mac took the stairs two at a time down to the ground level.

The crowd continued to scatter, but Pete was still there with the cops, not five feet from the bodies of the three terrorists.

"Get the hell out of here," he shouted.

Pete looked over her shoulder.

"Go, go, go!"

She turned back to the cops, who had their weapons drawn and were still looking up toward the catwalk.

"Christ," McGarvey swore.

He fired another short burst into the air, and this time Pete grabbed one of the cops by the gun arm and pulled him away.

She shouted something that McGarvey couldn't make out, then he headed in a dead run toward where he'd seen the couple standing, watching.

Worst-case scenario, create a back door. A path and a means for escape in a situation that has fallen or is about to fall apart. It was SOP, Standard Operating Procedure.

"What the fuck are we standing here for?" Miriam shouted.

People were streaming away from the base of the tower, but they were moving slowly, and there was still a big crowd around the south pillar of the tower. The explosive vests would detonate at any moment. No matter what else happened, there would be casualties.

Najjir phoned his backup, and the man answered on the first ring.

"Yes."

"Where are you?"

"Boulevard de Grenelle, near the Quai Branly. Do you need an extraction?"

"Yes. We're one block from the Parking Pullman on the avenue de Suffren."

"Two minutes," his contact said.

The Saudi contractor and four others in the anonymous Toyota van, all of whom had been members of special forces in one European country or another until they had been discharged for use of excessive force, were too highly skilled to waste on suicide missions.

Najjir had hired them and briefed them three months ago and had arranged for their accommodations in an apartment complex on the rue Saint-Denis, just to the east of Les Halles. The neighborhood was one of the seediest areas in all of Paris, and along with the Bois de Boulogne was the stomping ground for prostitutes, drug dealers, and the scum of the city.

His contractors felt at home there, in part because they'd been paid well and they had the real chance of shooting people.

Two massive explosions, coming nearly simultaneously, made the air dance and ripple directly down the long park filled with people, and the tower swayed toward the southwest, at least three or four feet off center.

There was no third explosion.

Yet watching the tower sway and then rebound gave Najjir hope that the son of a bitch would actually come down after all.

"Holy shit, holy shit," Miriam mumbled.

People were screaming, sirens were getting closer, car alarms were popping off, and an air raid or fire alarm on some building off to the left began to wail.

The crowd parted slightly, giving Najjir a brief glimpse of the man in the blue blazer, carrying a Heckler & Koch low at his side. He had to have taken it from one of the boys.

People trying to escape in earnest now that it was too late obscured him from view.

Time to leave, but Najjir hesitated. The bastard had put himself in the middle of something that was none of his business. But the fact that he had removed the threat to the tower had to mean something. He'd possibly known what was about to happen and had shown up to prevent it.

His being there, with the woman for cover, could very well mean that there was a leak in the organization in Riyadh. It was one piece of information that was too vital to leave to chance.

"Bleeding Christ, what the fuck are we standing here for?" Miriam demanded, pulling at his sleeve.

"Shut your mouth," Najjir told her, trying to catch another glimpse of the man who'd screwed everything up.

"Give me the keys and I'll get out of here on my own."

Najjir took his Glock 10mm pistol from the holster under his left arm and pointed it at her chest from a distance of just a few inches. The positions of their bodies concealed the gun.

She squeaked and started to move away, but Najjir took her arm and pulled her even closer.

"We failed, this time," he told her. "But the operation is not done with until I say so."

"You're fucking out of your mind."

"You're right. But if you want to survive to take the train back to London this afternoon you'll do exactly as I say."

She looked past him at the crowds moving directly away from the tower. "You won't shoot me, not in front of all these people, and the cops will be all over the place any moment now."

"Care to bet your life on it?"

It only took her a moment to back down. "I told you that I was in for the duration, so don't get your arse in a bundle."

Najjir glanced over his shoulder. The man was less than fifty meters away—out of the range of the room broom, but closing.

The fox to the hounds.

"Now," Najjir told Miriam, and he holstered his pistol as they started toward the parking garage.

At that moment two police vans pulled up on the avenue de Suffren and a dozen cops dressed in combat gear—ballistic vests, Kevlar helmets, automatic weapons at the ready—piled out.

EIGHT

☐

Pete was lying on her side with no immediate recollection of how she'd gotten there, except that something heavy and wet was on top of her. Her head was ringing and her stomach was flopping over so badly that she was sure she was going to throw up.

It was dark, dust or smoke so thick it was hard for her to make out much of anything farther than a few feet.

She shifted her weight and managed to shove the thing off her and sit up. The thing was the decapitated body of the cop she'd managed to pull around the corner of the south pillar, just before the flash of light and the concussion that had knocked her out of her shoes and had torn away much of her skirt.

Everything came back to her in a horrible rush: McGarvey had shouted at her to get away and then had disappeared in the crowd that had been moving far too slowly. There'd been an explosion, maybe more than one.

But the Eiffel Tower had not come down.

She got shakily to her feet, the nauseous feeling nearly overwhelming her. The cop had not lost his grip on his SIG Sauer pistol, and on instinct alone she pried it from the man's dead hand and staggered around the corner, out into the open.

Bodies and parts of bodies lay everywhere. Blood coated the pavement in a tremendous splatter pattern that stretched at least fifty feet to the southwest, as far as some body parts had been thrown.

It was like a scene from hell, or from some B-list horror movie. It was nearly impossible for her to take it all in.

She took several steps away from the jumble of bodies nearest to the south pillar. People were still running away. Screams came from all directions. Traffic on the Quai Branly along the river had come to a stop as police cars and SWAT team trucks, sirens blaring, came from all parts of the city.

Her legs and one arm and possibly her face had been cut up by the flying debris, but she was so covered with the cop's blood it was nearly impossible to tell how badly she'd been hurt. But she could move without much pain.

The last she'd seen of Mac he'd been running toward the west, but the smoke and haze in that direction were still too heavy for her to make out much more than ghostly moving figures.

But that's the way he'd went, which was good enough for her.

She started after him, moving as fast as she could on the extremely slippery blood-coated pavement.

Najjir holstered his pistol beneath his jacket before the first of the SWAT team reached him and Miriam.

"There's a man with a gun," he shouted, pointing back toward the tower.

He grabbed Miriam's arm and pulled her aside.

"He's shot some people!"

The crowd had still not completely cleared the park, and though the dust and smoke were dissipating, an acrid haze lingered, especially directly around the base of the tower. A lot of people were still screaming and crying, many obviously in pain, others out of fear and panic.

One of the cops stopped, but the others didn't slow down.

"Did you get a good look at this man? Can you give me a description?"

"My height, a little more husky, short hair, a dark jacket, I think."

"A white man or black?"

"White."

The cop glanced in the direction his team was heading and said something into the mike at his right shoulder.

"He was shooting? At who?"

"I don't know."

"What kind of a weapon?"

"A small machine gun, I think. It was very fast."

The cop turned and sprinted after his team as he spoke into his lapel mike, his Saint-Étienne M12SD submachine gun at the ready.

Pete pulled up short, well beyond the periphery of the blood spatter and gore. Mac had been straight out toward the west, toward the avenue de Suffren, but she had lost him. For a long moment she didn't know what to do.

People were everywhere, trying to get away from the tower and the horrific scene of death, and from the wounded people lying on the pavement, screaming for help in a dozen different languages. A few people, including a woman whose left arm had been blown off, wandered in circles.

She held the pistol behind her right leg so that it was partially concealed as a SWAT team squad, their weapons at the ready, rushed past her, and moments later another of the special operators came past her in a run. They all were dressed in black, with bloused boots, helmets, and Kevlar bulletproof vests, sidearms in holsters on their chests and submachine guns unslung.

She stepped aside, her left hand to her face.

Mac had disappeared.

Straight ahead, less than fifty feet away, she spotted the well-dressed man and woman who had caused the scene in the restaurant and had been escorted out by the police.

The man was looking at something behind him, but the woman was looking directly at her, and their eyes locked for the moment.

Four men in ordinary street clothes, jeans and pullovers, came from a windowless van that had pulled up on the avenue and went directly to the man.

The woman said something and the man turned and spotted Pete. He pointed at her.

Two of the men from the van broke off and started directly toward Pete. They were large, bigger than Mac, and she got the momentary impression that they might be from the Middle East, maybe Syria, or even as far east as Pakistan. Their skin tone was olive and their hair and eyes were dark, things she noticed even from the closing distance.

She sincerely wished that Mac had not insisted that they come into France unarmed. Anywhere unarmed, for that matter.

"We're on vacation," he'd told her on the flight over. "And it's getting tougher every day to take a weapon across international borders."

"Mark would have brought us something once we'd passed through customs."

Mark Kraus was the second assistant chief of Paris station. It was his job to be the direct contact with the CIA's assets in country—that included supplying their subcontractors and others with money, papers and, if need be, weapons.

He'd laughed. "Vacation means sleeping late, going to bed late, seeing the sights, eating rich food, and drinking too much. It does not include shooting people."

For them, she thought bitterly, the fact of the matter was that they were never on vacation.

She turned to the left and feinted moving away as the first man to reach her grabbed for her arm.

Swinging back suddenly, she elbowed him in the throat, and as he staggered backwards she kneed him in the groin and brought the cop's SIG up.

But the second man was there, and he jammed the muzzle of a large pistol—a silenced Wilson .45 caliber she thought—into the side of her head.

"Come with me, madam, or I will shoot you."

The first man recovered almost immediately. He snatched the pistol from her hand and slammed its handle into her left breast.

She stepped back, her knees weak. But what was more bothersome to her at the moment—more than the intense pain—was the look of absolute indifference in both men's eyes. Cause her pain or kill her outright. It didn't matter.

NINE

☐

Mac pulled up short about twenty-five meters away from the man and woman from the restaurant as four men who'd emerged from a van swooped down on Pete and hustled her away.

He had lost himself in the middle of the crowd that was trying desperately to get away from the carnage and he had no clear shot.

The French SWAT team had disappeared toward the tower, and the man and woman were gone too.

Shoving his way through the mob, he got clear as Pete was being bodily shoved into the van's open side door. At least one man had stayed behind and was pulling her inside, and another was behind the wheel as the four piled in the back.

He was less than twenty feet from the avenue when the van pulled away, its tires squealing. Someone in back started to close the side door when he spotted Mac. He brought up his pistol but lurched suddenly out of sight, and Mac got the fleeting impression that Pete was right there and had shoved her kidnapper out of the way, preventing him from taking the shot.

Reaching the street, Mac was in time to see the plain gray Toyota van turning to the right on the Quai Branly, against the flow of what traffic there was.

He raced out onto the avenue and headed in a dead run in the direction the van had gone, in time to see the driver turn left onto the bridge across the river.

A yellow Mercedes taxicab was pulled up at the curb.

McGarvey ran to it, pulled open the left door, and yanked the startled driver out onto the street.

Before the man could respond, McGarvey tossed the room broom onto the passenger seat as he got behind the wheel, slammed the car into gear, and floored the pedal.

Najjir and Miriam stopped just inside the doorway to the parking garage when the man from the restaurant raced past in a taxi.

"Persistent son of a bitch," Miriam said. "He has to be a cop."

At the restaurant Najjir had gotten the impression that the man and woman were perhaps husband and wife, or at least lovers, and that they were Americans, by their dress, their haircuts, and their mannerisms. But they didn't quite fit the mold, at least not in his mind, of cops. But who were they? And why the hell had they stuck their noses into the operation? It made no sense to him.

He and Miriam took the elevator up to the third level.

"What's going to happen when he catches up with your people?" she asked.

"They'll kill him," Najjir said. But he wasn't as sure of that outcome as he wanted to be.

When they reached the Peugeot he opened the driver's side door, then popped the trunk lid.

"There are some clothes inside for us. We need to change before we take the train back to London. Someone besides the couple from the restaurant might have noticed us."

"Whatever else you are, you do think of everything," Miriam said, reaching inside the trunk.

No one else was in sight on this level at the moment. Najjir pulled out his pistol as he walked back to Miriam, placed it an inch from the back of her head, and pulled the trigger.

The hammer slapped on an empty firing chamber.

She turned around, a small .32-caliber revolver in her left hand. "Everything except checking the spring in the magazine."

Najjir shrugged and holstered his pistol beneath his jacket. He could easily overpower her and take away her silly little girl's gun, but he was more curious about who she was than concerned about the pistol she was pointing at him.

"So now what?" he asked.

"We get back to the Gare du Nord and take the train to London."

"Why not shoot me right now, stuff my body in the trunk—the same as I intended for you—and take the train back yourself? You'll have your money. Mission accomplished. Or nearly so."

She lowered the gun. "Because we may have further use for you, " she said, first in English and then in Russian.

Pete's left breast was on fire, her skirt had been torn away in the blast, leaving her bare below the waist except for some flimsy panties, and she was pissed off, but she didn't let any of that show. Mac was somewhere back there, and with any luck at all he saw what happened.

The rear of the van was blocked off from the front, and there were no windows in the back, so she couldn't see where they were going, except that they had made one turn to the right—if it was onto the Quai Branly, it would have been against traffic—but they made a another sharp turn, this one to the left. It had to be the bridge over the Seine.

They'd snatched her for whatever reason and on whoever's orders—though she had a fair guess that it had been on the orders of the couple who'd made too obvious a scene in the restaurant.

What was even more ominous to her than the kidnapping was the fact that they had not covered their faces. It didn't matter to them that if she ever got free she would be able to identify them for the police. They had no intention of letting her escape, because they were going to kill her.

But then why had they taken her, unless it was meant to flush out Mac?

She managed to wet her lips, though her mouth was as dry as parchment, and she grinned. "If it was you guys who tried to bring down the Eiffel Tower, I have to say you did a piss-poor job."

The one who hit her in the breast with his pistol just looked at her, as if he was seeing a mildly interesting but completely harmless bug.

"Now that you have me, what's next? We're going to your hideout, where you're going to take turns raping me?"

None of them said a thing.

They had turned right again, most likely onto the expressway along the river, because they had sped up and she could hear traffic noises.

She wanted one of them to say something. All of them looked vaguely Middle Eastern, but that covered a lot of territory.

"Give a girl a break. How about it, fellas? The condemned gets her last wish before going to the gallows?"

The one she'd shoved away from the open door as he tried to take a shot turned on her. "Shut your fucking pie hole, bitch!"

One of the others motioned for him to shut up and he turned away.

Pete sat back and tried to keep the look of surprise from her face. The son of a bitch was Russian—from one of the former Soviet republics. Her guess was Kazakhstan, Uzbekistan, or farther south, Turkmenistan.

"My partner will find me," she said.

They looked at her but said nothing.

"I have a GPS chip implant."

The one who had hit her in the breast, and who had just motioned for the one by the door to keep quiet, reached back and took a small device that looked like a cell phone out of a bag, powered it up, and waved it in her general direction.

He shook his head after a moment or two, shut it off.

Pete figured that he was the operational commander and that he and his people were either intelligence officers or possibly military special forces. Spetsnaz, perhaps. No one else had such sophisticated equipment.

But it made absolutely no sense to her.

Only a terrorist organization like ISIS or al Qaeda would have tried to pull off taking down something like the Eiffel Tower. Responsible governments didn't do such things. The risks of blowback were simply far too great.

Even Putin with his grandiose desire to bring Russia back to the international stature of the old Soviet Union wouldn't order such a stunt.

These guys were pros, but working for whom?

TEN

□

Across the river, Najjir took the rue Saint-Denis toward the Gare du Nord in the tenth. It was not the fastest way to the train station but it was in the same direction his cleanup crew had taken the woman, and the same direction the hijacked taxi had gone.

He had the driver's window down, and even though traffic was very heavy and noisy, he could still make out sirens converging from all over the city toward the Eiffel Tower.

The operation was a failure; the tower had not come down. But people on the ground at the south pillar had been killed, and as another act of terrorism here, Parisians would not soon forget it.

"Why are we going this way?" Miriam asked.

"I want to find out what happens."

"If you mean the American couple from the restaurant, your people will kill them. Unless they fuck up too."

"I want to know who they are."

"Tourists."

"I don't think so," Najjir said. He phoned his team leader. "Where are you?"

"Coming up on the Forum," Bernard, who was driving, answered. The Forum des Halles was the huge underground shopping mall and Metro station that had replaced the old market. It had opened in 1986 and was always busy, though a lot of Parisians hated it because an important part of the city's history had been bulldozed.

The team's plan was the ditch the van a few blocks away and take the

Metro out of the city to an apartment in Saint-Ouen, just outside the Périphérique ring highway around the city proper.

From there they would change clothes—including Najjir and Miriam,
who were to have been extracted from a situation gone bad—pick up new
identification packages, and make their way out of France by separate
routes.

"What about the woman?"

"She's a pain in the ass."

"Have you found out who she is?"

"No, but Karim's guess is she's an LE from the States. She talks the talk,
and she won't back the fuck down." LE was law enforcement. "What do
you want us to do with her?"

"Take her to the *église*, find out who's she working for. Then kill her and
get back on plan."

The église was the thirteenth-century parish church of Saint-Leu-Saint-
Gilles in Les Halles, not far from the Forum. At this time of the day in
midweek it would be a safe haven, with a rat warren of chambers below
street level. They had set it up as a temporary safe haven in case something went wrong.

From a subbasement they could reach the Paris sewer system, which
would provide them with a nearly foolproof escape route. It would also
be a great place to dispose of a body.

"Will do," Bernard said.

"But you have another problem coming your way," Najjir said. "The
man she was with hijacked a Mercedes cab and he's right behind you. He's
armed with a room broom."

"Stand by," Bernard said.

Najjir figured that they were about ten minutes behind the van. But he
had no intention of getting into the middle of a shooting situation between
his extraction team and the American couple.

"I'm making a right."

Najjir waited. Bernard—which was an operational name—was one of
the better German contractors he'd worked with. From what had been
Berlin's east zone, but trained by Iran's Republican Guard, he'd gone

freelance about eight years ago. He was an extremely experienced forty and had contacts with practically everybody in the business.

"I have him."

"Use the woman to lure him into the church, and then kill him as quickly as you can. You can get what information we need from the woman before you kill her, and then get out of there."

"Are you joining us?"

"No need," Najjir said. "When you're clear, make contact through the usual channels."

"Will there be another op?" Bernard asked.

"Yes," Najjir said, and he switched off.

"You don't think their being there was a coincidence?" Miriam asked.

"I don't believe in such things."

"Neither do I."

The van turned right onto a narrow side street and McGarvey tucked in right behind them, closing the gap to less than ten feet.

They were in Les Halles, one of the most diverse arrondissements of Paris, with its neighborhoods of Turkish and Kurdish butchers and bakers, Pakistani and Indian restaurants, African and Alsatian businesses selling everything from wigs to sauerkraut, and whores on nearly every street corner. Traffic was heavy, but not many people were on foot right here at this moment.

Someone stuck a pistol out of the passenger side window and fired four shots in quick succession, starring the windshield inches from Mac's head.

He slammed the taxi hard to the right and fired the room broom with his left hand at the van's front passenger door. He was handicapped because he couldn't fire at the rear of the vehicle for fear of hitting Pete.

The van jogged hard to the right, sideswiping two parked cars.

Someone opened the sliding door and rapid-fired five shots from a pistol before ducking back.

McGarvey jammed the gas pedal to the floor and the taxi leaped forward. He hit the van's bumper on the left side and the driver lost control for a moment, swinging even harder right, skidding and nearly rolling, until it clipped the front end of a tourist bus coming on a green light through the intersection with the rue de Turbigo.

The bus slowed but kept coming. Even so, the van managed to get around the front as Mac slammed on the brakes, skidding hard to the left and slamming into the side of the double-decker, which finally stopped.

He backed up, jammed the gearshift into Drive, and floored the pedal again, but when he got around the bus the van was gone.

People at a sidewalk café halfway down the next block had gotten up, and they backed away as McGarvey passed. Two of them were on cell phones.

It wouldn't be long before the cops showed up, but the guys who'd snatched Pete were professionals. The local police wouldn't stand a chance against them.

Back on the rue Saint-Denis, McGarvey was in time to see the van pull in behind an ancient church with twin towers and stop. Only the battered rear of the vehicle was visible.

The street was narrow here and filled with pedestrians. Shops of all sorts lined both sides of the rue, along with sidewalk cafés, some of them beneath overhangs or broad awnings.

McGarvey pulled up a half block from the church and left the taxi in one of the few open spots. Recharging the compact submachine gun with a fresh magazine, he concealed the weapon beneath his jacket and headed on foot to the church.

Many of the women on the street wore scarves covering their hair, and most of the pedestrians were dark complected, a lot of the men with beards. The few Western tourists here and there stood out for their obvious differences, mostly in dress and skin tone.

No one this far down the block seemed to have noticed the battered van or the beat-up taxi or McGarvey walking up the street. Either that or they were not paying attention on purpose. Sometimes it was for the best to keep your nose out of other people's business and go about your own.

ELEVEN

The bottom of Pete's feet were cut up by glass that had littered the pavement beneath the tower, but she hadn't felt it until she was hustled inside the church. It was a cocked-up mess, and it was her fault for blindly stumbling into it. She'd been trained to treat situational awareness as the number one priority.

"It's not only your six you need to watch, but you damned well better know every other point of the compass, along with up and down, for as far as you can see," one of the tactical instructors at Camp Peary, the CIA's training facility, informally called the Farm, had lectured. "In an op, consider yourself inside a bubble that's filled with possible threats to your mission as well as your personal well-being."

"Heads up in case someone is taking a bead on your ass," one of the recruits had quipped.

"Something like that."

It was Mac on her six, otherwise the van driver would not have taken such evasive actions. It was up to her to help him help her, because she sure as hell wasn't going to end up on a slab in Paris's morgue—the Institut médico-légal.

Inside the église it was dark, the only light coming from the stained glass windows lining either side of the nave. To Pete it smelled only faintly of a church—wood polish, flowers around the altar, maybe incense—her nose was still filled with the acrid odor of the explosion, along with the sick smells of the cop's blood and body fluids.

The driver of the van, tall, dark, with cruel eyes and an old scar that disfigured his lower lip, was apparently the leader. He said something to his men in heavily accented Russian, and two of them stayed behind, flanking the doors, as he and the other four hurried up the aisle on the right side.

Ducking around behind the altar, one of them threw back the iron latch and opened the short but broad wooden door. The dank odors of what she took to be a sewer rose up from the darkness down a set of narrow stairs.

Mac was coming after her, and the two left behind had concealed themselves in the one of the pews a few rows from the entrance, waiting in ambush. If he appeared in the doorway, they wouldn't be able to miss.

One of the men prodded her inside, but she sidestepped him and shouldered her way past two others, back out to the side of the altar.

"Two men waiting on the left," she screeched.

One of the operators grabbed her arm and yanked her off balance, forcing her back to the open door. The leader was already a couple of stairs down, and he turned back, aiming his pistol at her.

But she pulled away again. "A door behind the altar!"

One of the men at her side smashed the butt of his pistol into the side of her head, just above her ear, and she fuzzed out, her legs buckling.

She was bodily dragged through the door and down the stairs.

Moments, or perhaps minutes, later, she heard the door slam.

A waste of resources, it came to her. *Leaving two men behind.*

The double doors to the church had been left partially open, probably as an invitation for him to come inside. But Mac had heard everything that Pete had shouted.

The narrow plaza around the front and sides of the church was empty. Parisians had become accustomed to acts of terrorism in the past few years, and at the first sign of trouble they scattered. A battered van and taxi, plus men dragging a woman into the church and another carrying a submachine gun, were more than enough.

"Hang on," Mac shouted, and he slammed the left door open with his foot and stepped aside.

A half dozen rapid-fire shots each from two pistols smacked into the door and door frame.

McGarvey waited for the lull, then thrust the H&K room broom around the corner and emptied the magazine.

Tossing the weapon aside, he ducked into the church, below the level of the solid wood seat backs angled to the right.

He caught the brief impression of one man sprawled backwards in a pew a few rows away and a second fumbling to reload his pistol.

Leaping up, he jumped over the seat back as if he were a high hurdler, and as the man was bringing up his pistol, Mac hit him high on the torso, shoving him backwards with such force that his spine broke with an audible *pop*.

Mac recovered his balance, snatched the pistol from where the dying man had dropped it, and raced toward the altar and the door behind it. The gun was a heavy-duty Glock 20 Gen 4 that fired 10mm rounds from a fifteen-round magazine, which the shooter had just reloaded.

McGarvey eased the door open a few inches and listened.

Someone was on the stairs below, but at least two levels down.

"Your friends are dead," McGarvey said.

Someone whispered something and Mac eased back, just out of the line of direct fire.

"The woman is my wife. Send her back up and we'll call it even. We'll leave and won't interfere with your escape."

No one answered, but the movement below had stopped.

"If you harm her, I promise that I will find you and kill you."

"Who are you?" a man asked. His accent sounded German to McGarvey.

"I used to be a US Navy SEAL close quarters combat instructor. I retired several years ago, but believe me, I haven't lost my edge. Send her up."

The darkness below was silent.

"We know about the couple in the tower restaurant. And we know about the bombers—all of them dead now. And of course the tower still stands. At this point you have nothing to gain by harming my wife, and only the possibility that I might get lucky and kill more of you."

In the very dim light coming from several low-wattage bulbs spaced at long intervals down the long stone tunnel, the four operators on the recovery team were all but lost in the shadows as they pointed their weapons toward the stairs.

The woman was still dazed, but she was already coming around. She was a tough bitch, but what bothered Bernard the most was the confidence in her voice and in the voice of her husband or partner or whoever he was.

They were professionals, but he didn't think the man was a retired SEAL instructor. The *pizda* was more than that.

At the very least the American was a fucking liar. And he was going to die down here this afternoon.

Pete became aware that she was in a small room with stone walls. An open door led out to the narrow, very dimly lit corridor.

She was on her tiptoes, her wrists bound together by a strap of some sort, tied to a pipe or perhaps an electrical conduit on the low ceiling.

Her breast still ached. She was sick at her stomach, her ears rang, and her vision was blurry from the blow she'd taken to the side of her head. Her mouth was dry and her tongue felt thick.

"All in all, not a good day," she muttered.

"What was that, my dear?" the man she took to be the lead operator asked from a dark corner. "A little louder, please, so that your friend can hear."

"You and your people are so fucked," she said.

TWELVE

□

Bernard walked farther along the tunnel and around the corner that led, ten meters away, to a second set of stairs down. His cell phone showed only one bar but his call to his control officer went through.

"We're in the first basement of the église. The woman is secure, but two of my people may be dead, and the man is here. He says that he's the woman's husband."

"Who are they?" Najjir demanded. "American FBI?"

"He claims to be a retired SEAL combat instructor."

"Yes?"

"He may be lying. But the situation is fluid. I suggest we kill the woman and get out of here."

"We're less than a block from your position. What are the chances that you can take the man alive?"

"Is he that important?"

"Possibly not, but I want to make sure," Najjir said.

"What about the woman?"

"I don't care about her."

"Then our chances are fair," Bernard said. It would be a relief to finally shut her up. "What about the conditions topsides?"

"No police yet. All their assets are at or en route to the tower."

"As you wish," Bernard said, and he broke the connection and pocketed the phone as he walked back around the corner.

He motioned for two of his people to take up positions on either side of the stairs. If it came to a gun battle, they would have the advantage of catching the bastard in a cross fire.

"What do I call you?" he asked, raising his voice.

"Your worst nightmare," McGarvey said. "Send her up to me and we'll leave."

"Fuck you," Bernard said. He went back into the room where the woman was hanging by her wrists from a water pipe in the ceiling and slammed his fist into her injured breast.

She bit off a scream and looked into his eyes. "How about untying me and let's try that on an even footing?"

Bernard raised his fist to hit her again.

"Fucking coward," she whispered.

He grabbed her throat with his left hand and squeezed, constricting her carotid arteries.

McGarvey stepped through the doorway and paused. Only a dim light showed from below, and the smells were definitely from the sewer. Their escape route.

It was a trap, of course. It was possible they'd taken Pete away, leaving behind one or two men, almost certainly at the base of the stairs, in the shadows, if there was room to conceal themselves.

He started down the stairs, making as little noise as possible.

Something moved directly below him and he stopped.

It was quiet again.

He looked back over his shoulder, realizing that he was outlined by the light coming from the altar door. He went back up, slammed the door shut, and then raced down the stairs, firing two shots at the ceiling near the bottom as a distraction.

A man popped up on the left and McGarvey fired one shot, hitting him in the face, and he turned as a second man rose up out of the darkness less than three feet away on the right.

McGarvey stepped directly toward the shooter, batting his gun hand away, and fired three shots in rapid succession into the man's chest.

Even before the bastard's body had hit the floor, McGarvey was off the stairs and down the tunnel in four quick steps, pulling up short at the doorway, just out of sight of anyone inside, flattening himself against the brick wall.

Bernard released his grip on the woman's throat. Her head lolled to the right and her eyes fluttered. She had lost consciousness, but he'd not held on long enough to kill her or cause her any brain damage because of the lack of oxygen.

But she was mercifully quiet for the moment.

He had to assume that his two operators at the base of the stairs were dead. It left only the last two of his crew, stationed now on either side of the doorway.

Bernard slapped Pete on the cheek, gently, only to rouse her.

Her head came up and she whimpered. "Kirk."

Bernard placed the muzzle of his Glock to the side of her head.

She moaned again, this time more loudly as she started to come fully awake.

"Won't you join us, sir?" Bernard said, his tone reasonable. He smiled.

The man the woman had just called Kirk came around the corner of the door frame, moving low and fast, a Glock pistol in his hand.

Bernard's remaining two operators were right there on either side of the man. "Drop your gun and your woman may survive the day," he said.

The man pulled up short.

He was a professional, that much was certain. But he wasn't a young man, and he favored his right leg.

"I'm sorry," Pete said.

The man was clearly evaluating his chances, but he finally bent down and laid the pistol on the stone floor, then straightened up.

"Your call, but we have people who know the situation," he said. "You might consider your position before you do something foolish."

"I'm listening," Bernard said, but only because it amused him. His control officer would be here shortly, and the responsibility would shift to him, though it was his inclination to kill both the man and the woman and get on with their plan of escape.

"My wife and I are contractors working for the Central Intelligence Agency."

It wasn't exactly what Bernard had expected, but he wasn't terribly surprised.

"Your attack on the Eiffel Tower failed, which might be your salvation, providing you and your operators put down your weapons and release my partner before the French police arrive. I don't think they'll be so understanding."

"What are you proposing?"

"A trade."

"For what?"

"Your counterintelligence value," Mac said.

Bernard almost laughed. "I'm not a terrorist. I had nothing to do with the attack."

"Bullshit," the man said. "Or didn't they teach you that word at School One in Moscow? Or was it with the ministry's spy school outside Tehran? We hear that a lot of disaffected operators from East Germany—where I'm guessing you came from—end up across that southern border." The Ministry of Intelligence—the MOIS—was Iran's elite secret intelligence service.

Bernard was shaken, but he didn't show it. "Actually I think that your counterintelligence value might be of more importance to my people than the other way 'round."

The man shrugged. "Have you ever been to New York City?" he asked.

The question was meaningless at the moment, and Bernard shrugged.

"Washington? Boston? Philadelphia, Chicago, Denver, Los Angeles?"

Bernard knew where the bastard was going. "Spare me . . ."

"You people don't have a fucking clue."

Bernard nodded and the two men flanking the American closed in.

THIRTEEN

□

Bernard raised his free hand and his two operators held up.

"No need for that," he said. "If the gentleman persists, his wife will die first and then I'll shoot him."

Pete whipped her head backwards, away from the muzzle of the terrorist's pistol.

McGarvey grabbed the man on his left by the gun hand, spun him around as a shield, the pistol pointed directly at the one to the right, and yanked off three shots center mass.

Bernard grabbed Pete by the hair and jammed the muzzle of his gun against the side of her head, above her ear. "I'm not going to fuck with you any longer. Step away or I'll pull the trigger."

"No you won't," McGarvey said. He twisted the man's gun hand inward, snatched the weapon from his hand, and yanked off two shots, both of them hitting the operator in the left side.

The man collapsed on the floor.

McGarvey raised the Glock and pointed it directly at the man holding the gun to Pete's head. "Same deal. Lower the gun and step away from my wife and I promise I'll keep you out of the hands of the French police."

Bernard's finger tightened on the trigger. "Then what? You'll shoot me?"

"We'll take you to the American embassy and turn you over to the chief of station."

"You mean Mr. Pickett? Harley Pickett? I think the CIA hired the wrong man to head up operations, and everyone knows it."

"You'll be safe with him until we can decide what to do with you. There are some questions about Russian policy we'd like answered."

"I'm not Russian."

"Like what happened to the nuke that has turned up missing. Maybe the ZBV3? Light enough for a couple of tough guys to handle." It was the Russian designation for a tactical nuclear weapon fitted to a self-propelled artillery shell. Ordnance security was still a big problem for the Russians.

"I have no idea what you're talking about," Bernard said. "But actually you're in no position at the moment to dictate terms."

"Behind you," Pete cried.

Something very hard, like the butt of a rifle, slammed into the back of McGarvey's head, and he went down to his knees, dazed but not out.

The pistol was taken out of his hands, and he fumbled to the left to reach the gun he'd laid on the floor, but a woman was right there, and she shoved it aside with her foot.

"How did you manage all this, you idiot?" Miriam demanded. She took off her shoes and removed her panty hose and gave them to Najjir as he holstered his gun.

"Help me, before he comes around," he ordered.

He and Bernard manhandled McGarvey over onto his back, secured his wrists over his head with the waist of the panty hose, and dragged him across the small room. With Miriam's help they managed to hoist him so that his feet were just off the floor, and she tied the stocking legs to a three-inch sewer drain line that came out of the wall near the ceiling.

"He claims they work for the CIA," Bernard said. "But it was you who called me for extraction. He must have been on your tail."

"Since the Jules Verne in the Eiffel Tower," Pete said. "They bungled it. Fucking amateurs."

Najjir walked over to the woman, took her jaw in his hand, and forced her to face him. "Are you CIA spies after all?" he asked, his tone pleasant.

"Actually I work for J. C. Penney and my hubby works for Sears. Makes

for some interesting dinner conversations with our eleven kids who pre-
fer to shop online. But you know how it is."

"How did you find out?"

"We checked the reservations list. Your names were on our hit parade."

"Is that how you knew about the missing nuclear weapon?" Miriam
asked. She eased Bernard aside and gently ran the fingernails of her right
hand down Pete's face, to her neck and then to her battered breast.

"Dyke," Pete said.

Miriam smiled. "You can't imagine the half of it, sweetheart. But let's
get back to the weapon."

"I don't know what you're talking about."

"But your friend does. So I'm betting you do too."

"The offer still stands. We'll get you to our embassy and you'll be safe."

"Safe, like in Guantanamo?"

"Beats hell of what'll happen if the DGSE catches up with you," Pete
said. "After what you guys tried to do at the tower, those guys are seriously pissed off."

Miriam turned away. "They can be made to talk, of course. Everyone
does at some point. But they're good, so it'd take more time than we have.
And I sure as hell don't want to drag them along with us."

"What about the nuclear weapon?" Najjir asked. "Is it true?"

"There've been rumors."

Najjir picked up one of the pistols near the door. He had the almost
overwhelming urge to kill Miriam and the extraction team leader and make
his way to the safe house at Saint-Ouen and from there disappear.

The money was important, of course, as were any future assignments,
but his life was more important. This situation had been well planned,
but it had fallen apart because of the CIA. And now he was being told about
a Russian nuclear weapon that might have gone missing.

He'd been lied to by his control officer outside Riyadh. Directly about
Miriam. And by omission about the weapon, if it was somehow relevant.

"Whatever you want us to do will have to be done soon," Bernard said.
"We made quite an entrance getting here with that son of a bitch on our
tail. The cops can't be too far behind."

Bernard and his team had been assigned to the operation in case things started to go south, which they had. And Najjir was grateful for the man's help. But he'd lost six of his supposedly well-trained operatives who knew the business—to one man. The only person he'd managed to control was the woman, whose smart mouth had to be an irritation to anyone.

"It's being treated as an accident with the tourist bus. The metro flics are on it."

"How can you be sure?" Bernard demanded. At six two, he towered over Najjir, and he was seriously angry at the moment.

"Look at this," Miriam said. "You let a cripple get the better of you and six of your operators." She had raised McGarvey's left pants leg. He was wearing a prosthetic leg from just below the knee.

Najjir was suddenly not so sure of himself and the operation. "I know this man," he said. "Unless I'm very much mistaken, his name is Kirk McGarvey. He was the director of the CIA a few years ago."

It was clear that Bernard had heard the name and knew the reputation. "Kill him and the woman now, and let's get the hell out of here while we can."

McGarvey's head lolled forward, his breath shallow.

Najjir stared at him for a longish moment.

"I agree," Miriam said. "I don't want this bastard coming after us. And he will."

"We'll have to answer for our failure."

"Your failure," Bernard said.

"You can use him as a bargaining chip," Pete said.

"Bargain for what and with whom?" Bernard asked.

"With our government, for your lives, you fucking imbecile," Pete said.

FOURTEEN

▢

Najjir considered his options. The Eiffel Tower had not come down, and he would be going back to face his control officer as a failure. Unless he brought something of value.

McGarvey was still mostly out of it, possibly with a concussion from the blow to the back of his head with the stock of the H&K. It was possible he would never recover, and if he did he would become a formidable piece of baggage to get out of France.

The woman, on the other hand, would be relatively easy to control, though she had a smart mouth. The urge to kill them both here and now was strong.

"Get the woman down, I'm taking her with us," he told Bernard.

"What the hell are you talking about?" Miriam asked.

"You're going back home, but I'm taking her with me."

"How, for bleeding sake? The first flic you come across she'll start screaming her bloody head off."

"I don't think so."

"She's right," Bernard said.

Najjir came close to the woman. "You'll promise to behave, won't you, sweetheart."

"Take it to the bank," Pete said, grinning.

Najjir brushed the tips of his fingers across her lips. "You will, in exchange for Mr. McGarvey's life."

"You're nuts," Miriam said. "He'll come after us."

"He'll come after me, so you have nothing to worry about. But by the time someone comes down here and finds him, and by the time he explains to the cops all the dead bodies upstairs and down here—his fingerprints are all over the murder weapons—the three of us will be long gone."

"He'll move heaven and earth to find the woman."

"I think he will," Najjir said. "He might even be willing to make a pact with the devil to save her. Might be interesting."

"When he catches up with us he'll kill you," Pete said, but it was obvious in her eyes and the tightness in her lips and how she spoke that she was more than a little concerned.

"He'll try," Najjir said. "In the meantime, McGarvey's life for your cooperation."

Pete didn't hesitate. "If you keep your word, I'll keep mine, because both of us know that once he gets out of here he will move heaven and earth to find me."

"He sure as hell will," Miriam said.

"And we'll take him alive on the ground of my choosing," Najjir said. "Cut her down."

Bernard and Miriam got her down from where her wrists had been tied to the electrical conduit and she stumbled toward McGarvey, but Bernard stopped her.

"Your cooperation, my dear," Najjir said. "Your complete cooperation."

Pete looked up at McGarvey's face, but he was still out of it. She turned back and nodded. "It's the worst mistake of your life," she said.

"Once we get you to our safe house, we'll get you something decent to wear," Najjir said. "Take her up to the car. I'll be right behind you," he told Miriam.

"We go together, including this asshole," Pete said, nodding at Bernard.

"No more bargaining," Najjir said. "Get her out of here."

"Goddamnit," Pete said.

Miriam took her arm. "You can take a nice hot bath when we get there, if you behave yourself."

"Christ," Pete said, but then she went with the woman.

"Right behind you," Najjir said, and as soon as they were out of earshot, he turned to Bernard. "Give us five minutes to get clear, then kill the bastard and get the hell out of here."

"You're going to the safe house?" Bernard asked.

"We need the get the bitch ready to travel."

"What about Miriam? She knows too much."

"Yes, she does. But she won't be a problem much longer."

As soon as Najjir was gone, his footfalls lost at the end of the tunnel, McGarvey opened his eyes.

Bernard, a Glock in hand, stepped back a pace, startled.

"What's it worth to you?" McGarvey asked. His ears were ringing, his vision was slightly blurred in his left eye, and he had a mother of all headaches.

Bernard pointed the gun at McGarvey's head. "For me not to kill you?" he asked.

"Whoever ordered the downing of the tower has to be pissed off right about now. Those kinds of people usually don't take kindly to failure."

"Shut the fuck up."

"Unless you go deep they'll find you, and once they do you'll end up dead."

"I think bagging a former CIA boss might be worth a few points."

"You guys fucked up today."

"Our job was extraction, in case something went wrong."

"Which it did."

"Because of you."

McGarvey laughed. "He had to blame someone. With me dead, you'll be next. Guys like that always have a way out. You oughta know that."

"Shut the fuck up," Bernard said, and his aim steadied on McGarvey's head.

"One million dollars."

"What?"

"If you have a cell phone I can transfer the money into any account you want."

Bernard's eyes narrowed. "So you can trace me. Yeah, right."

"It's a Chase account. I can give you an account number that you can use at any Chase bank in the world. Just walk in, give them the number, and walk out with one million US—or any currency you'd like—in cash."

Bernard hesitated.

McGarvey lowered his voice. "I can transfer it to a De Beers outlet and you can pick up a million US in diamonds."

"Someone would be waiting for me to show up."

McGarvey softened his voice even more. "Any Chase or De Beers office in the world."

"What?" Bernard asked, and he stepped closer so that he could hear.

McGarvey suddenly reared up, kicked the pistol away, and wrapped his legs around the man's neck. Before Bernard could recover, Mac twisted sharply to the left, using his body weight as a powerful lever to break the man's neck.

Bernard collapsed, his eyes open, his face turning red.

McGarvey swung around so that he faced the wall and, raising both feet above his shoulders, pressed with every pound of his body mass and every ounce of his strength against the restraints around his wrists.

The tough fabric of the panty hose did not give, but the knots the woman had used to tie the legs around the sewer piped slipped loose, and McGarvey fell back, his head bouncing hard on the stone floor.

He saw stars again, and fuzzed out for a moment or two.

Rolling over, he got to his hands and knees and remained in that position for another moment or two before his head cleared and he was able to remove the panty hose tied around his wrists.

He snatched the Glock from the dying man's hands, got to his feet, leaped out into the tunnel, and raced up the stairs to the nave.

The church was quiet, but sirens outside were very close.

The son of a bitch had Pete, which was the dumbest thing anyone had ever done. The bastard was a dead man walking.

Barely able to contain his rage, McGarvey raced up the aisle and burst out the main doors into the church's courtyard, into the nearly blinding sunlight.

A dozen French SWAT team cops were in positions behind two armored vehicles and a couple of squad cars.

"*Jetez vos arme,*" a cop ordered by bullhorn. "*Jetez vos arme, ou on fair feu.*" Drop *your weapon or you will be shot.*

FIFTEEN

□

Pete sat in the backseat of the Peugeot with Miriam while Najjir headed up the rue de Clichy, driving with the general flow of traffic, which in Paris always seemed to be at a manic pace.

The man was sharp, she thought. He did not stick out, even though cops seemed to be everywhere, on foot at street corners, speaking into lapel mikes, some in patrol cars or SWAT vans, sirens blaring as they raced past, and in helicopters coming in from the north, possibly from the airfield at Le Bourget.

Paris was astir as if someone had poked a hornet's nest, and there wasn't a damned thing she could do now to be of any help to Mac.

"You're goddamned lucky, you know," Miriam said.

Pete looked at her. "Funny, but I was just thinking the same thing about you," she said.

The woman was well put together, slender with a pleasant oval face and nice eyes. But her English seemed odd; she'd turned her cockney accent on and off, like an actress. And some of her gestures, especially the way she positioned her lips just before she spoke, as if she was about to say lines that she had memorized. And the set of her chin, the tilt of her head. None of it rang true for Pete. But she couldn't put her finger on why she was bothered.

"If it was up to me I would have killed both of you," Miriam said.

"I know the feeling, because if the tables were reversed—which they will be sooner or later—I'd kill both of you in a heartbeat."

They passed a cemetery off to the right, and Najjir called someone on his cell phone. Apparently no one answered, and he hung up.

Pete caught Najjir looking at her in the rearview mirror. It struck her that he had received bad news.

"You guys screwed up at the tower," she said. "But what I can't figure out is why the hell you took the chance of being right there in the middle of it. You don't strike me as the martyr types."

Neither of them responded.

"Unless you weren't sure that your idiots would actually go through with it. Maybe at the last minute they'd figure out that dying wasn't such a hot idea after all."

Najjir was watching the road, but Miriam was looking at her.

"Let me take a wild guess. You're starting to have a little trouble recruiting soldiers willing to die for Allah. That it?"

"Shut the fuck up, would you?" Miriam said. "Or maybe I'll help you."

Pete rested her hands on her bare knees. "Anytime, sweetheart," she said. She felt as if she had been hit by a battering ram, and it took an effort to nod her head and smile. "Take your best shot."

"Stand down. I need her intact," Najjir said.

"Good idea," Pete said. "Otherwise she might have a hard time getting back to London. Or, wherever."

"He meant you," Miriam said.

"Are you sure about that?"

Something passed in Miriam's eyes, only for a moment, but long enough for Pete to catch it. Her main job with the Company, before she and Mac had begun working as a team, had been as an interrogator. And she had been very good at it, because of a natural ability to read people by their gestures. It had been more about their silences than their confessions. During waterboarding, anyone would say just about anything that their interrogator wanted to hear. But it was when the prisoner wasn't saying a word that their inner secrets became most evident.

Miriam was troubled, and the way the woman had looked at the back of Najjir's head spoke volumes.

. . .

They crossed under the busy Boulevard Périphérique into an area of Paris that Pete knew absolutely nothing about, except that the place was even busier than it had been around the Eiffel Tower. They passed through what looked like a rat warren of shops and stalls, vendors selling anything and everything. A lot of the merchandise looked used to Pete, and she figured out they were in the middle of a gigantic flea market.

The entire place was filled with shoppers apparently unaware yet of what had happened at the Eiffel Tower, which struck her as odd, considering the instant news on smartphones.

Najjir turned down a narrow side street, and a block later pulled half up on the narrow sidewalk in front of a three-story apartment building and shut off the engine.

There were no shops back here, not even a sidewalk café, and the street was deserted of people and vehicles in either direction.

Otherworldly, the unbidden thought came to Pete. Bad things happened in places like this.

Najjir got out, opened the rear door on Pete's side, and took her arm to help her out.

She jerked her arm away, got out of the car on her own. and looked up at the roofline, as Mac had taught her to do first off in hostile territory. Look for a shooter on the roof, the glint of a sniper rifle scope.

"Home sweet home?" she said.

"Until tonight," Najjir answered pleasantly.

Miriam had gotten out on the other side, and she went across and unlocked the door to the tiny ground-floor landing. Six mailboxes were set into the wall next to the stairs—two apartments for each of the three floors. There was no elevator, and the building smelled very old, the paint peeling and the stamped tiles of the tin ceiling faded and water damaged in numerous spots.

"Peachy," Pete said.

Miriam prodded her up the stairs to the third floor, where she unlocked the door to the apartment at the rear and went in, Pete behind her and Najjir following.

The place was small. A tiny living room, a galley kitchen to the left, an open door to the single bedroom at the rear, the bathroom to the right. It was furnished minimally, with nothing on the walls or even a television.

"Lay out something for her to wear," Najjir told Miriam, who stood across the tiny room, her right hand in her jacket pocket.

"And?" she asked.

"Walk back to Les Puces, take a cab to the train station, and return to London."

"What about the woman?"

"I'm taking her back."

"I meant later?" Miriam asked. "What's to become of her?"

"That depends entirely on Mr. McGarvey."

"We'll want a share of the product," she said, her accent, for a moment, Russian.

Pete suddenly realized what had bothered her about the woman. She was a Russian operative. Almost certainly working for the SVR. "I'd expect that, with all of your problems in Ukraine and Syria, and lately in Belarus and Lithuania, you guys might want to stand down for a bit," she said, but the woman ignored her.

"I'm sure that it can be arranged," Najjir said.

"Yes, arranged," Miriam said.

"Trying to fuck with a former DCI might be a bit out of your league," Pete said.

"We know all about your Mr. McGarvey, and we've been waiting for a long time to have a private little chat with him," Miriam said. "But I never thought that he'd fall into our laps so easily."

"Careful what you wish for; it might jump up and bite you on your ass."

Miriam laughed. "Weren't you taught at your Farm that attachments are the bane of every operative? It's universal, ducky. Look at what it's done for your boyfriend. Every skirt he's ever got close to—including his wife and daughter—has lost their lives because of him. Didn't you know that going in? Or is he such a fantastic lover that you simply didn't give a good goddamn?"

"I'll be there when he puts a bullet in your brain, podruga," Pete said, hiding as best she could the fact that she couldn't feel Mac's presence. She was no longer sure that he was out there somewhere, coming for her.

SIXTEEN

☐

McGarvey, seated at a metal table in a small room with what he took to be a one-way glass, looked up as the door opened and a young, attractive woman in khaki slacks, a white blouse, and a blue blazer came in and sat across from him. She'd brought several thick file folders marked "*Le Plus Secret*"—Most Secret—which she placed on the table.

It had been one hour since he'd been arrested outside the church. His wrists and ankles had been shackled, a black hood had been placed over his head, he'd been hustled into the back of a van and driven off with no sirens. The hood and shackles had been removed in this room fifteen minutes ago.

"I was with a woman, has she been found?" he asked.

"Not at this time," the woman said. "I am Lieutenant Dominique Carrel and I have several questions for you."

"You hold a civilian, not a military, rank, mademoiselle. Those are DGSE files, which means you know who I am."

"Yes, Mr. Director, I do. What were you and Ms. Boylan doing at the Tour Eiffel during the attack?"

"Having lunch, of course," McGarvey said. "What is being done to find her?"

"A witness saw her being taken from a van into the church by several men. But she has disappeared."

"They took her away, probably in a car. There may have been another witnesses."

"Not to this point."

McGarvey looked inward for a long moment or two. It was bad. This was not going to happen. Not again. He would find her at whatever the cost. Anyone in his way would go down. But an all-out search had to begin soon. If her kidnappers were given more than a few hours they could easily get out of the city, or completely disappear in some neighborhood somewhere.

"Have the Sûreté issue an all-points. I'll give you descriptions of the man and woman who took her."

"We found the bodies of the seven men who you killed in the church—six with a pistol and one in hand-to-hand combat—nothing else."

McGarvey rose from his chair, his movements nonthreatening, his temper carefully in check. "If you know who I am, then you know what I'm capable of. You have questions, I want answers. Which I'll find on my own, if need be."

"You're not advancing your case. Sit down."

"I'll find her myself if need be."

"It is impossible."

"I've walked out of the Swimming Pool before, I can do it again," McGarvey said. The headquarters of the Directorate-General for External Security—the French equivalent of the CIA—was located on the boulevard Mortier. Insiders called it the Swimming Pool because it was located next door to the Piscine des Tourelles, which was the home office of the French Swimming Federation.

Carrel reached inside her jacket and drew a big SIG Sauer pistol.

McGarvey leaned forward and snatched it out of her hand before she had a chance to bring it into a firing position.

She reared back. "*Merde.*"

McGarvey, never taking his eyes off the woman, ejected the magazine and thumbed out all the bullets, letting them fall as they would. He ejected the round from the firing chamber and then disassembled the pistol before laying the frame and pieces in front of her on the table.

"I'm not going to let you shoot me," he said. "But you're going to escort me out of the building now."

The door opened and Milun Alarie, a tall, patrician man in his early sixties, gray at the sides, his suit rumpled, his tie loose, came in. "You may leave us now, Dominique," he said.

"I'm sorry," she said, and she went out.

"Old times, Mac, hein," Alarie said.

He and McGarvey went back together a number of years. And although they'd never been close friends, there'd always been respect for each other's abilities and judgment. During his brief tenure as DCI, McGarvey had unofficially consulted with Alarie, who by then had become a fairly high-ranking officer in the DGSE, on a number of developing situations in Europe. And the exchange of information, much of it very sensitive, worked both ways. As of two years ago Alarie had taken charge of the DGSE's Strategic Directorate, which operated much like the CIA's Clandestine Services.

"We don't have a lot of room here, Milun, but you're exactly who I hoped would turn up," McGarvey said.

Alarie motioned for McGarvey to have a seat. "All of Paris is being thoroughly searched for Ms. Boylan. On that you will have to take my word. You running around won't solve a thing. So it will not be allowed."

"Let me call Otto Rencke. He might be able to give us a lead."

Alarie smiled. "He's threatened to crash our mainframe if he wasn't allowed to speak with you."

"I'll need my phone."

Alarie took McGarvey's phone out of his pocket and laid it on the table. "My people tell me that's its encrypted, so I would ask only that you put it on speaker mode."

McGarvey did it, and Otto answered on the first ring.

"Oh, wow, Mac. How are you?"

"A man and a woman who were seated near the kitchen at the Jules Verne were the control officers. They have Pete."

"Just a mo," Otto said.

"What's he doing?" Alarie asked.

"I expect that he's checking the restaurant's security system. Something your people or the Sûreté have most likely already done."

"Got 'em," Otto came back.

A video taken at an oblique angle, possibly just below the ceiling, in a corner, came up on McGarvey's phone. It showed the man and woman being seated at the table.

"That's them," McGarvey said, showing the screen to Alarie. "They both spoke with British accents, but she's Russian—I'd bet just about anything on it. And I have a hunch that he's Middle Eastern."

"Our old friends the Saudis up to no good again?" Otto asked.

"He could be a merc working for just about anybody."

"Narrows it down a bit, but it could take a few minutes, maybe longer. My darlings will have to work through a range of disguises, maybe even plastic surgery, depending on how serious these people are."

"Taking down the Eiffel Tower is a big deal for anyone," McGarvey said. "But what I don't understand is what the hell they were doing at ground zero?"

"Creating a diversion with their staged out-of-control tête-à-tête," Otto said. "Check the background out the windows."

Two of the terrorists in white coveralls momentarily appeared in the frame, and then they were out of sight.

"I'll get back to you," Otto said.

"Pete's out there somewhere," McGarvey said.

"I know. I'm sending this to the Frogs."

The connection ended.

"That's an offensive term," Alarie said, but there was no heart in his remark. "What now, my old friend? If I release you, where will you go?"

"Back to the church."

"There is nothing else to be found."

"We'll see."

SEVENTEEN

☐

Miriam was only one size larger and an inch taller than Pete, so the cream pantsuit she laid out on the bed looked as if it would fit reasonably well. She'd been waiting in the tiny bedroom when Pete got out of the shower.

"If you behave yourself you might live long enough for the bruises on your breast to fade," Miriam said.

"You get your jollies looking at naked women?" Pete said.

Miriam shrugged. "I hope they send me pictures of your trial for spying, then your execution. I'm told that the garotte can be painful, even more so than the nail you lost on your hand. That would pique my jollies"

Najjir came to the door. "Leave us now."

"She's a handful," Miriam said. "Sure you can handle her alone? I wouldn't mind coming along to help out."

"I think she'll cooperate."

"I wouldn't count on it," Pete said, standing in the bathroom's door- way. She tossed the towel aside and went to the clothes on the bed. There was only her dirty panties, but she put them on, and then the slacks. "The instant we hit the street I'm going to start screaming my head off."

"No," Najjir said.

He handed a strip of C-4 about the size of a cigarette stub, and a roll of white surgical tape, to Miriam. "Just under her left breast, I would think. And use plenty of tape so that she won't be able to rip it loose so easily."

Pete stepped back and held out a hand. "There's no fucking way."

Najjir just looked at her, a half-amused smile on his elegantly shaped mouth. "What is the old saying? Where there's life there's hope? Refuse

this and I will shoot you in the head and leave your body here for someone to find. Eventually word will get to your Mr. McGarvey and he'll move
heaven and earth—as you said—to find you. It might take a little longer
for he and I to come face-to-face, but it'll happen with or without your
cooperation."

Pete spread her arms. "I'll do as you want, because I want to be there
when the two of you do come face-to-face. I want to watch him rip your
heart out."

Miriam positioned the explosive putty just below Pete's left breast, se-
curely taped it in place, and stepped back.

Najjir raised a cell phone. "All it wants is the proper code."

"Comes to that, I'll make sure we're very close," Pete said. She put on
the blouse and buttoned it up.

Najjir moved aside and pocketed the phone. "Get back to London now.
I'll contact you when the next phase is to begin."

"There are bound to be witnesses, who might remember our faces,"
Miriam said.

"Do something with your hair, and maybe your complexion, I'll leave
that up to you," Najjir said.

"Plastic surgery?"

"I suspect there won't be enough time."

"How will you get out of here?"

"A car is coming to take us to Le Bourget. We'll be across the border
before you are."

"It'll be an interesting trip home."

"Just keep a low profile. No shopping sprees for the time being. You
know the drill. Anyway, you'll be rich enough to go home again, if that's
what you want."

Miriam laughed and took one last look at Pete before she got her bag
from the living room and left the apartment.

The bodies were being removed from inside the church when McGarvey
arrived with Dominique Carrel. Plainclothes police were canvasing the

neighborhood for witnesses. Two forensic teams were in the church gathering evidence—one team of four in the nave and the second team of three downstairs in the room where he and Pete had been held.

"You are being expelled from France later this afternoon," Alarie had told McGarvey. "A special flight leaves at five from Orly. You will be on it. But first I'll need your word that you will not harm Mademoiselle Carrel. Unless you give it to me you will be kept in a holding cell until it's time for your flight."

"I won't harm her," McGarvey had promised.

Alarie nodded. "She's waiting outside with a car."

On the way over, the woman had been nervous sitting beside him.

"Don't worry, I don't plan on taking your pistol and shooting you with it," he said.

She looked at him skeptically. "What do you hope to accomplish that our investigators can't?"

"Maybe nothing, but I need to take a look."

"As you wish."

"Ms. Boylan and I were engaged to be married. Getting her back is very important to me."

"I understand," Dominique said, her tone softening. "And I'll do whatever I can to help."

McGarvey and the DGSE officer stood just within the doors of the nave as the last of the bodies from downstairs was trundled out on a gurney. Photographers were putting away their equipment, and even the fingerprint and DNA techs were finished gathering evidence.

"Efficient," McGarvey said.

"They know their jobs," Dominique said. "There's nothing for you to find here that they haven't already recovered."

"You're probably right," McGarvey said. He went down the aisle and stopped at the open door behind the altar. He had no real idea what he was looking for, but he caught a hint of Pete's scent in the still air.

She was gone now, taken away, but she had been here. He'd seen her hung by the wrists, tied to an overhead pipe. She had been practically naked, but there'd been no real fear in her eyes. Just anger that she had been caught.

"There's nothing here, monsieur," Dominique said.

McGarvey held up a hand and then went down the stairs.

At the bottom, a pool of blood was on the floor off to the right and a long streak of blood was on the stone walls to the left.

Again he stopped to listen, to test the air for any other smells, to try to feel what else had happened here. The man had taken Pete somewhere. The smug bastard had been sure of himself. He'd think by now that McGarvey was dead and it was just him and Pete.

But for the life of him McGarvey couldn't understand why the man had taken the risk of trying to transport her somewhere. He should have killed both of them right here and made his break with the woman. It had been the only logical move.

But he hadn't.

McGarvey moved down the stone corridor to the room where he and Pete had been trussed up. Vulnerable. There hadn't been a damned thing either of them could have done to prevent the man and woman from the restaurant from killing them.

Inside the small, bare basement room, McGarvey stopped again. Pete's scent was still here, just on top of the odors of blood and death.

The web belt that had been used to tie her to the electric conduit, along with the panty hose McGarvey had been trussed with, were gone. Removed by the forensics people for evidence.

He stepped closer to the spot where Pete had been tied up, and he reached up and touched the stone block, damp with water seepage.

For a longish moment he missed the faint scratchings on the wall at what would have been at the level of Pete's hips.

He made out a portion of an S and then possibly part of an L or a T. Then something else.

On the floor below where her feet had been was a portion of a finger-nail, the color of Pete's polish.

And then he had it.

"Saint-Ouen," he told Dominique. "That's where they took her."

EIGHTEEN

☐

Najjir's cell phone chimed and he answered it. "Oui."

Miriam had left nearly a half hour ago, and during that time Pete had sat across from Najjir, who watched out the window.

He had punched a seven-digit code into the phone he kept in his jacket pocket and then gave her a smile. "As I said, all it wants is for the pound key and you will no longer have a beating heart."

"Charming," Pete had said, deeply frightened now for the first time. She had hastily scratched a few letters of the name of the Paris district on the stone wall before she was trussed up to the ceiling pipe. Najjir and Bernard had mentioned it only very briefly, but she'd caught its significance without changing the expression on her face.

If Mac had gotten free, and had spotted the markings, and then had somehow traced her here, it would have been like looking for the right needle in a stack of needles. But if he did somehow get here, she'd left him another message.

"Merci," Najjir said. "We'll be right down." He pocketed the phone.

"Is the driver also on your payroll?" Pete asked.

"No, so I'll have to insist that you behave yourself. If need be, I'll kill both of you and take a cab to the airport."

"And the aircrew? Strangers too?"

"Fortunately for me, no. So once we're aboard and in the air you can scream your bloody head off. In fact, I'll even remove your pacifier."

"Kind of you."

Najjir held out a hand. "Shall we go, my dear?"

Pete got up.

Najjir stepped aside for her. When she was at the door, he went back and moved the small coffee table away from the couch she'd been seated at. "Really quite clever of you," he said. He scuffed out the word *bourget* she'd painstakingly marked with her toe in the nap of the rug.

Her spirits sank and she considered flinging open the door and racing down to the street to scream for help. But she had no doubt she would not get that far.

"Did you leave another clue at the église?"

She didn't answer.

"Well, if you did, he either didn't see it or he's too stupid to know what it meant."

Pete managed to smile. "I guess you'll find out about it. In an up-close-and-personal way."

The car waiting on the street was a black Citroën DS 5, the windows deeply tinted. The driver, a pleasant-looking Frenchman in his late fifties or early sixties, dressed in a dark business suit, opened the rear door for them.

"Good afternoon, monsieur and mademoiselle."

"Good afternoon," Najjir said pleasantly. He handed Pete into the car and got in after her, slipping his right hand into his jacket pocket.

The driver got behind the wheel and they took off. "The airport is just a few minutes away, and your aircraft is standing by on the terminal three ramp at Signature's facility."

"You're from the FBO?" Najjir asked.

"Yes, sir. Your flight plan for Istanbul has been filed and cleared."

"Very well."

Pete's heart sank again. Istanbul was a city teeming with rat warrens of narrow streets and narrower back alleys. Unless Mac could somehow stop the plane before it took off, or have it met at Atatürk Airport, the chances of him finding her would be very slim.

But then it occurred to her that Najjir *wanted* Mac to find them. But not until he was settled somewhere of his own choosing. He was going to pick his battlefield—something he'd likely do with great care.

When he was set he would get word to Mac: "Here I am with your woman. Come and get her."

"Saint-Ouen is a very large place," Dominique said on the way up to the district. "And usually very busy this time of day at the Marché aux Puces."

She'd not called her boss, who'd probably instructed her to go along with whatever McGarvey wanted, provided he did get into another gun battle.

"So what do you want me to do, monsieur, drive around looking for something?"

McGarvey got Otto on the phone and put it on speaker so Dominique could listen. She might have some ideas. "Wherever they are in Saint-Ouen, it'll only be a staging area," he said. "They'll either have another car to get them out of Paris or they're booked on a train for somewhere to a private jet."

"C'mon, Mac," Otto said. "Along with several thousand other people leaving Paris this afternoon, or tonight, or first thing in the morning."

McGarvey wanted to lash out at someone or something. At himself. He felt so goddamned incompetent. The situation at the tower had been so blatantly obvious, and yet he'd rushed off, leaving Pete behind to handle the evacuation.

If he lost her it would be all over for him. It was as simple as that. He didn't think he would ever be able to look at himself in a mirror again.

"It'll be an apartment in a predominantly immigrant neighborhood."

"You're profiling," Dominique said half under her breath, but McGarvey heard it.

"You're goddamned right I am," he told her. "Either a short-term rental—starting a couple of months ago—or a place that hasn't been occupied by the original renters for that same period."

"I'm feeding it to my darlings."

"They split up, so it'll be the woman as a lone traveler—maybe London, considering her accent—plus the guy and Pete. Do you have an ID on either of them yet?"

"Still working on it, Mac. But listen—"

"I'm betting that the man is Middle Eastern, or raised somewhere in the region. Maybe Saudi Arabia, which was my first impression. So if he wants to get home with Pete in tow—and she'll be a major pain in the ass to him every step of the way—I'm betting that he won't try to get out of France by train. He'll take either a car or a plane. I'm pretty sure that if it's by air, it won't be commercial."

"From Saint-Ouen, Le Bourget would be the nearest. And that airport is completely noncommercial."

"Is the apartment worth a try?"

"Waste of time, and so will be the train stations," Otto said. He had the bone in his teeth now. "Unless the son of a bitch wants to hunker down, which I seriously doubt he does, it'll be by private jet. I'll get back to you."

When McGarvey hung up, Dominique was on her cell phone, asking someone for private jet flight plans filed from Le Bourget.

"I'm betting eastern routes," he said.

She glanced at him.

"La Tour Eiffel is French, not American," she told him.

Dominique's contact was back seconds before Otto. "Do you have a tail number?"

"C H three seven three," she repeated. "Swiss."

Otto came on. "It's a Gulfstream 650, seven-thousand-mile range."

"Atatürk, Istanbul," Dominique said.

"I heard that. But what the Frogs might not know yet is that the aircraft is registered to Awadi bin Abdulaziz, the Saudi minister of foreign finance and communications."

"It's rolling," Dominique said.

"Can you stop it?" McGarvey asked.

"Not without creating an international incident. No, sir."

NINETEEN

Dominique drove them over to the Signature Flight Support facility at Le Bourget and showed her government ID to the girl at the front desk, who telephoned for the general manager.

A short, beefy man without a suit coat, his tie loose, came from a back office. "Claude Renet," he introduced himself, examining Dominique's ID. "How may I be of service?"

"A Gulfstream with a Swiss registration left for Atatürk just a few minutes ago," Dominique said.

"Yes, that's true."

"I would like to see a crew, passenger, and luggage manifest."

Renet sneered. "Come back when you have a court order."

McGarvey grabbed a handful of the man's shirt front and bodily shoved him back against the counter. "I'm not here to fuck with you, monsieur," he said in French. "But unless you answer the lady's question I will hurt you very badly. Am I clear?"

"Who the hell are you? You're not French."

"Actually he's an American CIA officer who is being kicked out of France for murdering at least five men," Dominique said. "But he's not leaving until later this afternoon. If he happens to kill another one, he's still being kicked out."

"*Merde*," Renet said, but he nodded. "A man and a woman. No baggage or packages."

McGarvey let go. "Didn't you think that odd? Two people on their way to Turkey with no luggage?"

"My job is to run this FBO by serving the needs of our obviously upscale clientele, who do not take kindly to questions."

"What'd they look like?"

"The man was taller than you, dark features. The woman was much shorter, she had red hair, and it looked like she might have been in an accident."

"Names?" Dominique asked.

"The man identified himself as Giles Worley."

"The woman?"

"He didn't say."

"You didn't check their passports?" Dominique asked.

"Not my job. That'll be up to the Turkish customs authorities."

"Thank you," Dominique said.

"I'll file a complaint," Renet said.

"It is your right."

"Did they list Istanbul as their final destination?" McGarvey asked.

The girl behind the counter was studying her computer screen. "Oui," she said, looking up.

"Thanks for your help," McGarvey said, and he and Dominique started to leave, but he turned back. "I was a little rough, but I needed some answers. The woman with the red hair is very important to me."

"I'm still going to file a complaint," Renet said.

McGarvey nodded. "I would if I were you. Goddamn Americans."

"*Salopard*," the FBO manager said half under his breath.

"For your information, the people this man killed were terrorists trying to destroy la Tour Eiffel," Dominique said. "He and the woman, who is being kidnapped, were the ones who saved the tower for us. You might give that some thought."

"It's couple of thousand kilometers to Istanbul, so time is on our side," Dominique said on the way back to DGSE headquarters. "We can have authorities waiting for them when they land."

"And hold them?" McGarvey asked.

"Of course."

"Thanks for sticking up for me in there."

"But?"

"They might not stop at Istanbul. It's possible they'll be returning to Saudi Arabia. You heard who owns the airplane."

"We can have people meet them at King Khalid Airport."

"They won't be landing in Riyadh either. It'll be a private strip somewhere."

"One with a long enough runway to accommodate such a jet," Dominique said. "Narrows the list."

"Not enough," McGarvey said. "I have to go there."

"Once you return to Washington you will be free to go wherever you'd like, as long as it's not back to France."

"There's no time," McGarvey said. It was taking everything within his power to control himself, to stop from disabling the young woman, dumping her somewhere, and making his way back to Le Bourget to hijack a plane and crew.

It was crazy, of course, but he'd never felt so goddamned helpless, his back against the wall, just about all of his options gone, as he did right at this moment. The image of Pete, nearly naked, strung up like a farm animal ready for slaughter, would not leave his head.

As they passed under the Périphérique he phoned Otto again and brought him up to speed. "I have to get to Istanbul, and possibly Riyadh, ASAP. Have we got anything here in France or nearby that I can borrow?"

"Nothing. I've already checked. That includes Ramstein. But you're right about the Saudi connections. The guy is probably Karim Najjir. Used to work in special operations for the GIP before he was kicked out for excessive force. I'm still working on getting the whole story, but if the Saudis cut him loose it must have been bad."

"What's your confidence level?"

"Seventy-five percent, give or take. But if it's him, he's had a lot of plastic surgery," Otto said. "But listen, *kemo sabe*, the big deal with this guy—and it may end up being one of the reasons he was kicked out—is that he's been in bed with the SVR."

"The Russians?"

"Yeah, makes you think. Anyway, if it's our guy he sometimes travels under the British work name of Worley."

"Giles Worley," McGarvey said. "It's the name he used to charter the Gulfstream at Signature. What about the woman at the tower with him?"

"Nothing so far. She might have been just a one-off hire for the op. But I'm still working with the DGSE to come up with IDs on the bombers at the tower, and the guys you took down in the church."

"Assuming just for a minute that the Russians are involved, what would make them try such a stupid trick as bringing down the Eiffel Tower? The blowback would be strong enough to topple even Putin."

"If we find the proof, which I suspect we won't," Otto said. "And if we try to accuse them of having a hand in it, they and the Saudis will claim that it was a rogue operation."

McGarvey glanced over at Dominique, who was watching him out of the corner of her eye as she drove. In a distant way, at that moment, she reminded him of his daughter, Elizabeth. She and her husband had been CIA agents. They'd been killed in the line of duty, and their daughter, Audrey, was being raised by Otto and his wife, Louise.

He didn't know how much more he could take. But to make matters far worse, each time he tried to bring up his wife, Katy's, image—she'd been killed in a car bomb explosion meant for him—he couldn't do it. And even when looking at photographs of her he had a hard time recalling the good moments they'd had together. Sitting in the gazebo behind their house on Casey Key on Florida's south Gulf Coast. Sailing in the Bahamas. Concerts at the Kennedy Center and other places in Washington and New York. Katy loved ballet, but he liked symphonies, and some opera, especially Italian—Aida, Madame Butterfly, and Turandot. Ballet was too stylized for him, and those operas were too sad for her. But they had made the compromise, and it had been easy.

"I need to get out of here," he told Otto. "One way or the other."

"I'll take it upstairs right now," Otto said.

TWENTY

□

Otto phoned Alice Jenkins, who was Marty Bambridge's secretary, to ask for a meeting with the deputy director of Central Intelligence. Marty had always been a pompous ass, though there were times when he'd acted almost human, even when McGarvey's name came up. Alice, on the other hand, was an older woman—actually a grandmother of three—who was an experienced hand in the Company and had fond memories of working for Mac.

"He's been expecting your call," she said. "And he's in a mood."

"He knows, then?"

"He got a call from Lacoste an hour ago."

Claude Lacoste was the deputy director of the DGSE—the man to whom Marty had given his word that neither McGarvey nor Pete would enter France with sidearms.

"On my way."

"Have you talked to Mac?"

"Just got off the phone with him."

"Trouble?"

"Serious," Otto said.

Marty's office was on the seventh floor, adjacent to the director's suite, a small private conference room between them. This floor in the Original Headquarters Building was never bustling. It'd always seemed to Otto to be more like a church on any day but Sunday rather than the executive floor of America's primary intelligence service.

Alice passed him straight through with a smile for good luck. She was one of Otto's favorite people in the Company, because she was completely without guile. She was who she presented herself to be, nothing more and nothing less.

Bambridge, who'd always been an officious little man who never seemed to smile and who always seemed to be worried about something, looked up from behind his desk when Otto walked in.

"I hope that you're bringing good news and not another update on the body count."

"What'd Lacoste tell you?" Otto asked, sitting down. He was dressed in his usual tattered jeans and his CCCP sweatshirt with the sword-and-shield logo of the old KGB. He dressed that way at work, over his wife's objections, because he wanted to make an antiestablishment statement. Though in deference to Louise his hair was tied in a neat ponytail.

"Only that McGarvey and Ms. Boylan were right in the middle of a terrorist attempt on the Eiffel Tower. Both of them were armed and McGarvey's being sent back in a couple of hours."

"What did he tell you about Pete?"

"Nothing."

"She's been kidnapped, and there's a good chance that she's being taken to somewhere in Istanbul on the way to Saudi Arabia."

Marty said back. "I suppose that I shouldn't be surprised," he said. "Bring me up to date, please. I need to know where we're at before I take it to Gibson."

Edward Gibson, who'd retired as a Marine Corps four star, had been appointed by the new president as director of the CIA. In part it had been because the president wanted someone with a strong hand to run the agency, and hopefully to heal the rift that had occurred shortly before the president had taken office. The man was tough—inside the Company he was being called Ironsides—but he was fair. He wanted action and results but he was willing to listen to all sides of an issue. There wasn't an ounce of touchy-feely in the man. If you took something to him, you'd best have all your ducks in a row.

Otto quickly ran through everything that he'd learned from his darlings, and from Mac himself, including the probable identity of Karim Najjir, who almost certainly had ties with the Russians.

"Gibson certainly won't give much credence to a Saudi–Russian alliance."

"They've agreed on more than one occasion to limit oil production."

"Different matter completely," Marty said. "And you know damned well that no one in their right minds—not the Saudis and definitely not the Russians—would attack something like the Eiffel Tower."

"The Saudis almost certainly had something to do with our Nine Eleven, and just last year the downing of the pencil tower in New York."

"Altogether different."

"The Gulfstream taking Pete to Saudi Arabia is owned by Awadi bin Abdulaziz, the deputy minister of foreign finance and communications."

Marty tried to dismiss the fact with a wave.

"Mac wants to go after her."

"To Saudi Arabia?" Marty shouted, nearly coming out of his seat. "Are you out of your mind? Because I sure as hell am not going to march next door and try to tell the director that this is what the agency should do."

Otto held his silence. It was almost always for the best to allow Marty to calm down and accept the inevitable.

"The most I'll recommend is that the general hand this over to the president, who can call the Saudi ambassador. But not until we get solid confirmation that one of our officers is aboard that jet, that it belongs to the prince, and that Ms. Boylan isn't just off on a joyride."

Otto shook his head. "Marty, do you even hear yourself sometimes?"

"That's as far as I'm taking this business. McGarvey is coming home and when he gets here I'll personally debrief him."

"Good luck with that."

"What the fuck are you saying to me now?"

"Mac is going to ask Pete to marry him," Otto said. "Do you suppose he's going to get on a plane, fly back here, and answer your questions while the woman he loves has been kidnapped?"

"I'll have the French arrest him. They can escort him to the plane."

"Real problem is that the DGSE is looking for a little guidance from us. Mac killed, or at least caused the deaths of, at least eight men—three at the Eiffel Tower and another five in a church in Saint-Denis—after you gave your word that he and Pete would not be armed."

"You're goddamned right."

"But they're going to want to pin a medal on him for saving the Eiffel Tower. So you and the general are going to have to make a decision within the next hour, tops. Help Mac get to Istanbul and maybe Saudi Arabia or turn your back on him. And, Marty, even if the general doesn't understand who Mac is, you certainly know what the man is capable of."

"I'll have Tony send some housekeeping muscle from our embassy to make sure he gets on the plane."

Tony Blair, no relation to the former British PM, was the CIA's chief of Paris station. His title was listed as cultural attaché.

"You're not listening to me," Otto said. "Mac will get out of France on his own as quickly as possible, and nothing or no one on this earth will stop him. Unless you mean to have him assassinated."

"Good Lord, what do you take me for?"

Otto got up and went to the outer office.

Alice had evidently been listening, because she was on the phone. She looked up. "The director will see you now, Mr. Rencke."

Marty came to the door. "Stop this at once," he shouted.

Otto marched down the corridor and entered the DCI's outer office. His secretary, a man about Alice's age, smiled. "You may go right in, Mr. Rencke," he said.

Edward Gibson was a small, very compact, fit-looking man with short-cropped salt-and-pepper hair, the sidewalls showing bare scalp. He wore his dark gray business suits with the same precision he'd worn his marine uniforms.

"Mr. Director, we have a problem."

"I know what the problem is, so have a seat and let's figure out what we can do about it," the general said.

TWENTY-ONE

They'd been airborne for less than ten minutes, Najjir just removing the C-4 from Pete's chest, when Miriam came forward from the head.

"I didn't want to miss the excitement," she said. She sat down across from them.

Najjir was vexed, Pete was sure of it, but he didn't let it show. "You're supposed to be on your way back to London," he said, mildly.

"Cost me five hundred euros to bribe the asshole and his secretary to keep their mouths shut," Miriam said. She gave Pete a smile. "Well at least you won't be able to blow us all to kingdom come. Anyway, has he told you where he's taking us?"

"Istanbul," Pete said, buttoning her blouse.

"I'd have thought back to the training base in the desert. I guess he really wants to go mano a mano with your Mr. McGarvey. But if you ask me that's his second biggest mistake of the day."

"The first?" Pete asked.

"Not killing both of you immediately," Miriam said. "He had the chance but he blew it. Too bad." She smiled again.

"You should have done as you were told," Najjir said.

"Oh, shut the fuck up. You're going to need help when her boyfriend shows up. And by all accounts of his—adventures—it's exactly what he'll do. So how about fetching us girls some champers, so we can get caught up on our gossip."

They had only the flight crew, but no steward, so Najjir, the expression in his eyes completely neutral, went forward to the galley.

Suddenly the situation struck Pete as totally surreal, as if she was caught up in some insane drama where nothing any of the players said or did made any sense to her.

"So why do you suppose he didn't?" she asked.

"Kill you both?" Miriam asked.

"Yes."

Miriam considered it. "Ego, I suppose. He's trying to regain his chops— as you Americans say. He blew this op, so I thought that it would be in my best interest to tag along and help him regain his cred."

"If not by killing us, then how? You've got me because I made a stupid mistake. But you can't seriously believe you'll bag Mac. If you think so, then you guys are either dumber than you look or you've lost your fucking minds."

They heard the champagne cork coming out.

"You know enough about us to ask the next question, I suppose," Miriam said. "Why Istanbul and not home?"

"I think the royal family might take exception about him luring the former director of the CIA back to home sweet home. In the first place it'd tie your attack on the Eiffel Tower to them. That wouldn't set well in Washington, let alone in France. Saudi Arabia would become an outcast country—almost as bad as Iran—maybe worse."

"Then why Istanbul?"

"It's a big city," Pete said, but then she knew why. "He has friends there."

Najjir came back with the bottle of Dom Pérignon and three flutes. "Clever girl," he said.

"An army, actually," Miriam said, taking a glass from Najjir. "You would be amazed how much is for sale in Turkey—especially now. Every Muslim fanatic—and there is a share of them there—would more than love to kill a couple of Americans."

"Kill one, actually, but save the other," Najjir said.

. . .

Marty had joined them in the DCI's office, and Carlton Patterson, who was a longtime general counsel for the agency and close friend of McGarvey's, had arrived moments later.

"The French have ordered him out of the country," Marty explained, and he looked at his watch. "Should be on his way to de Gaulle by now."

"But as I understand the situation, he wants us to get him to Istanbul as quickly as possible," the general said. "We could get something to him before the Gulfstream touched down."

"If that's where they're going," Patterson said. He was in his late seventies, tall, dapper, always well dressed and soft spoken. No director in the past twenty years had thought to replace the man.

"They've filed for Atatürk," Otto said. "But Mac thinks that it's possible they'll head to someplace inside Saudi Arabia."

"If they stop to refuel in Turkey we could have our people there to meet them," Marty said.

"Won't work if they remain aboard," Patterson said.

"Anyway the Gulfstream has a seven-thousand-mile range—no need to refuel," Otto said. "No reason for them to actually land there, unless they have something else in mind."

"And that's the problem Mr. Rencke has brought to us to solve."

"You're saying that McGarvey may be wrong?" Patterson asked.

"It's a possibility that Najjir is using Pete as bait to lure Mac into a trap. Istanbul would be the perfect place for it. If the guy's got money—and we have to assume he does—he could hire a lot of guns."

"Given enough muscle, assassinating even someone like Mac would be fairly simple," Patterson said.

"They don't want to kill him," Otto said. "Apparently they found out who he is and it could be they want to take him alive."

"All the more reason to make sure he makes it back here," Marty said. "At least it would give us time to figure some course of action. And for the moment I'm suggesting that we take it to Poynter."

Richard Poynter was the secretary of state.

"You're suggesting a diplomatic move," Patterson said. "But if it's explained to the Turkish authorities that they have a hostage situation on their hands—assuming the aircraft lands in Istanbul—then the police would move in and almost certainly there would be casualties. Ms. Boylan could be caught in a cross fire."

The general was looking directly at Otto. "Do you think it's likely that Mr. McGarvey will allow himself to be flown home?"

"Not a chance in hell, Mr. Director. And you can take that to the bank."

"Assuming the aircraft lands at Istanbul, and assuming the passengers, including Ms. Boylan, get off and go into the city, and assuming that Mr. McGarvey actually makes it that far, and assuming that they capture him alive—what then? What do they want?"

"Why the dear boy's intelligence value, of course," Patterson said.

"He's been gone from this office for a long time; he can't be up to date," the general said.

"Trust me, he is," Marty said, glancing at Otto. "He knows at least as much about what's been happening in the Watch as we do."

The Watch was a five-person crew housed in a highly secure and very high-tech office manned 24/7, just down the corridor from the DCI's office. They monitored every single US intelligence resource, from which they produced a comprehensive morning report that outlined all current threats against US interests—in progress or developing—around the world. In the old days the DCI would personally brief the president, but these days the report went to the director of national intelligence, who in turn briefed the president.

"How?" the general said, steel all of a sudden in his voice.

"He has friends who still trust his judgment," Otto said.

"You?"

"Yes, sir."

"And me," Patterson said.

□

TWENTY-TWO

McGarvey figured he had only two choices left. Either disable Dominique and make a run for it before they got back to the DGSE, or try to talk himself out of being put on a plane back to Washington.

He chose the latter, simply because the young woman seated beside him in the car was an innocent. And even if he didn't hurt her too badly, her career would be over if she lost him.

They were passed through a rear entrance by armed guards behind bulletproof glass in a gatehouse. The extra bunker mentality was something new, and Mac said as much.

"A lot has happened in France over the past few years," Dominique said, tight-lipped. But she was clearly relieved that she had gotten her prisoner back inside the intelligence service compound.

Alarie met at them at a side door to the main headquarters building. "Did you find her?" he asked, as Mac and Dominique got out.

"She's on her way to Istanbul aboard a private jet that's owned by a Saudi prince," McGarvey said as they went inside. "But I think it's possible they'll change flight plans before they get there and go direct either to Riyadh or, more likely, to a private airstrip out in the desert somewhere."

"Yes, we received a complaint from the FBO's director at Le Bourget, who said he didn't give a damn if you saved the Tour Eiffel, you threatened his life."

"Yes, I did."

Alarie inclined his head. "Would you have killed him?"

"No," Dominique answered first. "There was no need."

"Merci," Alarie told her. "You may return to your regular duties now. Mr. McGarvey and I are going to have a little chat while his and Ms. Boylan's things are brought over from their hotel. Afterwards he and I will drive out to de Gaulle to meet his flight. First class, as is his custom."

"Yes, sir," Dominique said. She gave McGarvey a resigned look and left.

Alarie and McGarvey took an elevator up to the top floor, quiet, almost as if the place was deserted. But this was where the DGSE's top officials, including the director's offices, were located. It had almost the same feel as the seventh floor of the OHB at Langley.

"Your flight back to Washington is only the first small measure—of many—to thank you for what you did for France today. Inestimable damage could have been done to us besides the destruction of a national symbol and the hundreds, perhaps thousands, of casualties. If the tower had come down, France could never again believe in its future. The blow to us would have been a thousand times worse than it was for you when your twin trade towers came down, even worse than Pearl Harbor."

"I have to go after her," McGarvey said.

"I understand and agree with you completely, my old friend. But you must understand that first we need to get you out of France and back to your people who are waiting for you."

"No, I don't understand. Let me leave France, but not on a commercial flight to Washington."

"Unfortunately my hands are completely tied," Alarie said.

They went into a corner office, where a man in a business suit, his jacket off, his tie loose, his collar undone, was on the phone. He hung up immediately.

"The director will see you now, gentlemen," he said, jumping up. He knocked once on Lacoste's door, opened it, and stepped aside.

Claude Lacoste looked up and got to his feet. He was a very tall man, with a square face and a large Gallic nose. Dressed in his gray Ministry of Defense uniform, all the buttons done up, he was a striking double for Charles de Gaulle.

He put out his hand. "Monsieur McGarvey, I am happy that we finally meet."

McGarvey ignored the gesture. "I need to fly to Istanbul and then likely to Riyadh or someplace in Saudi Arabia. And it has to happen as soon as possible. Before the Gulfstream lands at Istanbul, unless it changes flight plans."

"I'm afraid that is impossible. As I told General Gibson just a few minutes ago. You are being returned to Washington, where, once you arrive, you will be free to go wherever you wish. Provided it is not back here to France."

"You're welcome, sir," McGarvey said. He turned to Alarie. "Let's leave now. I'd like a glass of wine and something to eat at the airport."

"I'm welcome for what?" Lacoste asked, a tightness in his voice and manner.

"For the Tour Eiffel, you arrogant prick. And I hope that if the life of someone you love is ever threatened you won't simply sit here in your office and issue directives."

Najjir had gone forward to talk to the crew, leaving Miriam and Pete alone. The Gulfstream was plushly laid out, with a separate conference area forward and three swiveling seats on each side of the cabin, facing each other, each with its own super glossy table inlaid with what looked to Pete like ivory.

"Amazing what money can buy," Pete said. "Even in Saudi Arabia now that oil is down again. And of course in Russia."

"I wouldn't know," Miriam said, looking out the window at essentially nothing because of their altitude, only a few cloud tops in the distance off to the southeast, toward the Med.

"All SVR agents—or at least the good ones—are trained in the realities of geopolitics."

"You think that I'm a Russian."

"Of course you are, though you've got the cockney-trying-to-rise-above-her-upbringing accent pretty well down pat. But I expect that you've always been a quick study."

Miriam shrugged.

"What I don't understand is what purpose bringing the Eiffel Tower down would have done for the Kremlin."

Still Miriam held her silence, but she had an amused look on her pretty face.

"Of course it would be stupid of me to think that you staged the entire business only to snatch me in order to lure Mac. His intelligence value, if you could get anything worthwhile out of him, would be nothing short of stellar. A game changer for you and your boyfriend's careers."

"He is not my boyfriend," Miriam replied just a little too sharply.

Pete had struck a nerve. "Zero for the lions and one for the Christians," she said. "We're making progress."

"What nonsense are you talking about?"

"You were assigned to help him—for whatever reason—but once everything fell apart back there I suspect that he tried to kill you. Something you must have figured might happen, and you were ready."

"Bullshit."

"He sent you away—back to London—but you showed up here. The question is, why?" Pete asked. "Unless you talked to your handler in Moscow, who told you that the SVR wanted to share the product if a former director of the CIA were actually to be captured."

"Be careful that your guesswork doesn't become so accurate that we'd be forced to eliminate you."

"Are you really that stupid? Am I supposed to believe that if I cooperate you'll let me just walk away?"

"But what other alternative do you have, my dear?" Najjir asked, coming from forward.

Pete smiled. "The real question is, who are you working for? I mean the broad here is an SVR operative who you tried to kill. So whose orders were you following—her handler's or yours?"

Najjir was amused. "What makes you think that we're on the outs with each other?"

"The stupid bitch all but drew me a diagram of how you tried to kill her. But she was waiting for it, and she came back against your orders to return to London and change her appearance."

Miriam started to say something, but Pete held her off.

"Now, I have to admit that the CIA has made some colossal blunders. The Bay of Pigs comes to mind. But Jesus Christ, all of us aren't as brain dead as you two."

Najjir and Miriam said nothing.

"Come on, guys, the fucking Eiffel Tower?"

TWENTY-THREE

McGarvey had given his word to Alarie that he wouldn't try anything on the way out to the airport, so it was just the two of them, plus a driver, but no housekeeping muscle.

"Monsieur Lacoste has a very long memory," Alarie said. "He won't forget you."

"I expect he won't. He's just like every other guy in a high position who's been promoted because of political connections, beyond their level of competency."

"I can understand why you're bitter, my old friend, but you must understand where France finds itself. We're a nation at war, almost the same as in the forties. Only this time the occupying army has infiltrated our entire society, and it's hitting us from inside."

"It's happening in Germany too."

"Unfortunately, yes."

"And you poor bastards are at a loss trying to figure it out, when it's been there all along, staring at you."

"If you mean terrorists embedded with refugees from Syria and Afghanistan and even Iraq, you're correct. But you have the same problem in the US with the Mexican drug cartels."

"Not in the same numbers," McGarvey said. "Between you and the Germans you've allowed more than a million people across the border. So what do you expect?"

"Germany has admitted the bulk of them."

"Because your Front National party is holding the government's feet to the fire. But they're still here in Paris, in Nice, everywhere."

"What would you have us do, turn the *salopards* back so that they can continue to be slaughtered?"

"Yes, until complete background checks can be made of everyone you accept."

"Easier said than done."

"And once they've been admitted, allow them to stay as citizens on the condition they become French in their dress, habits, and outlook. You're losing your country, Milun. Wake up. If they don't want to lose their Syrian identities, then let them stay in Syria."

Alarie's manner was steady. He had not risen to the bait. "You sound like your new president."

They had crossed the Périphérique, Le Bourget off to their left.

"In any event, the attack was probably organized and directed by someone outside of France," Alarie said.

"The kids with the vests and in the church were Eastern. But they were directed by operators either from Saudi Arabia or Russia or both."

"But there would be no reason for them to back such an attack. It would be lunacy. Tell me why."

"It's what I intend to find out once I get to Ms. Boylan. And then I'll kill the bastards just like the ones at the tower, and the ones in the church. And that's a promise you can take to the Banque de France."

Alarie held his silence until they took the exit for Aéroport Charles de Gaulle. "Whatever you must think of how you are being treated, France wishes to thank you from the bottom of its soul for what you did. You are a true hero of the Republic. We are in your debt."

"If that's how you treat your heroes and repay your debts, keep the medals," McGarvey said. He could not get the picture of Pete hanging from the wall in the basement of the église out of his head. It was a fearful image that he knew would stay with him for the rest of his life, just like the image of the car that his wife, Katy, and their daughter, Liz, were riding in when it exploded. Both were permanently seared in his head as if he had been branded by a very hot iron.

"My hands are tied," Alarie said.

"Mine too," McGarvey replied.

Inside the airport, Alarie flashed his credentials and they were passed directly through security into the international terminal 2E. The place was busy with passengers and crew arriving for flights, along with Police Nationale in helmets and flak jackets, armed with pistols in chest holsters and submachine guns at the ready. Some of the ones patrolling had bomb-sniffing dogs with them. After what had happened at the Eiffel Tower, every LE officer in the country was on high alert.

"You have an hour and a half before your flight; do you want to have something to eat?" Alarie asked.

"We didn't have much lunch at the tower. How about Illy?"

"It's on the lower level and it's self-service."

"I don't care," McGarvey said.

Alarie gave him an odd look but nodded. "As you wish," he said.

They took the escalator down and went directly to the very busy café.

Alarie found them a table. "You may go first. I think I'll merely have a coffee."

"I'd like to have my passport and my phone," McGarvey said. He held out his hand.

"It's impossible."

"Just take them out of your pocket and put them on the table, along with my boarding pass."

"And then what?"

"I'll need to use the bathroom. Something has upset my stomach."

Alarie was very still. "How long will you need?"

"Thirty minutes. Tell them that you think I was trying to reach my embassy. I have friends there."

For a long time Alarie didn't say or do a thing, until he got Mac's passport, phone, and the Air France boarding pass out of his pocket and laid them down.

"Thank you, my old friend. Your debt for the tower has been paid in full."

Alarie nodded. *"Bonne chance,"* he said. "Tell them at customs and immigration that your luggage did not arrive and unfortunately you need to return to the city." He took out his DGSE business card. "If there is a question, show them this. They can call on my mobile."

The customs people checked his passport, and on the strength of Alarie's card passed him directly through. On the street level, just away from the taxi queue, he phoned Otto.

"I'm at de Gaulle, at the departure doors."

"Milun cooperated, or are you on the run?"

"Both. He's giving me a half hour. Has the Gulfstream's flight plan been changed or canceled?"

"It's Istanbul for sure, kemo sabe."

"I need to get there as quickly as possible, What are my options?"

"I'm working it," Otto said. "I can't get anything of ours to you from Ramstein. Are you secure for the moment?"

"Yes."

"Hold on a mo."

At least one flight had apparently just arrived, because people were streaming out of customs. Two taxi expediters were moving into position at the head of the line of cabs.

"Le Bourget," Otto said.

"They know who I am."

"Not at Dassault. A separate FBO, not even close to Signature. Take a cab there now."

McGarvey was the third in line for a taxi, and he told the expediter he wanted to be taken to Dassault at Le Bourget.

Even before they got back on the A1, Otto was on the line again.

"The crew is preflighting a Falcon 50 for you. Not the fastest bird in the sky, but there's no real rush to get you to Istanbul."

"There is if that's where they're taking Pete."

"It is," Otto said. "And they're expecting you."

"How do you know?"

"Because Giles Worley, in the company of two women, called ahead and booked a suite at the Ritz."

TWENTY-FOUR

□

Najjir had spent the last forty minutes forward, talking on his sat phone, and although Pete tried to overhear what he was saying he spoke mostly in hushed tones that, combined with the jet noise, made it impossible to make out more than one word in twenty. But at one point he had seemed angry.

He had glared at her, but then turned away and lowered his voice.

"Sounds like your boss is in trouble," she said.

Miriam, seated across from her, was drinking champagne and working on a crossword puzzle in Russian, no longer bothering to conceal her nationality, though she appeared to be having some trouble. It seemed to Pete that Russian might not be her mother tongue.

The woman looked up. "As you keep saying, we failed to bring down the tower. But we have you, and we'll soon have Mr. McGarvey, whose actual value is far greater than any stupid monument."

The Gulfstream began to slow down and lose altitude. Pete could hear the changed pitch of the engines and feel the descent in her ears.

Najjir got off the phone, nodded to Miriam, and went forward. He came back a minute later and sat down. "We'll be touching down in fifteen minutes."

"Have you arranged for the boat?" Miriam asked.

Najjir gave her a dark look.

"A boat ride, that'd be peachy," Pete said. "Except I suspect you'd rather get across to Russia, maybe Sochi, by air. But you're afraid that I might make too much noise."

"You're right about that part, though I'm more concerned about handling Mr. McGarvey without killing him. No one wants to buy damaged goods from me. And of course there are too many foreign tourists in Sochi, so we'll head to Novorossiysk."

"Clever," Pete said. She remembered a briefing a couple of years ago about a new Spetsnaz base abuilding there. It was near Crimea, which Russia had annexed a while back. It's where they had garrisoned the highly trained special ops forces who were just about as good as US SEAL Team 6 operators. They were in place, waiting for trouble.

"In the meantime, what to do about you?" Najjir said.

He and Miriam were staring at her as if she were some sort of exotic creature on display.

"Might be for the best if you just let me go."

"I think that she'll cooperate with no problem whatsoever," Miriam said.

"In a pig's rump."

"What makes you so sure?" Najjir asked.

"It's her American sense of justice. For the downtrodden and all that shit. Someone gets screwed over, or hurt, or needs a kidney transplant or something, half the population comes out of the woodwork as bleeding volunteers."

"Not for someone like you," Pete said.

"I expect not. But we have plenty of places in Istanbul to hide out, and we have plenty of gun hands who will to do a job of work for pay. Fanatics, actually, but fairly good marksmen with absolutely no moral compunctions about anything."

Najjir hadn't gotten it yet, but Pete had, and the woman was right.

"Your point?" he asked.

"We rent a car at the airport instead of taking a cab to the hotel. When we get there we ask the valet to hold it until we call down. If the bitch cries for help in the driveway, we'll shoot the valet, the doormen, and anyone else within earshot and make our way to point alpha. Same thing if she waits until we're in the lobby—only by then I think the collateral damage would be quite a lot greater."

"I'll keep my mouth shut," Pete said. "Honest Injun."

"Of course you will. Wouldn't do for your self-image to have the blood of innocent people on your hands. It's why you and your Sir Galahad interfered at the tower. Sweet."

The rental car was a Mercedes C-Class. Miriam sat in back with Pete while Najjir drove into the city from the airport. The day was warm and very sticky, and the traffic was horrendous. None of the drivers seemed to pay attention to any of the rules of the road, even driving on the wrong side of one-way streets. And inside the city it was even worse.

The Ritz was housed in a glass and steel tower that was sided by Maçka Park and overlooked the city, the Bosphorus, and the new bridge, the spires of which were bathed in blue at night.

They pulled under the canopy and uniformed doormen were right there, helping Najjir and the women out.

"Giles Worley," Najjir told them. "We have reservations."

A bellman took the two bags from the trunk. "Shall I unpack for you, sir?" he asked.

"It's not necessary, thank you."

Miriam had a subcompact Glock pistol in the waistband of her cream designer slacks, and she carried her bag over her left shoulder to keep her gun hand free.

A valet came over. "Shall I park your car for you, sir?"

"Leave it here for the moment, if possible. We may need to meet a friend."

"May I suggest that a cab might be the better option, sir?"

"You may not," Najjir said.

He was slightly ahead of where Pete stood next to Miriam. Pete considered shouldering the woman aside and bolting down the driveway and out into traffic on the busy Askerocagi Street. But Miriam, sensing something, stepped closer.

"Trust me, sweetie, I won't hesitate to put a couple of ten-millimeter rounds into your back if you try to run," she said, her voice low. "And I'm a very good shot."

"You'd lose your chance at Mac."

"He wouldn't know that you were dead until it was too late. Trust me, if you want to get along, just go along. Okay?"

Pete nodded. There would be other chances; she would make damned sure of it.

The suite was magnificent, with two bedrooms, separate palatial master bathrooms, and very tall windows overlooking the waterway in one direction, with balconies on the other side that faced the greenery of the park. Between the sleeping accommodations was a very well-furnished, upscale sitting room with a large flat-screen television, fabulous upholstered chairs, and two couches. Large, ornately woven Turkish rugs were scattered as if randomly on the wooden floors, and several pieces of fine art, along with gilded mirrors, decorated the walls beneath crown-molded pan ceilings, from which hung chandeliers.

Pete and McGarvey had stayed in some very upscale properties during deep cover assignments over the past couple of years, but she was impressed with this place. One more rug, one more bit of artwork, one more amenity, and the hotel would have come across as gaudy.

Najjir gave the bellman two hundred euros.

When he was gone Miriam went to the phone. "I'll order us some champagne."

"Later," Najjir said.

"I could use a drink," Pete said.

Najjir came toward her and she stepped back.

"Get the scarf from your bag, please," he told Miriam. "We're leaving."

She went into the bedroom.

"Take off your panties," Najjir said.

"You want to rape me, you'll have to rape a dead body," Pete said, moving back another step.

"That's a scenario some of my people might find interesting. Now do as I ask, please, and no real harm will come to you for the moment."

"No."

Najjir stepped toward her so quickly that she didn't have enough time to react before he smashed his fist into her face, knocking her backwards onto the floor. She hit her head hard and fuzzed out for a moment. Her jaw felt as if it had been dislocated and one or more of her teeth had been broken. She was extremely nauseous, so she rolled over onto her right side in case she vomited. She didn't want to choke to death. But that move was all she was capable of for the immediate moment.

"That must have hurt," Miriam said, her voice a long way off.

"Take off her panties, we'll leave them as a calling card for Mr. McGarvey. And soon as she comes around put the scarf on her head, to cover her hair and her face. We're going to do a little sightseeing now"

"We just got here."

"The man at the desk welcomed us," Najjir said. "By name. Mine, yours, and Ms. Boylan's."

"Shit."

He went to the phone. "I'd like to leave a message for Mr. Kirk McGarvey, who is coming to see us. Tell him that we'll make the exchange this evening." He gave an address.

TWENTY-FIVE

It was getting dark when the Falcon 50 started its descent into Istanbul's Atatürk Airport. McGarvey was tired but he'd been unable to sleep. Twice he'd nearly phoned Otto to find out what was going on, but each time he held back. When Otto had news he would make contact.

But it was difficult. He still couldn't get the image out of his head of Pete hanging on the wall in the basement of the church. And he'd had even more trouble tamping down his almost insane rage. He wanted to lash out right now.

The copilot called back. "You have an incoming telephone call, sir. But we'll be on final approach in five minutes. I'd like you to be off by then."

"You got it," McGarvey said. It was Otto.

"They're in Istanbul all right. Booked into the Ritz, but they went out and left a message for you. Said they'd make the exchange this evening."

"At the hotel?"

"No, they left an address. It's in a neighborhood called Tarlabasi. The north part of the city, around a place called Taksim Square in the Beyoğlu district. Lots of African immigrants, Kurds. Families mostly. It has a dangerous rep unless you belong there, then it's supposedly friendly."

"But?"

"The government is restoring the area lot by lot, but it's still mostly a dirty, run-down, ramshackle place of narrow streets and dark alleys. Not a lot of nightlife, though there are some places you might call outdoor cafés—two or three old tables on the narrow sidewalk in front of a tiny storefront where you can buy a coffee. Maybe a dilapidated couch and a couple of old chairs outside an apartment building, where people gather to smoke and talk."

"Cops?"

"Almost never, but because of the Kurds the military sometimes sends in a patrol or two, especially on weekends. And if there's trouble downtown, the patrols are stepped up, in case there's a backlash in the neighborhood."

"What's at the address?"

"That's the rub, Mac. The place is nothing more than the gutted-out remains of what once was a three-story apartment building, maybe a factory before that. Evidently had a serious fire in the past year or so. The next-door buildings show a lot of damage, but people still live there. My guess would be that the guy who took Pete has got muscle for hire right there, definitely in shooting range."

"What's my approach?"

"From a street called Tatli Badem, Sweet Almond, you should be able to make your way down a back alley and come in from the rear. I'll send a map to your phone."

"Shut it down, please, sir," the copilot called back.

"We're coming in for a landing. I have to go," McGarvey said.

"Mark Rowe, a Company rep from our consulate, will meet you at the airport with some equipment and papers. But he won't be along for the ride. You'll be on your own."

"Good."

Rowe, a tall, very large man with an olive complexion and dark hair, dressed in a Western shirt, string tie, jeans, and Tony Lama cowboy boots, was waiting at the FBO ramp with a dark blue Toyota Camry when McGarvey thanked the crew for a good ride and got off the plane.

"Mr. Director," he said, "welcome to Istanbul."

"Thanks, I'm told you have something for me?"

"Three things actually. First, if you're carrying a bag it won't have to go through customs."

"I'm traveling light."

"Second, the car is yours. Registered to Regis Pharmaceutical Distributors, GmbH. And third, there is a package on the front passenger seat."

"Will you need a lift back to the consulate?"

"No," Rowe said. "And for whatever reason you came here, good hunting. And I sincerely mean that. But watch your six, sir, this is the Wild West."

"You're a Texas man?"

Rowe grinned. "Hell no, sir. This is just a clown suit to misdirect the opposition. I'm actually a seventh-generation Connecticut Yankee." He turned around and went back inside.

Otto was on the phone when McGarvey got into the car.

"I've programmed the address into the car's nav system," he said. "But listen to me. We can bump this up to the ambassador through State. He can take it to the Turkish authorities. Tell them that a diplomatic representative of the US government has been kidnapped and is being held for ransom."

"They won't do anything about it, at least not until the White House puts some pressure on them."

"We won't ask them to do anything like that. Just cordon off the neighborhood until our negotiator—you—can get on the scene. Might stabilize the situation long enough for you to get inside."

"It's me they want."

"And it's you they'll get."

"I have to do this alone. Najjir spots Turkish soldiers moving into place, he'll call it a day and bug out."

"Then I don't know what the hell you want, Mac," Otto shouted. "Goddamnit, what are you going to do?"

"Exactly what the bastard wants me to do. Turn myself over."

"Once he has you, he'll kill Pete—she won't be of any further value to him, and you'll be screwed."

"Things have a way of working themselves out," McGarvey said. He started the car's engine. "I'm going over to the hotel first, to see if Pete managed to leave something behind again."

Pete was awake, but in pain, when they stopped, and she couldn't see a thing because the scarf was over her eyes.

Miriam got out of the car and Pete heard what sounded like a rusty gate being opened. A moment later the car moved forward a few feet, stopped again, and Najjir shut off the engine.

The gate was closed, then Miriam pulled Pete out of the car and they marched somewhere for what seemed like a long distance, up some stairs and down a corridor, the wooden floors creaking as they walked.

Pete let her feet drag as if she were still only semiconscious, but she had come around enough to take some stock of her surroundings.

They were on the second floor of some very old building. It smelled of mildew and backed-up toilets and maybe machine oil or something else that could mean they were in a machine shop or factory of some sort.

In the distance the Muslim call to prayers echoed over the city; it had to be sunset.

Closer, she could hear a baby crying, two people with high-pitched voices arguing in what sounded like Arabic, and a small motorcycle or moped roaring past on the street downstairs. A cobblestone street, she thought.

They came into a room through what sounded to Pete like a metal door, and there were men here. At least two of them. They smelled like garlic and something else unpleasant, plus strong body odors.

"Tie her to a chair for now," Najjir said.

Kirk, Pete muttered to herself. His strong face, clear eyes, and smile came into her head and she almost cried.

He was coming. It was all she had to hang on to.

PART
TWO

Istanbul

TWENTY-SIX

□

McGarvey drove over to the Ritz Hotel, the blue lights on the Bosphorus Bridge across the Golden Horn hanging like a necklace above a laden freighter heading inbound to the Black Sea. Traffic was still very heavy and he had to concentrate on his driving lest he get into an accident or be stopped by a cop.

Rowe's package had contained five thousand euros—from some Company slush fund at the consulate—a well-used Walther PPK in the rare heavy version, of which only two thousand were ever manufactured, and three magazines of 9 × 18mm Ultra PP Super cartridges—one in the handle and two spares.

Otto didn't think that a new passport and false papers were necessary; Najjir knew who he was, knew that he was coming and had left a clear message for him. There was no need for stealth.

He reached the hotel a few minutes after nine, left the car with the valet, and went directly up to the suite booked under the Worley name.

The bastard had buried Pete in Istanbul, but he knew that Mac would have to come here first, on some off chance that Pete had left a clue. It was also possible that he and the woman had returned and were waiting in ambush. Force the battle here and now.

The corridor was deserted, and listening at the door, the gun in his right hand, Mac could hear very faint voices that might have been from a television, possibly a newscast in English. The cadences and intonations were wrong for ordinary conversation.

A door halfway down the corridor was open and an older man in a bellman's uniform emerged. "May I help you, sir," he asked, approaching.

"I forgot my key," McGarvey said.

The man took a cell phone from his pocket, but before he could call anyone, Mac snatched it from his hand.

"I need to get inside. A friend of mine was here, and she may have left something for me."

The bellman stepped back and glanced over Mac's shoulder at the elevators down the hall.

Mac raised the pistol from where it was concealed behind his leg and stuck it in the man's face. "Open the door, please."

The bellman shook his head.

"Right now, or I will shoot you."

Still the man hesitated. At any moment someone could show up on one of the elevators, or emerge from one of the rooms, and it would be game over. The police would be called, and he would be on the run.

Mac pulled back the hammer, an unnecessary action, but the soft click impressed the man.

He whipped out his universal key and unlocked the door. His eyes were wide, his mouth half open.

"Go," McGarvey said softly, and the man took off in a run down the corridor, toward the stairs.

The door to the suite was only ajar an inch or so. Leading with his gun hand, Mac pushed it open the rest of the way and ducked into the entry vestibule and then into the sitting room, moving low and fast to the right, sweeping his pistol right to left.

He ended in a half crouch

Large wall-to-wall windows looked toward the illuminated bridge, and doors left and right opened to separate bedrooms—one with glass doors to a balcony facing the city, the other with doors opening onto a balcony overlooking Maçka Park.

No one was here. Straightening up he lowered the pistol, muzzle off to the side, tossed the bellman's cell phone on the couch, and went into the bedroom on the left.

The panties Pete had been wearing when they'd left the hotel for the tower, torn, a little blood on the waistband on the right side, were lying on the bed. He stared at them for a long moment, trying to work out the significance of the message Najjir had sent.

We have your friend, and she is under our control. Our total control. Come get her if you can.
But there was more.

Mac holstered the pistol and picked up the panties. Maybe she'd been raped, either by Najjir or one of his people. Maybe they'd made a show of it. To infuriate him so hard that he would not be thinking straight. They wanted him to come barging in blindly, gun blazing.

They'd set a trap and the panties were part of the bait, like the first in a trail of bread crumbs leading where they wanted him to come.

Pocketing the panties he went back into the sitting room as a short, thickly built man with deep-set black eyes, a dark complexion, and black hair appeared in the doorway from the corridor. He was wearing a neatly pressed gray linen suit, the jacket unbuttoned, the bulge of a pistol on the left side obvious.

"I expect that you are Mr. McGarvey, here seeking the whereabouts of your friend, who was recently a guest with Mr. Worley and another woman."

"I was looking to see if they left anything behind."

"I understand perfectly, but you must also understand that we cannot tolerate a display of weapons, and especially not the threat against an innocent employee who was merely doing his duty."

"I meant no harm," McGarvey said. "But I have to leave now."

The man was pained. "Unfortunately that is not possible. The authorities have been called and have asked that I detain you until they arrive."

"You're the house cop?"

The man nodded. "My name is Mehmet Demir. And you are the former director of the American Central Intelligence Agency, for which you have my utmost respect, sir."

"The easy way would be for you to step aside and allow me to leave."

"I am truly sorry."

McGarvey pulled his gun, but did not point it at the house cop.

Demir smiled and spread his hands. "Do you actually mean to shoot me?"

"One of the women is my fiancée."

"Congratulations, sir."

McGarvey holstered his pistol and held out his right hand as he went across the room to the cop. Demir raised a hand to shake, but McGarvey reached inside the cop's jacket, snatched his gun, and stepped back.

"Now you have two guns with which to shoot me. But it doesn't matter."

"Do you understand my situation?"

"Perfectly," Demir said. "But do you understand mine and that of the hotel?"

"An impasse, then," McGarvey said. He holstered his Walther and returned the house cop's pistol. "Will you shoot me in the back if I leave?"

Demir inclined his head. "No, not a man in love." He stepped aside. "The public elevators are locked, but the stairs will be faster than the service elevator. But first, hit me, please."

"I won't hit a man who helped," McGarvey said.

Mac took the stairs down eight flights to the service level one floor below the lobby. The laundry area was off to the right, down a broad corridor from two service elevators, and straight back was the receiving area where deliveries such as food, wine, and other items, including twice-daily mail deliveries, were made to three loading docks.

He made his way to one of the overhead doors, then outside onto the dock, from where he jumped down to the driveway. The few employees in sight at the moment paid him no attention, nor was anyone looking from the second-floor office windows.

Up on the street level he turned left and walked directly away from the hotel's main entrance. A block and a half away he hailed a cab and directed the driver to take him to Taksim Square.

The driver, an old man with a gray beard, wearing a Chicago Cubs baseball cap, looked in the rearview mirror. "This is very bad place. Beyoğlu. Do you understand?"

McGarvey handed a hundred-euro note to the driver.

"Is impossible."

McGarvey handed over a second note. A moment later, a third.

The driver finally took them. "Your funeral," he said, the expression very American.

TWENTY-SEVEN

☐

Najjir stepped off the freight elevator on the third floor of the ramshackle building that had once held the Allied Tin Manufactory Co-op of Beyoğlu and went to a door with a frosted glass window, at the end of the broad corridor.

The only noise here this evening was the badly warped wooden floor that creaked under his footfalls.

Miriam, wearing jeans and a short-sleeved sweatshirt, several pieces of rope in hand, came out of the room that had once been the office of the co-op's bookkeeper. She looked tired. "Do you mean to starve us, or did you come to tell me that dinner is served?"

"Downstairs. But no alcohol. I want everyone sharp."

Miriam shrugged. "Do you think he's stupid enough to actually come for her?"

"He hasn't called for help."

"But someone from the American consulate met his plane."

"Almost certainly a CIA officer by the name of Mark Rowe. But he drove himself to the hotel, where he apparently pulled a gun on a bell-man and the house cop. The metro police are there now, but he managed to slip away."

"If they're looking for him, and trace him here, we'd have trouble explaining what the fuck we're doing."

"The cops are treating it as nothing more than a simple assault. No one is making any serious effort to find him."

Miriam nodded, but it was clear she was worried. "I'd just as soon kill her right now and get the hell out of here," she said.

"Soon enough. But for now she's the bait for McGarvey. And you know what bringing him in would mean for us."

"Hate to be a stickler for details, love, but you were the incident commander for the bloody tower op. You fucked up, not me. So if I make a quick fade into the woodwork, no one will come looking for me. At least not in the short term."

"Your career would be over."

"Better than getting my nine ounces," she said. It was the old KGB euphemism for a 9mm bullet to the back of the head.

Najjir was truly fed up with the slut. He'd warned his control officer from the beginning that hiring amateur help was a bad idea. Of course he'd not been told that she was a Russian intel officer, only that in the end she would be expendable. In fact, eliminating her would be the most desirable outcome. The details had been left to him. He only had to wonder what instructions she had been given about his own expendability.

For now, however, she was riding herd on the woman, something that was becoming more difficult by the hour. But once they had McGarvey in hand, it would be his pleasure to kill both women.

"Maybe in the end it'll be me coming for you," Najjir said. "But for now I need your help with her. Scratch my back and I'll scratch yours."

"Your American is showing. Won't play so well back in the Rodina," Miriam said. She held up the short pieces of rope they'd used to tie Pete to the four legs of the metal cot that one of the shooters had found somewhere and brought up. "She managed to get loose, and I caught her trying to pry open the window."

Najjir stepped around her and looked inside the room. Pete's hands, raised above her head in what appeared to be an extremely uncomfortable position, were handcuffed to the crossbar at the end of the metal cot.

She was awake and she glared at him and Miriam, but said nothing.

She was still wearing the slacks and blouse that Miriam had dressed her in, and a fair amount of blood had run down from her mouth onto her right shoulder. Her face was red and badly swollen, as was her right eye. She had to be in a lot of pain, but she wasn't showing it.

"Where'd you get the cuffs?"

"From one of your goons," Miriam said. "They're police issue, but I didn't ask how he came by them."

"Best not to ask too many questions. All of them are a little jumpy. The army has done a lot of sweep-and-clear operations down here."

"Christ, you didn't say anything about that."

"Nothing in the past ten days."

"Not to say they won't start up again at any minute."

"We'll be out of here before morning," Najjir said.

"We'd better be," Miriam said. "Now let's eat."

"What about something for her?" Najjir asked, just to see what her reaction would be.

"You've got to be kidding."

Her attitude was exactly what he'd thought it would be. She had a total lack of humanity. Which made her as perfect an operative as a dangerous one.

Mark Rowe pulled up and parked a battered dark blue Toyota Corolla a half a block behind where the cabby had dropped off McGarvey at the edge of Taksim Square.

He'd almost lost the former DCI, who by happenstance he'd spotted walking down the street, away from the hotel, at the same time the Turkish National Police had shown up in front. Something apparently had happened inside the hotel—almost certainly McGarvey's doing—and the TNP had sent two radio units, with two cops in each car.

It was after ten in the evening, and the park and most of the streets around it were all but deserted. Most families were barricaded inside their mean apartments for the night, while the bad guys for the most part wouldn't be out and about until after midnight. Oddly enough, this time of the evening, when the small sidewalk cafés and other businesses were closed or closing, was just about the safest time of the day or night.

His mobile rang, and he recognized the number. "Yes, sir."

"Have you lost him?" DDCI Marty Bambridge demanded.

"He just got out of a cab on the south side of Taksim Park. It's in the Beyoğlu District."

"I know where the fucking park is located. No matter what, you need to stick with him, am I perfectly clear?"

"I'll need help, sir. This definitely is the wrong side of Istanbul's tracks."

"You're on your own. Just don't lose him."

Pete waited until the door was closed and the sound of their footfalls faded down the corridor before she pulled her shackled hands down far enough so that when she craned her head upward she could make out the cuffs, the holes for the key and, more importantly, her slender wrists.

She'd managed to wriggle one hand from the length of rope holding it to a bed leg and quickly untie her other hand and ankles.

The steel mesh covering the window had been so rusty that she had managed to pull one corner loose and was certain she could get a second corner undone. From that point she figured it would be fairly easy to pull the mesh far enough away that she could open the window, or at least break the glass, crawl outside, and make it down to the street.

One of the barely housebroken baboons, about the size of a small house, had come in at that moment, batted her in the side of the head, and slammed her down on the bed. He'd had her trousers down around her knees when the woman had shown up and shoved him aside.

She had feigned semiconsciousness, so that when the bitch had put the handcuffs on her it was fairly easy to bunch up her muscles so that her hands, wrists, and lower arms had increased just enough in size that now she was reasonably sure she could wriggle her hands free, as she had done with the rope ties.

TWENTY-EIGHT

□

Otto was at one of his monitors, trying to track Bambridge, who had left his office two minutes ago. He called Mac's mobile but it rang four times before it was answered. "Are you in a position to hold up for a few minutes?"

"I'm in Taksim Park, next to a statue."

"You could have trouble coming your way. Rowe is right behind you. Evidently he's been following you since the airport."

"I don't know who's the chief of Istanbul station, but have him order the son of a bitch off my back."

"There's more, kemo sabe, and you're not going to like it."

"I'm listening."

"He's working for Marty."

"Christ."

"I intercepted a phone call he made to Rowe. Ordered him to stick with you, no matter what."

"If they call for help, this thing will go south and they'll kill Pete and bail out. Did you tell that to Marty?"

"He left his office as soon as he talked to Mark. I'm working on finding him. I'll get back to you."

"Soon as."

"Right," Otto said.

He'd programmed one of his darlings to search the building by sampling conversations with a reverse search algorithm. The Company's entire campus was shielded from any sort of eavesdropping from outside—mechanical, electronic, or by laser beams sampling windowpanes for vibrations made by conversations inside all of the hundreds of offices, even the library, the Starbucks on the first floor, and the cafeteria in one of the covered walkways.

No one discussed classified information outside any of the buildings—not even in the interior courtyards—so picking up conversations with a parabolic dish would yield nothing. Every building on campus was shielded from the inside by Faraday cages, which blocked electronic signals from coming in or going out. And every window was doubled, with white noise pumped between the panes.

The outer layer of glass in each office did not vibrate, but the inner panes did, which Otto's program monitored.

Marty was talking to someone named Oscar in a second-floor office of the George H. W. Bush Center for Intelligence, in what was known as the New Headquarters Building.

Otto pulled up a directory. Oscar was Oscar Cowen, the liaison officer from the Department of State. He tapped into the office as Cowen was offering Marty coffee.

"*Later, but thanks for agreeing to see me on such short notice,*" Marty said.

Otto phoned Mac who answered immediately. "Yes."

"Is your situation holding?"

"For now," Mac said.

"Marty just showed up in State's liaison office. I'll switch it over so you can listen in."

"*. . . situation is developing about the way I thought it would,*" Bambridge said. "*The son of a bitch is predictable.*"

"*Do you want me to go ahead then?*" Cowen asked.

"*You have someone you can call?*"

"*I set it up as soon as you asked for my help. Army Major Aydin Yilmaz.*"

"*How soon can he get his troops over there?*"

"*They've done a number of raids in the district over the past several months. He promised that he could have his people mobilized and in place within twenty minutes.*"

"He understands the situation?"

"Completely."

"Do it."

"Can you patch me in to Cowen's speakerphone?" McGarvey asked.

Otto made an entry. "You're on."

"Mr. Cowen, if you call for help from the Turkish army it will result in the death of someone very close to me," McGarvey said.

"Jesus Christ," Marty swore. "Rencke, you bastard!"

"Do not call for an army raid. If Ms. Boylan is harmed I will come for both of you."

"Is that a threat?" the State Department liaison demanded.

"Yes."

"Who the hell do you think you are?"

"You don't want to know," Marty interjected.

Otto hurriedly found the password for Cowen's computer and hacked into his system. He turned on the monitor's camera as Marty finished writing something on a pad of paper and passed it across the desk, into clear view.

DO IT ANYWAY. WE'LL DENY IT.

"Marty passed Cowen a note to go ahead with the raid anyway," Otto said. "They'll deny it later."

"You're a fucking dead man, Bambridge," McGarvey said, and the connection was broken.

"He's gone," Otto told them.

"Have your major go in and take the bastards down, rescue Ms. Boylan, and take McGarvey into custody, by force if necessary," Bambridge said. "I want him back here."

"Bad idea, Marty," Otto said.

Mr. Rencke, you're terminated. You no longer worker for the CIA You'll surrender your identification and badges to security, who will escort you off campus."

"Good luck with that."

. . .

Otto entered a seventeen-character alphanumeric code into the system that rode herd on all of his darlings, then walked out of his office and got to the stairwell as a pair security personnel from housekeeping showed up on the elevator.

He managed to duck through the doorway before they spotted him, and hurried up four floors to the seventh, where he had to use his special security pass to gain entry.

The director's office was halfway on the right down the long corridor, and Otto barged in.

"Mr. Rencke, the general is busy at the moment," Gibson's secretary said, half rising.

But Otto charged straight through without stopping.

Marty Bambridge was just coming through the connecting door from his office, and he pulled up short, his face red. "I just fired him, Mr. Director."

"In thirty minutes the mainframes of all fourteen intel agencies in town, including ours, will freeze up for ten seconds. Thirty minutes after that they'll go down for twenty seconds, and at every thirty-minute interval they'll go down for double the previous time."

Bambridge went to Gibson's desk and reached for a telephone, but the DCI held up a hand for him to stop.

"Unless?"

"Unless I ask my programs to hold off."

"For what ransom? Your job? You'll not lose it as long as this is my office. Or is this about McGarvey again?"

"You're goddamned right it's about McGarvey," Bambridge shouted, but again Gibson held up a hand and Marty shut his mouth.

Otto quickly explained McGarvey's situation and what Bambridge and Oscar Cowen had decided to put into action.

"Mr. McGarvey believes that this would be the wrong thing to do at the moment?" the DCI asked.

"Yes, sir."

Gibson picked up the phone and buzzed his secretary. "Telephone

General Daichi Osman in Ankara, with my compliments and apologies for the lateness of the hour, but I have a matter of some urgency to discuss."

Osman was in charge of the Turkish Joint Chief of Staff Intelligence Bureau, which controlled all sensitive military intel operations in the country.

TWENTY-NINE

□

Najjir sat with Miriam at one of the tables on the first floor in what had served as the factory's break room. A half dozen of the fifteen contractors were there playing cards and smoking. The room stank of unwashed bodies and something greasy that had burned in a pot on the stove.

The nine others—four of them snipers—were set up on the roof, with clear sight lines in every direction that McGarvey might approach from, as well as on the ground floor, watching Tatli Badem, where it was likely McGarvey would make his initial recon approach. Their strict orders were shoot to disable, not to kill.

Miriam had found a couple bottles of beer in the fridge along with a Styrofoam carton that held an untouched order of ground lamb *koftes* someone had picked up earlier from a small bakery around the corner. They ate directly from the carton with plastic forks while the contractors kept to themselves across the room.

Najjir switched his phone to the walkie-talkie mode. "Unit one, base."

"Base, unit one," Nikolai Turkin responded from the roof facing Taksim Square. He was a former Russian Spetsnaz operator who'd officially resigned from the service in order to gather contractors for unsanctioned missions—such as capturing a former director of the CIA.

"Give me a sit rep."

"Clear."

"He should be close now."

"We're frosty," Turkin replied.

A number of years ago, when he was still a serving lieutenant, his

Spetsnaz platoon participated in a joint training mission with an American SEAL Team 6 unit in Libya. They'd worked, ate, and slept together for two weeks, and he'd picked up a number of American battlefield expressions. Among them were "Incoming rounds have the right-of-way"; "If everything seems to be going well, you're probably running into an ambush"; and "A sucking chest wound is nature's way of telling you to slow down."

"I want him alive," Najjir reminded.

Turkin didn't bother to reply, which was only slightly bothersome. The man was damned good, one of the best in the business, and he'd never screwed up. Yet Najjir couldn't keep himself from muttering, "But."

Miriam gave him a sharp look. "Trouble?"

"I don't think so," Najjir said, but he had a definite feeling between his shoulders that the bastard was out there, about to do something completely unexpected.

Najjir sent Miriam back upstairs on the freight elevator to check on the woman. "I'm going to look around outside."

"Something's bothering you. What is it?" she asked. "You're starting to worry me."

"The man has a reputation, which includes leaving a trail of bodies behind. At least that's the warning that comes up in his file."

"Do you want to share it with me, for Christ's sake? He's only one man and there're seventeen of us."

"He's apparently faced worse odds."

"So let's kill the broad and cut and run," Miriam said. "Whatever his Intel value might be, it's simply not worth our lives. If you think he's a superman, what's the bloody point?"

"The Eiffel Tower," Najjir said. "I won't report in with two failures."

Miriam looked at him. "Is it really as simple as all that for you?"

"You can't imagine."

.   .   .

Pete had been working for a full fifteen minutes trying to get free of the handcuffs, but they were tighter than she'd thought they would be, and she was stuck just at the base of her right thumb.

The building had been quiet for the past half hour or so, and at one point she thought that she'd heard a siren far off in the distance. She'd held her breath, listening, hoping it was coming this way, but the sound slowly faded and was finally lost, and she'd sunk into despair.

Kirk was across the table from her in the Eiffel Tower before the shit had hit the fan. She'd almost laughed out loud, just about certain what he was going to say next, but not helping him. She'd liked the look of fear in his eyes. Not fear of some force that he thought was overwhelming— she didn't think he'd ever felt something like that—but a genuine fear of what he was about to say and of all the consequences.

She could feel her face against his chest, feel his body against hers in bed, and an almost overwhelming sense of love and security with it. Kirk was at her side and he would always be there for her. You and me. Together.

The metal bracelet cut into her right hand, tearing the flesh. Blood began to well up and suddenly her hand was out.

She pulled the empty cuff free of the bed frame, and lubricating her left wrist with blood was able to pull it free.

Jumping up from the cot, she went to the door and opened it just a crack. One of the goons was at the end of the corridor, about thirty feet away, where the freight elevator opened, his back to her, a shoulder up against the wall.

She shut the door and, careful to make no noise, went to the window and started work again on the rusty steel mesh.

She suddenly stopped and looked over her shoulder. The service elevator had just arrived at the end of the corridor.

Miriam crashed open the service elevator gates and stepped out into the corridor. One of Najjir's operators leaned insolently against the wall, a freshly lit cigarette dangling from his fat lips.

The look on his broad Slavic face was bothersome to her for some reason. Najjir was okay, even urbane, though much of the time he was an arrogant prick and a pain in the ass. And Turkin, the group leader, was okay, but the rest of them were barely human.

"When's the last time you checked on the woman?" she asked in Russian.

"She's not going anywhere," Dimitri said. His accent was Far East—from somewhere in or around Vladivostok. Those guys were only half a step away from being uneducated nomadic Siberians.

"That's not what I asked."

He shrugged indifferently and took a pull from his cigarette.

Miriam slapped it from his lips. "Come to attention, you *pizda*," she said. It roughly meant "pussy."

Dimitri reached inside his jacket for a pistol as he pushed forward. But Miriam had her Glock out first and jammed the muzzle into the man's left cheek, forcing him back against the wall.

"The American coming here will probably manage to kill several of you stupid bastards before he's taken down. If you choose instead to die here and now, it will make no difference."

Dimitri glared at her.

"No one will weep at your graveside."

"Or yours."

Miriam withdrew her pistol. "And I wouldn't want it," she said. "Come with me; we'll check on the woman. Who knows, maybe she's trying to escape and we'll have to shoot her."

Dimitri cracked a slight smile.

A muted *twang*, almost as if an out-of-tune bass string had been plucked, came from one of the rooms down the corridor.

Miriam and Dimitri raced down to the room, but Pete was gone, the screen pulled back, the window open.

THIRTY

☐

Directly ahead of McGarvey's position was the shattered ruins of an apartment building, next door to which was a complex of five-story buildings that looked as if they might have been the site of a factory at one time. He'd been given the address of the apartment building, but he was almost certain the shooter would be in and around the complex.

No lights shone from the windows or openings of either place, but if he had mounted the operation he would have put his people on the roof and at several positions on the ground floor of the factory.

They had Pete and they knew that he would come for her. They also had probably guessed that his likely approach from the hotel would be through the park. A couple of shooters in the shadows on street level and a couple of snipers with night vision scopes on the roof would be plenty.

But to the left, and a full block from the factory, was a nightclub, a dim red light just within the recess of a doorway marking it for what it was. The seedier sections of Istanbul, according to what he'd read on the flight from Paris, were studded with clip joints that were called *pavions*, or glitter bars, where gullible tourists looking for some action would be hosted by good-looking women drinking watered-down cocktails for huge prices, while the tourist would be served full-strength liquors. The idea was to bilk the guy—or in some cases the woman—out of a lot of money with the vague promise of sex later. Of course, the sex never came, and the tourist was kicked out of the place once they were tapped out.

In some instances the tourist would be mugged once they left, but only if it seemed like a worthwhile risk to take, and if the cops on duty in the district that evening had been paid off.

Keeping to the shadows, McGarvey worked his way back into the park, where he was definitely out of sight of anyone on the roof of the factory, before he crossed the street to the club. A small sign over the door in German and English said "Seligkeit and Ecstasy," which was a typical name for this kind of a place, as was the fact the signs were not in Turkish, which would have been deeply offensive to the Muslim population.

The club was less than half full at this early hour, but as soon as he walked in, a good-looking young woman wearing a sheer white blouse and a skirt slit up to the curve of her butt approached him. She had an oriental cast and a broad smile.

"Good evening, welcome to Ecstasy," she said, her accent French. "You're American?"

McGarvey grinned. "Does it show, sweetheart?"

"Yes, but in a good way."

Fifteen or twenty tables for two and four were arranged around a dance floor. A small jazz combo was playing something soft on the small stage, and three couples were dancing to the music.

"I am Sophie. What may I call you?"

"Dicky."

The girl laughed. "Not your name, but I get the joke."

They sat at a table on the left side of the dance floor just as the combo was taking a break. The three musicians disappeared through a door at the rear of the stage, giving Mac a glimpse of a short corridor, at the end of which was an EXIT sign.

A waitress, much older than Sophie and the other hostesses, came over for their drink orders. McGarvey laid down two hundred euros. "This'll do?"

"Yes, sir," the woman said, scooping up the bills.

Sophie ordered a champagne cocktail and McGarvey ordered a Maker's Mark.

"Make it a double, and keep 'em coming, would you, darlin'?"

The waitress and Mac's hostess exchanged a glance.

"So, tell me about yourself," Sophie said.

"Nothing much to tell."

There had to be bouncers in the place, because there would almost always have to be trouble later in the evening, when the tourist realized what kind of prices he was paying. But for the moment the only people in sight were a couple of cocktail waitresses, a lone male bartender off to the right, and the customers and their hostesses.

"Have you come to Istanbul for business or simply pleasure?" Sophie asked, spreading her legs. She was seated next to him, not across the table, and her panties were as sheer as her blouse. Her pudendum had not been shaved, which meant that she was nothing more than a hostess, not a prostitute.

"Actually business," Mac said.

Their drinks came, and when their waitress was gone he pulled out ten hundred-euro notes. Keeping them out of sight under the table, he offered them to the girl.

She glanced over at the bartender. "Not here," she said. "Maybe when I get off. It's the police regulations."

"What's outside the rear door?"

She shook her head, confused. "Buildings, apartments, I think. An alley. Garbage."

"I want to get thrown out of here, but I don't want any real trouble. Do you understand?"

"No."

"I'm going get up and call you a name and go out the back way."

"Security will stop you."

"You're going call me a cheap bastard. No money, no credit card."

The girl took the money, and nodded slightly.

McGarvey jumped up, knocking the chair over. "You fucking whore!" he shouted.

Sophie got to her feet as two very large men came from somewhere out of the darkness across the room next to the bar. The other customers looked up.

"The *salopard* has no fucking money! Just the two hundred! I want him the fuck out of here!"

McGarvey winked at the girl, who cracked a momentary smile, and he was across the dance floor and out the rear door before the bouncers could reach him.

He didn't think they'd be too hard on the girl. They hadn't served him a drink yet, and they had his two hundred.

McGarvey held up in the shadows at the end of the squalid alley, the three-story buildings leaning over at such extreme angles that the roofs almost touched, nearly forming an arch.

One of the bouncers had come out, and although it wasn't likely he could see Mac, he held up a middle finger before he turned and went back inside.

From here he was just across a narrow street from a block of similar apartment buildings and what appeared to be a small bakery, closed at this hour. A moped, without its tires, was chained to an old-fashioned iron light post—the light on top missing. A delivery van was parked at the corner to the right. Beyond that intersection the street led to the front of the club and, the other way, toward the ruined apartment and abandoned factory.

Once he was across the street he would be out of any sight line from the roof of the factory.

His phone vibrated.

Nothing was coming from behind him, and at the moment the street he faced was empty of traffic.

"Yes.

It was Otto. "Are you clear?"

"I'm fifty meters from the apartment and factory.

"Gibson called someone in Istanbul and stopped the military from interfering. If that's what you still want."

"What about Rowe?"

"That's the problem. I've lost him."

"What do you mean?"

"He's a smart bastard. I'll give him that. He knows we're on to him and he's taken the battery and SIM card out of his phone. Could be he's probably still on your ass. So watch your six."

"Have the chief of Istanbul station call him off."

"Already tried, but the guy is apparently out of the city. No answer on his cell or at his office or home, just answering machines."

"How about the number two?"

"For the moment Rowe is acting deputy chief of station," Otto said.

"Marty hired him."

THIRTY-ONE

□

It seemed like forever to Pete, hiding in the shadows underneath the cot, her back against the wall, before the guard Miriam had ordered to remain in the room stepped out into the corridor.

There had been little or no noise since the woman had used her phone to sound the alarm and then raced down the corridor and took the stairs. Down, Pete thought.

Sooner or later they would realize that she might not have left the room after all and would come back to look for her. In the meantime the son of a bitch in the corridor was the one who had tried to rape her.

Keeping her eye on the open door, she eased out from beneath the cot, just about every bone and muscle in her body aching because of the several beatings she had endured. But she'd had enough of being the helpless victim. Kirk was coming for her, and she wasn't going to lie around waiting for him.

Anyway, it was time for a little payback.

Taking great care to make absolutely no noise, she picked up the handcuffs and crept to the door. She could smell the goon's body odor, and garlic on his breath.

Holding her breath, she took a quick peek around the corner. The big bastard was standing right there, his back to her, his left shoulder up against the wall. He was a good ten inches taller than Pete and outweighed her by at least one hundred fifty pounds. His massive neck was short, and dirty. She could see the grime in the folds of his skin.

Holding her head against the door frame for just a moment, she took a deep breath, then swiveled around at the same moment the Russian pushed away from the wall and started to turn.

She jumped on his back, looping the handcuff chain around his neck, a bracelet in each hand, and she reared back, her left knee in the small of his back, and pulled with every ounce of her strength.

The goon reached for the chain as he lurched forward, but he couldn't get a grip on it.

Pete continued to hold with everything she had, the side of the man's face starting to turn beet red as he bucked to the left and then right, trying to dislodge her.

She pulled even harder.

He slammed backwards, mashing Pete's body against the wall, nearly dislocating her knee.

She started to fuzz out but rode the man down as he slumped to one knee. He reached down with his left hand on the floor to steady himself from falling, his jacket open.

Pete had lost her grip on the cuffs, but before the Russian could recover she snatched the big pistol—an Austrian-made Steyr 9mm, the thought came to her—leaped to one side, and without hesitation fired a shot at point-blank range into the man's head.

Dimitri pitched forward onto to his face, on both knees as if he were a Muslim at prayer.

The building was suddenly very quiet after the sound of the gunshot. Pete stumbled away, almost falling, the leg she'd jammed against the Russian's back nearly giving way.

Shooting the bastard had been the last thing she'd wanted to do, because Najjir and the broad and just about everyone else in the building were going to come up here on the run. But she'd been no match against the Russian's bulk and she'd lost her grip on the handcuffs.

Keeping the pistol in both hands, down and away, she sprinted to the stairwell door at the end of the corridor and, switching to a one-handed grip, opened it with her left.

At least two people, but probably more, were coming up from below, making no effort at stealth. Up was the only way for her, but as she stepped into the stairwell she heard a door above slamming open and at least one person start down toward her.

McGarvey had pulled up at a back corner of the shattered apartment building. From where he'd been standing in the darkness, he'd made out one sniper on the roof of the factory, and two figures—one of whom had come out of the building minutes earlier—were apparently in deep discussion. The light was uncertain and the distance was too far for a positive identification of the one man, but Mac was almost certain it was Najjir.

The single pistol shot, when it had come seconds ago, seemed to have been fired from somewhere deep inside the factory complex, and higher up, but not on the roof.

Whoever had fired, and for whatever reason, it had come as a complete surprise to the two men on the ground.

The one Mac thought was Najjir turned and hurried back inside, his hand raised to his left ear as if he were talking on a phone.

The second man rushed up a driveway and disappeared through an open iron gate.

The sniper on the roof had disappeared as well, and from where Mac stood he could spot no other guard.

He took out the Walther that Rowe had given him at the airport and started to climb over the remnants of a concrete block wall, but then stepped back. He ejected the magazine, cycled the round out of the firing chamber, and mostly by feel started to disassemble the pistol, finding the problem almost immediately. The gun had no firing pin.

Marty had set him up, for whatever reason. In the old days he had blamed Martyisms like this one on plain stupidity. But this now was something else. The DDCI wanted Mac and Pete dead.

The question was, why?

McGarvey holstered the useless pistol, checked the approaches to the factory for shooters, then climbed over the wall and, keeping low, moving in a zigzag pattern, made his way through the apartment building to the doorway where the two men had been talking.

. . .

Pete held up short on the landing just below the door to the roof as whoever was coming down stopped.

"She's just below me," the man from the roof spoke softly.

"Hold your position, One, we're on the way up," a woman replied. It was
Miriam and they were on walkie-talkies or cell phones in speaker mode.

"I'll take her."

"We want her alive."

Pete's heart rate slowed, just as she'd been taught at the Farm that it
would. Trust in your training combined with your instincts. Take advantage of your openings. The advantage had shifted to her. They wanted her
alive as bait for Mac.

Moving swiftly and as silently as possible on the balls of her feet, she
sprinted up the last half flight of stairs, and when she came into view,
the sniper on the landing above started to bring his Heckler & Koch MR7
rifle with infrared scope around, but she fired two shots, hitting him center mass, and he collapsed.

Shoving the pistol into the waistband of her slacks, Pete went the rest
of the way up, snatched the cell phone from the dead man's hand and
the MR7 from where it lay at his side, and went to the roof door, where
she held up.

She eased the rusty metal door open just a crack, in time to see one of
the snipers with the same weapon in hand racing her way.

Shoving the muzzle of the rifle through the opening with her right
hand, she fired a sort burst, the sniper going down.

"What the fuck is going on up there?" Miriam demanded.

Pete raised the phone and hit the Send button. "Why don't you come
up and take a look for yourself, bitch?"

The woman didn't respond for a full three seconds. When she did, she
sounded unconcerned. "You're only delaying the inevitable, sweetheart."

"Three down," Pete said. "The odds are getting better for me."

"But not for Mr. McGarvey. We have him covered from this side as well
as behind."

Pete glanced out the door. The sniper she'd downed wasn't moving, nor had anyone else shown up.

"Where there's life, there's hope, isn't that what you people are fond of saying?" Miriam radioed.

"You might think about that for yourself."

"We don't give a damn about you, but we really don't want to kill your boyfriend. So why not help us save his life, like a good little mum."

THIRTY-TWO

☐

Najjir reached the landing between the second and third floors, where Miriam and two of the operators where hunched down. Mistakes he could abide, but not gross negligence, and especially not incompetence. But everything that had happened in Paris, and now here, reeked of an amateur operation.

"What the hell happened?" he demanded, keeping his voice low.

"I'm not sure, but she took out two of your lookouts topsides and probably got the drop on Dimitri."

"You had her handcuffed to the bed."

"So she got loose," Miriam practically shouted. "If you still want McGarvey, get over it."

Najjir got on his phone. "Unit One, Base. What's your situation?"

"The woman is just inside the doorway," Turkin responded.

"Casualties?"

"Yevgenni was in the stairwell, and I'm assuming she took him out, because she has his weapon and she used it to hit Arkadi."

"Are they dead?" Miriam asked.

Turkin laughed. "Arkadi isn't moving," he said. "Why don't you come take a look for yourself?"

"Who's covering the southwest approach from the park?" Najjir demanded.

"No one."

. . .

"Oops," Pete said.

"What are your orders?" Turkin asked.

"Shove the rifle up your ass and pull off a round," Pete radioed. "Even a tough Spetsnaz operator isn't likely to miss."

"I need that approach covered," Najjir said. "Take her out now."

"Stun grenade?"

"Do it."

Pete had to figure her chances. She couldn't go back downstairs. Najjir would no longer hesitate to kill her. But if she did nothing and the Russian on the roof tossed a stun grenade through the door, she would go down. But first he had to get the grenade, probably off a utility belt, and he would have to pull the pin.

All that went through her head at the speed of light.

She brought the rifle up as she swiveled through the doorway.

Turkin was ten feet away, a stun grenade in his left hand, the rifle in the crook of his arm. He looked up, realizing his mistake, the instant before Pete fired one short burst, hitting him center mass, and he went down hard.

Two seconds later the grenade went off with a tremendous flash and a *bang*.

"Four down, and counting," Pete radioed.

McGarvey was halfway through the ruins of the apartment building when the second burst of gunfire erupted from the roof, followed by the noise and light of a flashbang grenade, and he pulled up short.

Some sort of a battle was going on inside the factory—possibly a faction fight. But he wanted to think that Pete was still alive somehow and had taken the initiative.

He raced to the crumbling outer wall, which faced an empty lot strewn with bricks, boulder-size pieces of concrete, some with rebar sticking out at all angles, and held up as something or someone behind him made a noise that sounded like a cough.

Whipping out the useless Walther, he slid to the left and dropped into a shooter's stance.

"By now you have to know that the pistol I gave you has no firing pin," Rowe said from deep in the shadows, perhaps fifteen or twenty feet away. "I followed you on Mr. Bambridge's orders."

Just to Mac's left was a section of brick wall about four feet tall. To reach it he would have to expose himself to fire from anyone in the factory, and to Rowe. At the moment a practically no-win situation.

"I picked up a new gun at the club."

"No," Rowe said. "But I'm here to warn you that something is going down in Washington. Bambridge is involved, though to what extent I'm not sure. But I do know that if you somehow survive this mess you'll be a marked man when you return to Washington."

"Why tell me this?"

"Because it's wrong, and because I'd rather have you as a friend."

"Makes you a marked man."

"I'll disappear tonight," Rowe said. He stepped out of the shadows and carefully set a pistol on the ground. "I didn't think I'd be at this point, so unfortunately I didn't bring an extra mag or two. But it's a ten-millimeter Glock, fifteen rounds in the handle, one in the receiver, and an intact firing pin."

McGarvey glanced over his shoulder at the factory, and when he turned back, Rowe was gone. "I'll look you up when this is over."

"Do that," the CIA officer said from the dark.

McGarvey stuffed the Walther into the belt at the small of his back, then retrieved the pistol, checked that a round was in the firing chamber, and went back to the wall. He held up for a second, to make sure nothing moved, then sprinted across the open field.

Pete ducked inside the freight elevator equipment room just a few meters from the open stairwell door. From where she crouched she had a sight line through some rusty louvers on the doorway to the left and the downed

Russian's legs on the right. But she had no clear view of the other positions on the roof, where she was pretty sure snipers had been placed.

But they would have to come into view if they wanted to get to her.

Propping the rifle against the tin wall, she took a closer look at the phone. It was a Russian-made YotaPhone that used the Rostelcom network. It was old, and slow, but very sturdy and reliable. They'd been introduced to a variety of cell phones and services around the world at a five-day technology seminar taught by Otto.

She switched it from the walkie-talkie mode and entered Otto's number. He answered in Russian on the second ring.

"Da."

"It's me," Pete said. "I took down four of their people and I'm armed and hiding on the roof of what I think was a factory. Where's Mac?"

"Oh, wow. You okay?"

"For now. But I'm talking on one of their phones; can they listen in?"

"No. Mac is close, but something else has come up."

"First, can you let him know that I'm holed up in a freight elevator equipment room?"

"Yes, I have you pinpointed. Are you secure?"

"I don't think for long."

"I'll let him know. But in the meantime it looks as if Marty has got a hand in the situation. Don't know what, yet, but he may be calling some of the shots."

Pete was incredulous. "Was he involved in the Paris thing?"

"I don't know, but something else is going on that I haven't got a handle on either. Except that the number two guy at our station there in Istanbul has apparently been piping Marty with intel—above and beyond the station's normal output."

A man dressed in all black, the same as the two Russian operators she'd killed, appeared on the right for just a moment, before he ducked down and disappeared in the shadows.

"I've got company. Gotta go," Pete said, breaking the connection.

THIRTY-THREE

□

McGarvey flattened himself against the wall next to the driveway that led through an open iron gate into the factory complex. Since the gunshots and flashbang grenade a couple of minutes ago, there'd been no sounds from inside.

He took a quick look through the gate and pulled back. One man, with what looked like a Heckler & Koch MP5 room broom at port arms, stood just inside the overhang of a doorway. A dark blue Mercedes sedan was parked off to the left, beyond which were three windowless vans with some markings in Turkish but a Latin-based alphabet.

The sounds of traffic in the distance, a siren somewhere, and the mournful blast of a ship's whistle, out in the Bosphorus but close, could have been New York or San Francisco. But they sounded foreign, ancient, a thousand or more years of history even before Columbus sailed to the New World.

He checked again, but the guard hadn't moved from his position. He cleared his six before he phoned Otto.

"I'm at the front gate. Do any of them have cell phones you can access?"

"Yes. But the situation has changed. Pete is barricaded on the roof. I talked to her."

"I heard automatic weapons fire and a flashbang grenade. Is she okay?"

"For now. She took down four of their people, and she's armed with one of their rifles and a Russian-made cell phone. But they know where she is, and there are at least two other operators on the roof with her, plus someone on the stairs, so she's cut off."

"Connect me with Najjir."

"Goddamnit, Mac. If you let yourself be taken, they won't need her. You know that."

"Link her with the call."

"They know you're coming," Otto said. He sounded desperate. 'It's not too late to call for help. Gibson will go along with just about anything we want, at this point."

"Do you think he's suspicious of Marty?"

"That's fringe, but no, I don't think so."

"Good, then we'll leave it at that for the moment. Make the call."

"You're not thinking straight."

"If Marty is somehow involved with these people, an attack in France was nothing more than a diversion. Something else is going on that we need to know about."

"Okay, but what?"

"Could Marty have known that Pete and I would be at the Jules Verne at that moment in time?"

"I don't know, but I doubt it."

"Unless he has some other intel sources you don't know about?"

"If it's non-electronic, and is off campus—face-to-face—then sure."

"I'm going to find out. But in the meantime I need to get Pete away from here and on a flight out of the country."

Otto was silent for a longish moment. When he returned he sounded forlorn, as if he'd just lost a good friend or he'd learned that just about everything he'd come out of the cold for had been false.

"If you're going to do what I think you're going to do, I'm going to link the call with every cell phone in the building," he said. "I don't want some twitchy son of a bitch getting nervous and taking a potshot when you show yourself. Stand by."

Najjir and Miriam were holding, just two steps down from the open door, when Viktor Lipasov, one of the two remaining operators on the roof, made contact.

"She's inside the elevator machinery room. What do you want me to do?"

"Can you get her out with a grenade?"

"No. The door's closed."

"Stand by," Najjir said. At the same moment his phone buzzed, and he switched to speaker mode.

"Mr. Najjir," McGarvey said.

Pete was also receiving his call. "Don't mean to be a pest, sweetheart, but what the hell has taken you so long?" she said.

"I'm here," McGarvey told her. "You okay?"

"Peachy. What's the plan?"

"Yes, Mr. McGarvey, what is the plan?" Najjir asked.

"You want a trade? Here I am."

"Might be that you're a little late. There's already been a considerable amount of collateral damage done."

"Your call. But that's just Ms. Boylan's doing. Maybe you should think about what I'm capable of."

"You didn't come into this country armed."

McGarvey didn't respond.

"Where are you at this moment?"

"At the front gate."

"Show yourself."

"Your operator will shoot me."

"He will not, you have my word on it. We want you alive," Najjir said. "Give me a moment and I'll call him."

"No need. Every one of your people who has a phone is hearing us," McGarvey said. He cleared his six again and, holding the Walther in plain sight, stepped around the corner.

The man in the doorway came to attention, his assault weapon pointed at McGarvey.

"Step forward," Najjir said.

McGarvey started toward the operator, who raised a phone to his lips.

"He is carrying a pistol."

"I know, but do not shoot him," Najjir said.

It was a mistake. The bastard knew about the Walther with a missing firing pin.

"Send my friend down now," McGarvey said. The Walther was in his right hand, the phone in his left.

"Stop where you are, Mr. McGarvey," Najjir said. "Someone is coming to take you into custody."

"My friend," McGarvey said, less than ten feet from the operator.

"He is not stopping," the man in the doorway said. He was getting nervous.

"Shoot him in the legs," Najjir radioed.

McGarvey made a show of laying the pistol on the cobblestones.

"He put his gun down."

"It doesn't matter," Najjir shouted.

The confused operator started to raise his weapon, when McGarvey drew Rowe's Glock and fired one shot into the man's forehead from a range of less than three feet.

He left the phone on but jammed it into his jacket pocket and snatched the H&K from the dead man's hands.

Armed now with the pistol in his left hand and the assault weapon in his right, Mac rolled through the doorway into what had been a marble-tiled lobby fronting the business section of the concern, swinging the H&K to the right as a pair of black-clad operators came down a corridor in a dead run.

Firing two short bursts, center mass into each of the men, Mac swiveled on his heel toward a broad stairway from above as a third man descended, firing the same make of weapon as the man in front and the two in the corridor had been armed with.

But his aim was off because of his footing on the stairs, the bullets pinging off the marble floor, giving McGarvey the chance to fire another short burst, catching the man in the left shoulder and then the right side of his head.

Two more men came down the stairs and Mac turned toward them.

A third man came through the front door. "Put it down, or I will fire."

THIRTY-FOUR

☐

Pete heard everything that was going on in the lobby through Mac's phone, though it was muffled. Someone had evidently come up from behind him.

"I will shoot you, Mr. McGarvey," the man said. His accent was definitely German, which made almost no sense to her, except that Mac was in trouble.

She raised the cell phone. "I'm coming out."

"About time, my dear," Najjir said.

"What about this bastard?" the German demanded.

"Shoot, but only in self-defense. I want the man alive and transportable."

"Ja. I'm at the front door. Vlad and Paul are on the stairs. We'll disarm him, but if he moves so much as a millimeter I will put a round in the base of his spine. He'll never be able to walk, but he will be able to talk."

"Good enough," Najjir said.

"The deal is off," Pete screamed. "You'll have to dig me out of here, and it'll cost you."

"I've always loved old American movies," Miriam interjected. "Frankly, my dear, we don't give a damn. You can stay up there until hell freezes over, because we have what we want."

The black-clad operator who'd briefly appeared through the louvers came into sight again, and Pete emptied the H&K's magazine on him, and he flipped over on his back.

Without hesitation she dropped the weapon, slammed open the rusty steel door, and moving low and fast reached the downed man, snatched the assault rifle from his dead hands, and hit the deck, flattening herself behind the man's body.

So far as she could tell, she was now alone on the roof.

She raised the phone. "One more down," she said. "Najjir and the broad are in the stairwell, but I have the door covered."

McGarvey lowered the room broom by its strap to the floor, then held the pistol away from his body. "I'm going to put it on the floor too."

"With care," the German said.

Moving slowly, McGarvey bent down and laid the pistol on the floor, then straightened up.

"Tell him to kick them away, Hans," Najjir said.

"Do as he says."

McGarvey kicked the pistol away, then the submachine gun.

"Is it the Walther?"

"It's a Glock," Hans said.

"Where the hell did he get it?" Miriam demanded in the background.

"He may be armed with other weapons," Hans said. "We'll search him to make sure."

"Send Ms. Boylan down, unharmed, and give her the keys to the Mercedes," McGarvey said. "When she's gone, you'll have my full cooperation, and no one else needs to get hurt here."

"I'm not leaving without you," Pete said.

"Yes, you are."

"No, goddamn it."

"Pete, listen to me. I'm going to need yours and Otto's help once I'm taken. And right now the only guarantee for your safety is for me to cooperate with them. Do you understand?"

Pete did not reply.

"Good advice, sweetheart," Miriam said.

"Fuck you, dyke," Pete shot back.

"It's the easiest choice," McGarvey prompted. "Trust me."

Again Pete held her silence for a long moment or two. "Okay," she said, resigned, her voice soft.

McGarvey spread his arms. "Get it over with. I want her out of here right now."

"Turn around and face me," Hans said.

McGarvey did as he was told. "KSK?" It was the German Army's elite special forces group—the Kommando Spezialkräfte.

Hans didn't bother to reply. "Paul, search him, but first give your weapon to Vlad."

McGarvey smiled, but the German remained expressionless.

A man about the same height and build as Mac came from behind. "Nice and easy now, okay, mate?" he said. His accent was British.

He turned Mac around so that they faced each other, and began to frisk him, starting at the shoulders and chest.

The man had been armed with a room broom, which he had turned over to the other man on the stairs. But like all special operators in every military organization in the world, he also carried a sidearm in a holster strapped to his chest. In this case, a SIG Sauer P226—one of the most common pistols in the British Secret Air Service's arsenal. Old habits died hard.

"*Verdammte Scheisse*," Hans shouted.

McGarvey snatched the man's SIG at the same time he bulled him around so that his back faced the German, who fired at the same time Mac fired one shot at the man on the stairs. As the Brit's legs gave out, Mac followed him down to the floor, using his body as a shield, and fired two shots.

The German, light on his feet and incredibly fast, sidestepped to the right. Mac's first shot went wide, but his second hit the man high in the throat and at an angle, the 9mm round plowing into the man's brain, killing him almost instantly.

McGarvey went to the operator who had pitched face-forward down the steps, snatched both room brooms, plus two spare magazines of ammunition, and started up the stairs, slinging one of the compact submachine guns over his shoulder and stuffing the mags in his pockets.

"Soon as I clear the ground floor I'll meet you topsides," he said as he reached the second-floor landing, which opened into a wide space that had once been one of the manufacturing floors in the factory.

He pulled up short, sweeping his weapon left to right. The room was littered with old wooden crates, pieces of dirty cardboard, broken bricks, and trash of all sorts. Straight across, about forty meters away, half the wall and windows were gone, that side of the building open to the night. But nothing moved, nor were there any sirens in the distance.

With all the gunfire and the grenade on the roof, McGarvey figured that by now someone must have alerted the police. Unless Gibson's call had put a hold on raids down here. Actually it was one less complication to the situation. With the cops or military crawling all over the place it would be to Najjir's advantage to simply kill both of them and slip away.

But there were still too many holes in the operation. Something was going on that he couldn't get a handle on. Something or someone was pulling or causing strings to be pulled. Downing the Eiffel Tower had been an insane objective, especially because the apparent chief architect of the attack had been right there on-site.

And unless they had somehow known in advance that he would be there at the Jules Verne, at that exact hour, snatching him and Pete made even less sense. But they had set up the church as a fallback, the flight here to Istanbul, and this place, with a fair amount of firepower—apparently pulled from the ranks of former special military forces from at least four countries: Russia, Germany, Britain, and France.

All of that took a lot of advance planning and money. And for what objective? For the life of him he couldn't fathom what it might be.

And on top of all of that, Marty Bambridge apparently had some hand in the mess. He'd never liked the man—and the feeling had been mutual—but he'd never in his wildest imagination taken the man for a traitor.

He raised the phone. "Can you get your hands on a flashbang?"

"Right in front of me," Pete replied immediately.

"Give me thirty seconds, then toss it into the stairwell."

"Will do."

McGarvey turned and started up the next flight, this time making enough noise that Pete and everyone else in the complex was certain to hear him.

The hounds to the hare, but with a decoy.

Ten seconds later, Pete heard the sounds of someone tromping up the stairs, which she took to be Mac's signal that the thirty seconds had been a ruse.

She started to pull the pin on the flashbang grenade she'd taken from the downed man's utility belt, when the muzzle of a rifle was placed on the back of her head.

THIRTY—FIVE

□

Otto hesitated for just a moment outside Bambridge's office on the seventh floor.

He had reprogrammed the entire electronics suite in the deputy director's Lincoln Navigator so that the GPS would report the vehicle's every movement and real-time position, the phone system would report every call made, and the stereo system would relay anything said inside the car—engine and systems running or not.

And with a flesh-colored earbud, all but invisible to anyone unless they were standing a foot or two from his left side and pushing his long hair aside, he continued to monitor the phone conversations at the warehouse complex. As Najjir and the rest of them had to be realizing about now, it was a very bad idea to underestimate Mac. Or Pete.

It was Marty's turn to learn the same lesson.

The inner door to the deputy director's office was open, and before his secretary could intervene, Bambridge looked up, resigned, and motioned Otto in.

"You've come to tell me that McGarvey and Ms. Boylan have been shot to death— something I warned you and the general would happen—or your hat is in hand and you want my help after all."

"Neither," Otto said, not bothering to sit down.

The last transmission he'd heard from the factory was Najjir's voice speaking only two words in English: "Come now." There'd been nothing further from Mac or Pete since, and it was more than bothersome.

"Well?"

"Mac has made his way into the factory complex, he's there now, and he's apparently taken down several of the bad guys."

"How do you know this?" Bambridge demanded, a little too sharply.

Otto suppressed a smile. "I've managed to monitor some of the cell phone conversations."

"And?"

"He told me that before he went inside he had a chat with Mark Rowe—he's our guy from the consulate station who gave Mac papers, money, and a weapon. Evidently there was something wrong with the gun. Maybe a manufacturing defect. But Mark brought him a replacement just in the nick of time."

"Where did this take place?"

"Within sight of the factory."

"I thought they were holed up in an apartment building."

"An abandoned factory next door."

Bambridge was disturbed, and he took a moment to respond. When he did he was angry. "What the hell do you want from me? You've already turned down my help. Or am I suddenly supposed to go back to General Gibson and tell him to ask for assistance from the Turkish Army after all?"

"Not yet. But I wanted to keep you informed. You might want to give Mark a recommendation. Maybe a commendation."

Again Bambridge took his time answering. "I'll consider it."

"Thanks," Otto said, and he turned to leave, but Bambridge stopped him.

"So what's the bottom line over there? What the hell is going on?"

"I don't know, Marty. Mac says he's on top of it."

"But he wants no help from us?"

"No, nothing else. He says something else is going on that he needs to get a handle on."

"This is fucking crazy, do you know that? You're all certifiable. McGarvey is finally going to get himself and his girlfriend killed, and I'll be here to say I told you so."

"That, and the Company will deny any responsibility for what he tried to do."

"You're goddamn right!" Bambridge said. "Now get the fuck out of my office."

"With more pleasure than you can imagine."

McGarvey held up in the stairwell, one landing below the roof. Everything above was silent, but he thought he could hear someone coming up behind him.

No one was using the phones now, not even Pete, and that was the most bothersome to him. But there'd been no sounds of gunfire in the past few minutes, nor had she tossed a flashbang through. The best-case scenario was that she'd understood his ruse and was waiting for him to show up, or at least to tell her what to do next. The worst-case scenario was that she had been denied the use of the phone, possibly even killed.

A half mile away Rowe phoned Bambridge's encrypted cell phone. The deputy director answered on the first ring, as if he had been expecting the call.

"Yes."

"I followed him over to the apartment building and made the weapons exchange as you suggested. But it's only a fifteen-round mag, so there's no way in hell he'll survive. The odds are too great, even for him."

"Are you nearby?"

"No, but I stuck around long enough to hear one hell of a gunfight."

"Don't write him off just yet," Bambridge said.

"The man's fifty years old and he's got a peg leg. Christ, he's not Superman."

"Tell me, Mark, when you had the chance, did you have the possibility of a clean shot?"

"Actually, yes."

"Why didn't you take it?"

"Wasn't in my brief."

"If he finds out that you've been working with me, I think you'll regret that decision."

"I brought him the pistol. He thinks I'm his friend."

"He doesn't have any real friends. Men like him can't afford them."

"What do you want me to do?"

"Start on a text, sending your regrets that the former DCI was involved in a shoot-out with as yet unidentified criminal elements in Tarlabasi that resulted in a number of casualties—including his death and that of his fiancée, who was an employee of this agency but was, at the time of her death, on vacation."

"What if he survives?"

"You'd best hope that he doesn't," Bambridge said.

Pete was on her knees, her hands laced behind her head, and she felt incredibly stupid. She'd been in this position for what seemed like an eternity to her, but she figured it couldn't have been much more than five minutes. An eternity for fluid situations like these.

After what sounded like an intense firefight, somewhere below, the building had fallen silent. No one, not even Mac, had used the phones in all that time, and her heart was hurting. She thought that there was a very real possibility that he was dead.

They'd discussed that very thing one night six months ago. They'd been walking along the beach at his house on Casey Key on the Gulf south of Tampa. It was early evening, the stars out, the night air soft.

"Have you ever thought that it was game over?" she'd asked.

He'd chuckled. "Damned near every time."

She'd stopped and looked at his face. "You're kidding."

"No."

"Then, why?"

He'd shrugged. "It's who I am—or maybe *what* I am."

A car went by on the narrow island's only road, behind them. Some-one heading somewhere. Maybe dinner, Pete thought. But not into a situation that could very possibly lead to their deaths by violent means.

She was at his side at that moment, but she thought that it was perhaps the loneliest and most frightened she'd ever been in her life. Until now.

THIRTY-SIX

□

McGarvey slipped into the third-floor corridor, where he paused for a moment, holding the door open and listening with all of his senses to the sounds of the building.

There was nothing from above, but at least one person, maybe two, was moving on the stairs below, very quietly, making almost no noise.

Easing the door shut, Mac raced down the corridor to the freight elevator, where he hit the call button. Moments later the car, which was somewhere below, started up with a clatter.

He took the phone out of his pocket. "Otto, are you still with me?"

"Here," Rencke came back immediately.

"I haven't heard anything from Pete in at least five minutes. They may have taken her phone."

"I can't pinpoint it closer than a couple of feet, but it's still active."

"Then she's either unconscious or someone is holding a gun to her head, threatening to kill her if she opens her mouth. I'm going to give them some room, try to defuse the situation long enough to let everyone cool down."

"What's the plan, kemo sabe?"

"I'm going to take the freight elevator to the ground floor. There's a car and a couple of vans parked just outside. Soon as I get to them I'm going to try for a trade again. But if Pete's down, you can go ahead with the general's suggestion."

"The army?"

"I'll cover the front. Najjir and his people will have to get past me, and it won't be easy."

"Pete's not dead," Otto said. "I'd feel it."

"I hope so. I just want this to be over with."

"You're not actually going to turn yourself over to them, Mac. Think it out."

"If Pete is still alive and they let her walk free, I'll keep my word."

The elevator arrived and Mac sent it back down to the first floor.

A minute and a half later gunfire erupted from below.

McGarvey went back to the stairway and headed down to the next landing, where he crouched low on the stairs, from where he would have a clear shot on anyone coming up or down.

"He wasn't on the elevator," one of the operators from below radioed.

"I think that he's one floor below us, so watch yourselves," Najjir said.

"Roger."

Najjir stood at the open door to the roof, Pete on her knees glaring at him. He held the phone in his right hand, blocking the microphone, and turned to Miriam. "He's on the floor just below us," he said softly. "Go down and talk to him, but leave your pistol here."

Miriam caught what he was doing, so she whispered, "Have you lost your fucking mind?"

"As soon as whoever's left downstairs gets up here we'll have him in a cross fire."

"With me as a fucking hostage."

"That's the point, isn't it, my dear. The man wants to trade, so let's do it."

"We're not bargaining with my life."

"How does it feel, bitch?" Pete shouted.

The operator holding the rifle on her slammed the butt of the weapon into the side of her head and she went down on her face.

"I'm not fucking around," Najjir said. "We need him alive. Whatever the cost."

"No."

"As long as he knows that his girlfriend is still alive, and there's a possibility we'll trade for her, he won't kill you," Najjir said. "Look, she's our

hostage; you'll give yourself up as his. The longer we can keep him occupied, the more the advantage will swing our way."

"We underestimated the man, didn't we," she said.

"Yes," Najjir said, but just to appease her. His people had been sloppy
at the tower and church in Paris and here. But this op, with McGarvey,
was an unexpected bonus. Actually a lifeline, worth even more than the
Paris–Washington thing.

The only thing that bothered him was the man's being there at the Jules
Verne at the very moment the attack was starting up. It was an improbable
coincidence, a thing he'd never trusted.

"Your choice," Najjir said.

Miriam shook her head. "I'm probably facing my nine ounces no matter
what I do."

"I'm in just about the same boat."

"Unless we bring the former CIA director back with us."

"Alive," Najjir said.

Miriam handed over her pistol. She turned and started down, but then
looked back. "Something else is going on, isn't it? Him and the broad at
the tower just then."

Najjir nodded. "It's one of the things I'd like to ask him about."

"Me too," Miriam said. She headed down, the operator who'd been
holding Pete at gunpoint on the roof just behind her.

McGarvey, crouched on the landing between the third and second floors,
had heard only some of Najjir's conversations. The man had apparently
done something to his phone to mute out most of his transmissions.

Whoever was coming from below had held up, but they were close.
Someone else started down.

"Mr. McGarvey, I want to talk to you," Miriam said. "I'm unarmed."

"Someone is in the stairwell below me. Send them away."

"I can't do that, but I just want to talk, that's all."

"Send Pete down to me."

"I can't do that either."

Making as little noise as possible, Mac went back up to the third floor, holding up at the open doorway.

"May I come down?" Miriam asked. She'd stopped on the next landing up.

"All I want is a trade. Send Pete down, and once she's away I'll turn myself over to you."

"What guarantee do we have?"

"None."

"Goddamnit, we want you alive, not dead."

"Then why did your operators opened fire on the freight elevator when they thought I was on board?"

"When you have a chance to take a look for yourself you'll find that they didn't actually fire into the car."

"Then come," McGarvey said. "But if someone is tagging along, I'll shoot you first. Are you clear on that?"

"One operator is on the stairs behind me, and two are below you. They won't come any closer."

"Your life depends on it."

Miriam turned the corner on the midfloor landing and, her hands in plain sight, moved down the last few steps, but then stopped, confused. McGarvey wasn't there.

"Mr. McGarvey?" she called softly.

McGarvey appeared at the open doorway, the room broom pointed in her general direction. "That's close enough."

"I've come to offer myself as a hostage."

"I don t take hostages."

THIRTY-SEVEN

☐

Bambridge had driven over to Turkey Run Park just north of the CIA's main entrance on the GW Parkway, which followed the Potomac River, and parked at the start of one of the footpaths. It was a weekday, and just enough people were present to make his arrival nearly anonymous. Another visitor taking a break from a busy day.

The man he knew as William Rodak, a midlevel aide to President Weaver, had been friends with an old college buddy of Marty's. He'd been introduced a couple of years ago, in the middle of Weaver's incendiary presidential campaign, as a man who might prove useful to the agency if the impossible happened and Weaver won.

Rodak's specialty was Russia. He'd actually lived and studied for his Ph.D. in Moscow and Vladivostok and had gone back to do a couple of research papers for the State Department. The media had viewed him as the most likely link between the White House and the Kremlin.

Marty had always considered him a valuable resource.

He was a powerfully built man with broad shoulders, a sturdy frame, and a no-nonsense, all-business demeanor. It was said that he never smiled, because he felt that he carried the fate of American–Russian relationship on his shoulders.

"Rapprochement is our only viable option," President Weaver was fond of saying. They were Rodak's words.

Marty had three favorite soft-porn sites that he visited on his personal tablet from time to time. Rodak had the means to hack all three sites. One meant Marty wanted to set up a meeting at the Lincoln Memorial at noon in two days. Another meant Marty wanted to meet at the bar in the Watergate the same evening at ten. And the third was the most urgent: Marty wanted a meeting immediately, this time at Turkey Run Park. Wherever they met, they would agree on the next meeting place, never using the same places twice.

Rodak was sitting on a park bench, smoking one of his ever-present unfiltered Camel cigarettes.

Marty sat down next to him, and for a minute or so neither of them spoke, until Rodak broke the silence.

"What has you bothered, my friend?"

"The Paris thing may be spinning out of control."

"Because of the possible connection with Moscow? If that's the case, you needn't worry. From what I've learned, the entire business was directed from the lowest possible level."

"Deniable?"

Rodak looked at him. "Of course. Your hands remain clean, Martin. In that you have absolutely nothing to worry about."

Some of the man's mannerisms and occasional turns of phrase sounded almost Russian. The media had picked up on it during Weaver's campaign and Rodak had merely laughed it off.

"I suppose that too much of my formative youth and zeal was spent over there in my studies."

"A girlfriend?" a *Washington Post* reporter had asked.

Rodak had smiled good-naturedly. "Maybe more than one."

Marty was startled. "What do you mean my hands will remain clean? I've done nothing to be ashamed of. Nothing contrary to my charter."

"No one, least of all me, is saying anything to the contrary. But you did ask for an emergency meeting."

"It's possible that Kirk McGarvey has gotten himself into a situation that I never foresaw."

"He has that history. But he did save the Eiffel Tower, which was in your original plan. What has gone wrong?"

"They captured his girlfriend."

"Ms. Boylan, one of your employees."

"They took her to Istanbul, and McGarvey followed them."

A squirrel came across the grass and began digging in the dirt. Rodak watched for a moment or two. "Inventive animals. When the time to harvest acorns is in full swing, they bury them just an inch or two deep. Shallow enough so that when they want to dig them up they can smell where they are."

Marty was irritated. "What're you talking about?"

"Have you ever eaten a squirrel?"

"No."

"Neither have I, nor would I care to do so. They're nothing more than rats with bushy tails, after all. I think they would taste very bitter. Like your Mr. McGarvey. He can sense where the acorns are buried, and has the habit of digging them up. But I think that killing him would be a very bitter experience."

"Well it just may be worse than that," Marty said. "There's a decent chance that he's going to trade his freedom for that of Ms. Boylan."

Rodak was visibly startled. "Trade with whom?"

"The more important question is, why? And the answer is, to appease their failure in Paris."

"If they have him, then what?"

"Take him to Russia and trade with the SVR," Marty said. "You have to admit that his intelligence value would be considerable."

Rodak said nothing.

"Maybe you should give Weaver the heads-up."

"No," Rodak said. "You should have had him killed."

"I tried. It didn't work."

"Try again, Martin. Believe me, it wouldn't be in your best interest if Kirk McGarvey survived long enough to actually make it into the hands of the SVR."

"Nor in your best interest, William. Or the nation's."

The chameleon drone, about the size of a package of cigarettes, had turned green just before it landed in the tree just above where Marty and Rodak were seated. Its speed was much slower than an automobile's, but at altitude it could overlook a very large area.

Sitting in his office, watching a monitor, Otto had landed the drone in time to catch the last of the conversation.

He got on the phone with Mac, switching off the common channel and speaker functions. "What's your situation?"

"I've been offered a hostage."

"In exchange for what?"

"We haven't established that yet. But I think she's about to tell me."

"How's Pete?"

"So far as I know she's alive, but they recaptured her on the roof," McGarvey said. "Do you have something I can use?"

"Could be, but you have more trouble coming your way, and Marty is in the middle of it."

"Rowe is on his way back?"

"I don't know. But Marty is working some sort of a deal with Bill Rodak, who suggested that you be killed before the SVR got its hands on you."

"Weaver's Russian expert?" McGarvey asked.

"The same. So if you're going to pull something off to get out of there, do it right now."

"Before I'm surrounded."

"That's the idea."

"Too late," McGarvey said.

THIRTY-EIGHT

□

The interval from the time Miriam had shown up in the stairwell was less than two minutes, but listening to Otto on the phone with one ear while listening to the silence of the building with the other and watching the woman, he made his decision.

He pocketed the phone and lowered the compact submachine gun. "One of us has to make the first move."

Miriam started to reach behind her back but stopped as Mac raised the room broom again.

"First move, but not a stupid one."

She said nothing.

"I suppose I can kill you, then take out whoever is just above, before I kill your boss."

"He is pointing a gun pointed directly at your girlfriend's head."

"And mine is pointed at you. My offer of a trade is still on the table."

"How do you want to handle it, Mr. McGarvey?" a man said from the next landing up.

"Bring Ms. Boylan down to where I can see her."

"Then what?"

"We'll all go down to the ground floor, where you'll let her get in one of the cars and drive away."

"Afterwards?"

"I'll lay down my weapons and go with you."

"What guarantee do I have?" Najjir asked.

"My word."

"Other than your girlfriend's life, why should I trust that you'll surrender peacefully?"

"Because you have only one choice," McGarvey said. "Do as I say or I'll kill the woman and the rest of your people, including you, in the next thirty seconds—and you can count on it."

"I think that you would try, but the odds are still against you."

"What do I have to lose?"

"Besides your life, why, your freedom, of course."

"So you can take me to Russia?" McGarvey asked. "Can you imagine the shitstorm that's going to rain down on you when my people find out where you've taken me? And do you actually believe that the Kremlin will thank you for bringing them a former head of the CIA?"

"You're not making a very good case for yourself," Miriam said.

"They'd only need you for twenty-four hours, after which you would be released relatively unharmed," Najjir said from the flight above.

"I'm tired of standing here. Bring her down or I'll start with the woman."

"She doesn't mean a thing to me."

McGarvey motioned for Miriam to move to one side, out of the direct path from the stairs leading up. She did it.

"Take out your gun, lay it on the floor, and shove it toward me with your foot."

"Not a chance."

"You don't mean anything to him, nor to me."

"Do as you're told, my dear," Najjir said. "I'll have the woman brought down as he asks. I don't care about either of you."

Miriam withdrew her compact Glock pistol and, keeping her eyes on McGarvey's, bent down and laid it on the floor. She straightened up and shoved it a few feet away.

"Do it now, but slowly," McGarvey said, and he stepped back so that he was at the fire door to the corridor. From his position he had clear sight lines not only on the woman but also on the stairs leading up and those leading down.

"Watch yourself," Pete called down. Her voice was shaky.

"You okay?"

"Peachy, except that Mr. Najjir is holding a pistol at my head," she said. She let out a yelp as if she had been hit. "One other shooter with the broad, plus whoever you didn't already kill downstairs."

"She'll need to be able to walk down the stairs and out to the car under her own steam," McGarvey said.

One man dressed in black came into view on the landing above. When he spotted Mac in the doorway, he hesitated, but then came slowly down the rest of the way, stopping again. His room broom was pointed down and away, but his finger was on the trigger. He was ready to shoot at the slightest provocation.

"Does the situation hold?" Najjir asked. He and Pete and were still out of view, but closer. Almost certainly just a few stairs above the landing.

"Ja," the shooter standing next to Miriam answered. He was German.

Keeping his gun pointed between the stairway and the operator, Mac raised his phone with his left hand. "Otto?"

"Here."

"Switch back to networking and speakerphone modes."

"Done."

"How many shooters are left in the building?" McGarvey called up the stairs.

"The one in front of you, and two on the landing one flight below," Najjir said. "Our misjudgment that we allowed you to take out the others."

"Count me in for three on the roof," Pete said.

"Can you verify any other active phones in the building?" Mac asked Otto.

"A bunch, but all of them on the ground floor, and three on the roof are not moving. Chances are he's not lying."

"No need at this point," Najjir said.

"Tell your people on the landing below me to go downstairs, start one of the cars, pull it in front of the door so that it faces the open gate, then step well back."

"Their weapons?"

"Won't matter at that point."

"Do as he wants," Najjir said.

"The advantage will be his," someone called from below.

"Just do it, Sergei."

The two shooters on the landing below started down, not bothering with any efforts at stealth.

"I'm coming down now, with Ms. Boylan," Najjir said.

"Otto?"

"Two phones below are moving downward, two are stationary at your level, and the one just above you is heading your way."

"The rest of you switch off," Najjir said over the phone.

The shooter lowered his weapon, got the phone from his pocket, and took the back off and removed the battery. He tossed everything aside, and Miriam followed suit.

"Everyone but you is off-line," Otto said.

Najjir appeared in the stairwell with Pete, hesitated a moment, then came down to the landing. "The phones were a nuisance. I thought it would be to my advantage to level the playing field."

McGarvey had the nearly overwhelming urge to shoot the bastard, but something nagged at the back of his head and he held up.

"Here we all are, one big, happy family," Najjir said. "I suggest now that we do as McGarvey says, but carefully; we don't want any further excitement." He made a show of placing his pistol on the floor. "I want everyone to lay their PDWs on the floor and push them out of reach." The personal defense weapons were the Heckler & Koch compact submachine guns.

Pete moved her head slightly to the left and then to the right, as if she were trying to ease a stiff neck.

The shooter on the landing placed his room broom on the floor and pushed it aside.

"Mac," Pete suddenly cried, when the muzzle of a pistol touched the back of McGarvey's head.

THIRTY-NINE

□

"Shall I kill him?" the man holding the pistol to McGarvey's head asked. He was Russian.

"No, he's more valuable to me alive," Najjir said.

In that instant the gunman's attention had turned to his boss.

Mac feinted left, then suddenly swiveled to the right. Bringing his pistol around, he fired one shot at point-blank range into the side of the man's head.

"Kill the son of a bitch," someone shouted.

McGarvey shoved the body aside and stepped out into the corridor as Miriam started for her pistol lying on the floor.

Najjir had stepped back at the same instant Pete dropped to her knees, exposing the shooter who had the muzzle of his pistol jammed against her head.

The man brought his weapon around, but before he could get off a shot, McGarvey fired, hitting the operator center mass, dropping him.

Miriam had just reached her pistol when Mac turned on her, while watching Najjir and Pete out of the corner of one eye. "Touch it and I'll kill you."

She hesitated.

"Stand up and back away."

Miriam did as she was told, and Mac turned most of his attention to Najjir, who hadn't drawn a weapon, and to Pete, who was still on her knees.

"Come on down; we're getting out of here."

"I can't stand up," Pete said. She was battered, her face badly bruised, and she spoke with a slur, as if she were missing teeth.

Najjir seemed almost amused. "What to do now?" he asked.

"Two options," Mac said. "Either I kill you and the woman right now and help Ms. Boylan down the stairs. Or the two of you help her."

"As you wish," Najjir said, and he helped Pete to her feet. "Almost done, my dear."

"Otto, any other shooters below me?"

"No signal from anyone but you."

"There were two men coming up."

"Nothing my darlings are picking up."

"Stand by. We're coming down," McGarvey said. He motioned for Najjir to start down.

Miriam had a look almost of wonder on her face. "You're actually going to give yourself over once your missus is clear?"

"Something like that," Mac said.

"That's providing he doesn't see any opening for the two of them," Najjir said. He had to all but carry Pete the last couple of stairs to the landing. "But then he'd be operating under a handicap. The poor girl is in desperate shape. What will he do?"

"I'll kill you sooner or later," Mac said.

Najjir shrugged. "You'll try."

"Call your man, tell him that we're on the way down."

"Sergei, copy?"

"Da," the man replied. It sounded as if he was on the first landing below them.

"We're coming down with the woman."

"What are your orders!"

"Go downstairs, move the Mercedes around to the door so that it's pointed toward the gate, then leave the engine running, the driver's side door open, and take up a defensive position, with a good sight line. Do you have that?"

"Yes, sir."

"We're making a trade, so I want no shooting unless the situation deteriorates. Do you understand that as well?"

"Da."

"Do it now," Najjir said. He turned back to McGarvey. "What if your girlfriend is incapable of driving away by herself?"

"I can work a shifter, turn the wheel, and push on the gas pedal, you fucking moron," Pete said through clenched teeth. She was looking directly at McGarvey. Telling him something.

"Your new love, so willing to save her own ass by sacrificing yours?" Miriam smirked.

"Only because he's going to kill both of you, bitch."

"Shall we go downstairs?" Najjir said. "I want us to be at the airport and on our way before midnight."

The color on one of Otto's monitors turned lavender, which indicated that something the program deemed to have a low percentage of probability was unfolding, and he looked up.

The drone that had followed Bambridge to the meeting at Turkey Run Park had risen from its perch in the tree as soon as he and Rodak were clear.

The White House staffer was headed back to Washington, but Marty had turned west on the Parkway, away from the city, and away from the CIA's main entrance.

Miriam went first down the stairs, followed by Najjir, who was holding Pete's arm to keep her from falling.

"Wait," Pete cried, and her legs started to buckle.

Najjir stopped short and Miriam, just below them, turned and looked up.

"I can't walk," Pete said. She tried to put her right arm over his shoulder, around his neck, but he pulled back. "If you think I like this any better than you do, you're living in a dream world. But I need some help here."

Mac was a few steps above them.

"As you wish," Najjir said, and he helped her stand upright and put her arm around his neck.

"Let's go," Mac said.

Miriam started down, and Najjir and Pete followed.

They held up for just a moment or two at the second-floor landing, then made the turn and continued down.

The going was slow, and McGarvey got the distinct impression that Pete was feigning her disability to slow them down. But he couldn't be sure.

It took a full four minutes to make it the rest of the way to the ground floor. The entry hall led straight across to the open front doors, a distance of twenty or twenty-five feet. There was a lot of blood on the stone floor, and shell casings were scattered everywhere. But the bodies had been moved, skid marks in the blood leading off to the left.

Najjir's people had been well trained. They had policed up the close-quarters battle zone so if it came to another firefight they would not be slowed down by a debris field.

The gray Mercedes diesel started up and pulled into view in front of the doors. A black-clad shooter got out, looked back, then left the driver's door open and disappeared from view to the right.

Najjir looked over his shoulder at McGarvey. "Your girlfriend has a free pass. You have my word that so long as no one makes a hasty move we'll have this done in the next two minutes."

Otto came on Mac's phone. "Is your situation fluid?"

It was Rencke speak for: Did Mac have any options open or was he backed into a corner?

"Limited."

"Marty just dropped off the grid. You probably have trouble coming your way, kemo sabe."

FORTY

Pete dragged her feet as they crossed the entry hall, causing Najjir to hold almost all of her weight to keep her from falling.

Miriam went ahead to the open doors and stepped outside. "Sergei's in place," she said, over her shoulder.

"Step out of the line of fire," Najjir told her.

She disappeared to the left.

Najjir turned. "The ball is in your court, Mr. McGarvey. But if you stay here I'll walk your girlfriend to the car, and when she's gone you'll put down your weapons and come outside."

"Trusting," McGarvey said.

"I'm told that you are a man of your word. I'm saving Ms. Boylan's life and I promise to deliver you to the SVR intact."

Pete suddenly lurched against Najjir's side as if her legs were completely giving way.

He grabbed her shoulder, leaving his right side exposed, his jacket pulled open.

At that moment Pete snatched the pistol from his shoulder holster, then shoved away from him, raising the gun so that it pointed directly at the side of his head.

"Tell your man to toss down his gun and back the fuck up, or I'll kill you," Pete screamed.

Najjir turned, seemingly unconcerned, and smiled. "I thought that you were playacting, my dear. But you should have checked that the gun was ready to fire. Full magazine, but no round in the chamber."

McGarvey had raised his room broom, but Pete stood directly in his line of fire. "Down!" he shouted.

Pete worked the slide back, jacking a round into the firing chamber at the same moment Najjir sprinted forward, out the door. She fired just as he disappeared from view.

There was little doubt in Marty's mind that Rencke had somehow traced his movements to the meeting with Rodak at Turkey Run. Maybe his freak of a wife had managed to retask one of the spy birds in geosync orbit. But it would have been impossible—even with the latest technology, which allowed their satellite to read the fine print on a line of stock quotes in a newspaper, even under low-light conditions—to read their lips. And the angle would have had to be perfect in any case to read what they were saying.

He was safe in that respect, but Rencke would have to know, or at least strongly suspect, that the meeting with Rodak had to involve McGarvey's current situation.

What Rencke couldn't possibly know was that Bambridge had purchased a throwaway cell phone at each of three convenience stores over the past two months against just this possibility.

As soon as he merged with the I-495 Beltway south, he used one of the throwaways to call a number in New York.

It was answered after the first ring, as if the officer had been expecting the call.

"Da."

McGarvey reached Pete just as a shooter outside opened fire, the rounds ricocheting off the stone floor, bullet fragments flying everywhere.

One plucked at his shoulder, and another, much larger fragment smashed into his prosthetic leg a few inches above where his ankle had been, nearly knocking him off his feet. He had only an instant to think that if he hadn't lost his leg last year, the round would have hit live flesh and bone and he would have been down.

Half shoving, half pulling Pete, he ducked into the long corridor that ran the width of the building, from the entry hall, past rooms that had been used as offices—one of them most recently the staging room for Najjir and his operators—all the way to the broad manufacturing floor.

Most of the walls in the big space—perhaps eighty or ninety feet on a side—were intact, but there were large gaps where windows had once existed, and the high ceiling here was open to the night sky in several places. All of the machinery and everything else of value had been long ago removed or looted, leaving behind only debris, much of it ceiling and roof materials that had fallen down.

A dark figure appeared at an opening in the wall straight ahead, and McGarvey got off two short bursts from the room broom before it went dry.

He angled sharply toward the deeper darkness to the left as Pete opened fire with Najjir's pistol.

The shooter at the far wall opened fire again, but the shots went wild, far to the right.

Pete's left knee gave out and she went down hard on the other, but immediately struggled up, obviously in a lot of pain.

"They're concentrating back here, so we're going to turn around and try for the car," McGarvey said. "Are you okay?"

Pete grinned. "You sure know how to show a girl a good time."

McGarvey took the spare magazine from his pocket and recharged the room broom. As he did so, Pete reached over and gave him a kiss on the cheek, then took the gun from him and handed Najjir's pistol to him.

"You can drive, and I'll slow down anyone coming from our six," she said. She grinned. "That is, if you can keep up."

Keeping low, and making as little noise as possible, they made their way in the darkness to the corridor, then, watching the corners and keeping an eye out for anyone coming up behind them, made it to the entry hall.

They held up at the front door. The Mercedes, its driver's side door still open, its engine still turning over, sat unattended, so far as McGarvey could tell.

But there was no time to make sure. It wouldn't take Najjir and his people very long to realize that he and Pete had doubled back.

"On me," he said.

"Right."

McGarvey sprinted out the door, directly to the driver's side of the idling Mercedes, Pete right behind him.

She was in the passenger seat as he got behind the wheel.

"We have company," she said, and started firing toward the rear.

Without closing the door, Mac slammed the car in Drive and accelerated down the short driveway, through the open gate, and toward the park, beyond which were busy streets leading toward downtown.

"Anyone following us?" Mac asked.

"Not yet, but we have a slight problem."

"What?" McGarvey asked, glancing at her.

"I think I'm going to pass out."

"Are you hurt?"

"I think one of the bastards taking potshots into the lobby got lucky," Pete said. "Hurts like hell, in my side. Like a stitch. Maybe my liver."

McGarvey reached for her with his free hand when she slumped over against the door.

He made a hard right, passing Taksim Square, and got on the phone with Otto, while checking the rearview mirror. So far no one was behind them.

"You're out," Otto said.

"Pete's been shot, maybe badly. Vector me to the nearest safe hospital. Someplace very public."

"The Vakfi Amerikan Hastanesi, but it's too far. You're better off trying to make our consulate—they have a good med staff on call."

"Are you tracking me?"

"Make the next right," Otto said.

Four military troop transports appeared from a street to the right and came to a screeching halt, blocking the main street.

McGarvey had no recourse except to slam on the brakes, one hand preventing Pete from pitching forward, and crank the wheel hard left, sending them careening down a side street.

FORTY-ONE

Marty Bambridge got off I-495 a mile south of the interchange with the GW Parkway and headed down Georgetown Pike, which led to the CIA's rear gate, three miles away.

His phone chimed. It was Otto Rencke.

"As soon as you get back we're meeting with the general. I'm in his office right now."

"Fine by me," Bambridge said. "It's about time we get this shit straightened out."

"What shit is that, Marty?"

"Who's in charge of the Company's operations."

"It's certainly not someone stabbing two of its people in the back."

"McGarvey no longer works for us," Bambridge said, realizing his mistake at once.

"You're wrong, you son of a bitch."

"At any rate I don't give a flying fuck what kind of shit he and his girlfriend have gotten themselves into this time. But it has to stop. Now!"

"Is that what you discussed with Bill Rodak?"

"That's none of your goddamned business," Bambridge shouted

"But it is my business," General Gibson said. "I'll see you in my office. And just so you won't be blindsided, I've asked Carlton to join us with the usual nondisclosure agreement, in case it needs your signature."

Carlton Patterson was a personal friend not only of Rencke but especially of McGarvey. And employees holding classified information were required to sign the agreement at the time of their dismissal.

"That would require the consent of the president."

"No," Gibson said. "But depending on what you'll tell us, we may go over to the White House for a meeting to see if we can mitigate any damage that might be coming our way."

"Mr. Director, I can't begin to guess what nonsense Mr. Rencke has been telling you, but as your deputy director I have to advise you that this is a can of worms that you might wish to step away from. For the good of the agency."

"In my office, mister. Now!"

Otto's phone vibrated.

"I have what looks like a unit of the Turkish military on my ass right now," McGarvey said over the noise of an engine at top speed and wind noise from an open window or windows.

"Are you clear?"

"Four troop trucks showed up and baricaded the intersection just a couple of blocks from the warehouse. They knew we were coming. Is the consulate out?"

"Depends on Pete's condition," Otto said.

"She's unconscious, but still breathing. Lot of blood on the seat."

"Mr. McGarvey, this is General Gibson. I need you to pull over right now, turn on your headlights and flashers, and attend to Ms. Boylan before she bleeds to death."

"With all due respect, Mr. Director, the only way the Turkish military could have shown up so soon was as if they had been warned by Najjir. We stop here and they'll take us."

"If you don't, Ms. Boylan won't make it. I've seen my share of battlefield wounds. You take care of Pete and I'll take care of the Turks. But don't shoot at anyone, no matter what happens. Do you understand?"

"Yes, sir," McGarvey said.

. . .

Bambridge slowed down at the entrance to the Langley Fork Park, which was just adjacent to the CIA's property. He pulled off to the side of the road and parked as a dump truck rumbled past.

From here he could see the turnoff to the agency's back gate, but not the guardhouse itself. In his mind he only had two choices open: he had to bluff his way past the director or take a runner. Neither was an attractive option.

Otto Rencke was a fucking freak, but he had the respect of just about every intelligence agency in town, and he was feared for what he could do to the computer infrastructure. In fact it was he who had repeatedly warned not only Gibson but even the White House about Russian cyber attacks, and about the trouble that WikiLeaks was giving all of them.

His suggestion was to hurt the Russians so badly that they would back off, and to mount a full-court press—in secret, especially out of the eyes of the media—to track down whoever was feeding the information to Julian Assange and his people. And once that person or persons were identified, his advice was to have them killed.

Of course, the media would find out sooner or later and there would be hell to pay. Bambridge's advice was to leave well enough alone, investigating in the same way they had been doing. Stay the course and sooner or later the traitors would be outed and the problem would be solved.

The real problem was the Russians, of course, and Putin himself. It was a situation that he was intimately familiar with.

He waited for a car to pass, then headed down to the back gate. Running wasn't an option. Not yet at least.

McGarvey pulled in to an empty parking spot just past a coffeehouse, the sidewalk tables mostly filled with couples who looked more like tourists than locals.

He went around to the passenger side of the car and opened the door.

Pete almost fell out, and he had to hold her back to keep her from tumbling onto the sidewalk.

She had lost a fair amount of blood, but when he lifted her shirt he could see that the jagged entry wound just above her right hip wasn't bleeding profusely. Nor was the fluid that had come from the wound black. She was hurt, but not mortally.

He took off his shirt, folded it into a square, and pressed it against the wound. She moaned and looked up at him, her eyes open.

"Is it time to go home?" she asked, her voice ragged.

"Just about."

First one siren started up to the east, the direction of the roadblock, and then another, and then a third. All them headed this way.

McGarvey pressed her right hand over the makeshift bandage. "Hold this," he said.

She did as she was told, but then cocked an ear, the sirens much closer now. "That's for us?"

"Probably. But you need help, and Gibson said he'd take care of the Turks for us."

"Don't worry about the Turks, this is a Russian op."

"You're right. But I'm not going to drive around Istanbul while you bleed to death. So keep still, and let me do the talking."

"Sexist," she mumbled, and she drifted off.

Making sure that Pete was slumped back away from the door, McGarvey took the room broom from the floor, where she had dropped it, and laid it on the sidewalk, along with the pistol.

The sirens were very loud now, just around the corner, and people in the coffee shop were becoming alarmed. Many of them were walking away, while others had gotten to their feet but clearly didn't know what to do, which direction was safe for them to run.

A UAZ, the Russian jeep, came around the corner and screeched to a halt about twenty feet away. A man in military camos, officer's pips on his shoulder boards, jumped out, a pistol in his right hand. He made eye contact with McGarvey.

"Are you Mr. McGarvey?" he asked, in passable English.

"Yes. The woman in the car needs medical attention."

The Turkish officer pointed his gun at Mac as the three trucks came around the corner.

"Put up your hands, please, or I will be forced to open fire."

McGarvey did as he was told.

The trucks pulled up short, and a dozen armed soldiers piled out of each of them.

"The woman in the car is badly wounded," McGarvey said loudly enough that the soldiers could hear him. "She needs to be taken to a hospital."

"We will see to it," the officer said, but he didn't lower his weapon.

Najjir got out of the jeep.

FORTY-TWO

□

McGarvey stood loose as Najjir said something to the officer, who lowered his pistol. The civilians had fled from the café, and all that was left were the three dozen soldiers standing in a tight perimeter around the car, their rifles at the ready. No avenue of escape was even remotely possible now.

"Otto, are you copying?" McGarvey said softly.

"Yes."

"The Turkish Army is here; no way out."

"The general is working on it; stay frosty."

"Najjir is here too. He just got out of a jeep with a Turkish officer in uniform. Looks like army intel bureau markings."

"Stand by," Otto said.

Najjir walked over and stopped a few feet away from the side of the car, out of reach of McGarvey but where he could see Pete. "How bad is she?"

"She needs help."

"I can see that. The major assures me that an ambulance is en route, should be here momentarily."

"Where will you take her?"

"I'm told that a medical team is standing by at your consulate, and as soon as she's stable she'll be flown to Ramstein. How about you?"

"I'll live."

"That's good, because I've honored my part of the bargain and now it's time for you to cooperate."

"To Russia?"

"Out of Turkey," Najjir said. He held out a hand. "Toss your phone to me, please. There is no need for Mr. Rencke to listen to the rest of our conversation, or to track your movements."

"We will find you," Otto said.

"I don't think so."

"You can't go deep enough."

"We'll see," Najjir said. He gestured for Mac to toss over the phone.

"He's right," McGarvey said, but he held up the phone.

The major raised his pistol and the soldiers sharpened up.

"With care," Najjir said. "We don't want an unfortunate accident now."

McGarvey tossed the phone to Najjir, who took off the back plate and removed the battery and SIM card, both of which he dropped to the ground and crushed with the heel of his shoe.

"If you're ready, let's go," Najjir said.

In the distance they could hear an approaching siren.

"When she's aboard the ambulance and on her way," McGarvey said.

"You're in no position for any further bargaining."

"You can't imagine the trouble I'll give you personally. Once she's on her way I'll cooperate with you. My word."

Najjir hesitated for a moment, but then nodded. "As you wish."

The bar code in the windshield of Bambridge's car was still valid, and once the automatic scanner read it and the facial recognition program identified him, he was passed through the rear gate without having to stop and show an ID.

On the way up to the OHB he used another of the throwaway phones and called Rowe, who answered after four rings

He sounded stressed. "What?"

"What's your situation?"

"It's all fucked up. McGarvey's not dead, like you wanted. In fact the son of a bitch apparently took out a dozen or more shooters at the factory. The guy's a fucking machine."

"Calm down, and tell me what's going on, goddamnit."

"We got word a half hour ago to get a medical team over from the American hospital to take care of a serious gunshot wound."

"McGarvey?"

"You're not listening. The incoming is the broad he was with."

"Boylan?"

"Yeah. One of ours, and I don't know how the fuck you're going to explain what's going on if she wakes up and starts talking."

"We might have caught a break."

"I'm all ears. Because if you go down, so do I."

"You don't have to disappear just yet," Bambridge said. "Where are you at this moment?"

"I'm on the way to my apartment to get a few things in case this goes south."

"Get back to the consulate right now."

"What's the fucking point?"

"Thompson is still in Ankara, right?" Stu Thompson was the chief of CIA ops for Istanbul.

"He left this afternoon, soon as he found out that McGarvey was going to show up. Trouble follows the guy wherever he goes, and Stu wanted no part of it, so he dumped it on me."

"Good," Bambridge said. It had been his suggestion that Thompson get out of the city.

"What are you thinking?"

"Ms. Boylan works for the Company, which means the only people she will be allowed to talk with, if she wakes up, would be someone from the Company. Since you're the ranking officer in Istanbul, it'd be you."

"Then what?"

"You didn't hear me, Mark. I said if she wakes up."

Rowe was silent for a longish moment or two. "In for a penny, in for a pound, that it?"

"No other real choice now."

Again Rowe hesitated. "McGarvey better not survive."

"He won't," Bambridge said, that exact worry gnawing at his gut. "Guaranteed."

He broke the connection, and a few minutes later he was pulling in to his underground parking spot at the OHB.

The Boylan broad was a done deal; now all that needed to be done was to convince the DCI.

A white-and-red ambulance with the crescent moon on the sides pulled up behind the Mercedes and a pair of emergency medics pulled a gurney out of the back and rolled it over to the open passenger-side door.

McGarvey stepped close as Pete came around and looked up at the medics and then at him.

She smiled.

"They're taking you to our consulate," Mac said.

"What about you?"

"I won't be far behind."

She spotted Najjir and reacted. "Don't let them take you!"

He edged one of the medics aside and leaned in closer. "Won't be for long, Pete, trust me."

She managed a slight smile. "The silly bastard still doesn't know what he's gotten himself into, does he?"

"Whatever happens, don't talk to anyone but Mark Rowe."

"He's one of the good guys?"

"Yeah."

She managed to give him the thumbs-up, but then faded again.

McGarvey stepped back, and the medics checked her wound, then eased her onto the gurney.

One of them said something into his lapel mike while the other stuck a needle connected to a bag of clear fluid into Pete's arm.

"She's on her way, or will be in just a minute or two," Najjir said.

"Then let's get it over with," McGarvey said. "Actually I'm more curious to see what sort of a reception the SVR gives you, rather than me."

FORTY-THREE

☐

Otto was on the phone with the duty officer at the consulate in Istanbul when Carlton Patterson came in. General Gibson was on his phone, too, and he motioned for Patterson to take a seat.

"An ambulance transporting Ms. Boylan is on its way to you," Otto told the duty officer.

"Yes, sir, we just got word. The medical team is standing by."

"She's one of ours, so I want her treated well."

Bambridge walked in at that moment and sat down next to Patterson. He was scowling, but he was holding back something that was frightening him. Otto could see it in the man's eyes.

"Will do," the OD said.

"Is Mark Rowe there?"

"Not yet, sir, but I gave him the sit rep just two minutes ago. He said he was on the way."

"Good. Have him call me when he shows up," Otto said.

Bambridge turned away, but not before Otto caught the faintest glimmer of a smile on the man's thin lips. It seemed odd at just that moment.

Gibson hung up his phone, and gave Bambridge a hard stare, before turning to Otto. "That was General Osman, who assures me that none of his units have been deployed in the city at this moment."

"But they're there," Otto said.

"I told him that we had an eyewitness on the scene. He promised to look into it personally."

"Pete's on her way to our consulate; the OD just confirmed it. Which means Mac has been taken."

"Alive?" Gibson asked.

"Presumably. He was disarmed when he gave his phone to the man who we think is—or was—a midlevel Saudi intel officer by the name of Karim Najjir. The phone went dead moments later."

"And McGarvey thinks they mean to take him to Russia and hand him over to the SVR?"

"As crazy as it sounds, that's apparently what he and the woman plan to do."

"I'll give Subotin a call." Vladimir Subotin was the new director general of the Russian Foreign Intelligence Service, which had been the First Chief Directorate of the old KGB. Nothing much had changed in the past twenty years—not the methods, not the officers, not the training at School 1 or at Moscow State University—only the name of the mammoth intelligence service.

"He'll deny knowing anything about it," Otto said.

"At least until they're ready to send McGarvey home," Patterson broke in.

"He's likely to suffer an unfortunate accident at some point," Gibson said.

"Unless we send help first," Otto said.

"Who?"

"A contact of Marty's in the White House."

They all turned their attention to Bambridge, who pursed his lips. "Bill Rodak, the president's special adviser on Russian affairs," he said.

Otto glanced at Gibson, who gave him the nod.

"A friend of yours?" Otto asked.

"As a matter of fact, you he is. We go back a number of years, long before Weaver decided to run for president. I was the one who suggested Bill would be just the man in the White House."

"You met with him earlier today at Turkey Run Park. Why there and not in your office? Or at the White House?"

"Both of us wanted privacy. You bug my office and Weaver's people do the same to all of his staff. Common knowledge."

"What was so important you had to meet in private?"

"McGarvey, of course, who got himself and Ms. Boylan into the middle of an operation that had been in the works for some time."

"The terrorist attack on the Eiffel Tower?" Patterson asked.

"We knew about it, or at least we had some glimmerings. My chief of Paris station gave the DGSE the heads-up months ago. In fact we all thought that it was going to be a Russian-directed operation—which we're now almost certain it was. But of course Mr. McGarvey got himself involved, and the Russians we thought we were going to bag—with their trousers down around their ankles—walked away. But McGarvey and Ms. Boylan gave chase, of course, and the bodies started to mount as they usually do when he gets involved."

Gibson was angry. "This operation of yours, of which I was told nothing, was Rodak's idea?" he demanded.

"No, sir. It was mine from the start. But as I said, Bill and I go back a long ways together, and I asked for and received his input."

"Then besides your fear of being overheard in your office or his, why the secret meeting off campus?"

"Plausible deniability, Mr. Director," Bambridge said with a straight face. "For both of us. We thought that there was a better than even chance that this thing would go south—only not as far south as has happened because of McGarvey—and we wanted the White House, in the person of the president, as well as the Company, in the person of you, sir, to be off the hook."

"What was to have been the end result?" Patterson asked. It was clear that he wasn't buying Bambridge's story. "What did you hope to accomplish?"

"It was supposed to be a three-bagger. Nail the cyber spies, back off the SVR, and show Putin's ambitions for what they are."

"Which are?" Patterson asked.

"The creation of a new Soviet Union, of course."

"Jesus, Marty, do you even hear yourself talk sometimes?" Otto said, unable to contain himself any longer.

Bambridge turned to him. "Why don't you take a good look at yourself in a mirror, you long-haired fucking freak. McGarvey rescued you from your self-imposed exile in France after you fucked some nun—or was it an altar boy?—and the diocese fired your ass. So you figure you owe him, right? He lets you play with your fucking toys scot-free—because just about everyone on the planet is afraid you'll go even more berserk than you already are. In turn you feed him classified information that he's no longer cleared to receive, and the body bags get filled. Everyone is happy, right? You play, he kills."

Patterson sat with his mouth open.

Bambridge looked from Otto to him and then to Gibson. "Then we have the two femme fatales. Pete Boylan, who apparently will do just about anything—let me amend that—who will do *everything* for a good fuck. If that's what McGarvey is, though just about everyone woman he's ever been close to, including his wife and daughter, were murdered because of him. And then there's Louise, a super geek in her own right, who must like to get down in the mud and fuck with the hogs."

Otto was off his seat in a shot and, before Patterson or Gibson could say a word, slammed his fist in the side of Bambridge's face, knocking the deputy director off his chair and onto the floor.

Shoving the chair aside, he began kicking Bambridge in the ribs and the leg and the shoulder. Spittle flew from his mouth, and every fiber in his being wanted to destroy the smug bastard. Wanted to knock him down. Break all his bones. Cause him so much pain that he would beg to die, just so that he would no longer be in misery.

Gibson was there at his side, pulling him away, and Patterson was there a moment or two later.

"Easy, my boy, easy," Patterson was saying over and over.

Gibson's secretary was at the door, and the general looked up. "Get the medics up here," he told her.

Marty sat up, and he rubbed the side of his face. "No need, but call security and have this fucking freak arrested. And if he tries to escape, you have my authorization to shoot the bastard."

FORTY-FOUR

□

The American-made SUV was a Dodge Durango with three rows of seats. McGarvey was placed in the center row, while a shooter sat in the rear seat and Najjir, armed with a pistol, rode shotgun, turned in the seat so that he could keep an eye on McGarvey while another of the shooters drove.

They were on the European side of the Bosphorus, heading north well within the speed limit. It wasn't the way to the airport.

"It's a long drive to Russia," McGarvey said. "I thought that you'd want to get rid of me as soon as possible."

"Believe me, nothing would give me greater pleasure. But Atatürk is out, for obvious reasons, so we're going to take a little boat ride. The Black Sea isn't quite so pleasant as the Med, but it's less public for our purposes, and the yacht is comfortable."

A couple of years ago McGarvey had Pete had been involved in an undercover operation where they mingled with the superrich aboard their mega yachts off Monaco.

"The terrorism, kidnapping, and assassination business must be more lucrative than I ever expected."

Najjir smiled. "The yacht is a lease, not mine."

"Russian?"

"No. They know that we're coming, but I've kept your identity a secret for now. Less complicated."

McGarvey had to smile. "You're taking a big chance, springing me on them out of the blue."

"On the contrary. I assured them that I was bringing a valuable asset. One that they couldn't refuse."

"I have friends there."

"So I'm told. But enemies also."

The yacht was tied up at the istmarin about halfway up the Bosphorus, less than ten miles from where the waterway opened onto the Black Sea. A lot of big cargo ships steamed by in both directions, many of them Russian but a fair amount Chinese, most with registrations from places of convenience, such as Liberia and Cyprus.

She was a Dutch-built boat, just under one hundred feet, with the Arabic name Farashatan, or Butterfly. It was one of the lesser yachts owned by a Saudi prince, which had been moored at Monaco for the Grand Prix race.

"The poor man must be down on his luck," Pete had commented when they'd first seen it there. "Looks like a real yacht's dinghy."

McGarvey recognized it now, but said nothing.

It was past midnight and the marina was deserted, except for a night watchman in uniform.

The driver pulled up a few feet from the gate, and Najjir got out and walked over to the guardhouse, where he had a few words with the man.

The gate swung open and the watchman walked off, along the line of boats up out of the water and secured to cradles for storage or maintenance. As soon as he was out of sight, Najjir motioned for the driver to come through, and then he closed the gate behind the Dodge.

For just that brief interval, when it was only the distracted driver and the man in the rear seat, McGarvey thought that it would be fairly easy to take out the shooter and order the driver to do a 180.

But what was still puzzling was what the entire operation had been about in the first place. Taking down the Eiffel Tower would have been spectacular, but the ringmaster being right there on-site made no sense. Nor did the woman. Nor did taking him to Russia to trade with the SVR. Trade for what?

He wasn't going to make it easy for them; the Russians would be suspicious. But he was almost looking forward to meeting with whomever would be assigned to conduct his debriefing.

Najjir got back in and they drove over to the yacht and parked beside the gangway lowered from the aft deck. Najjir and the driver got out first, then Mac, and finally the shooter from the backseat. Again he thought that he had another chance to make an escape and get back to Pete at the consulate, but he stood there, his hands loose at his sides. She was safe now.

The diesels were idling, but only a dim light shone from the pilothouse. The night air smelled of diesel fumes, burned oil from the passing freighters, and something else. Something odd, foreign, like a combination of jasmine and sandalwood and a dozen other scents. Turkey was a place from another time. It smelled ancient.

Miriam, wearing jeans and a light sweater against the cool evening air, came out from the salon. "I didn't think that you'd actually make it," she said. She was holding a bottle of champagne in one hand and a flute in the other.

"Are we good to go?" Najjir asked.

"Of course. But what about his woman?"

"It became a trade after all."

"Maybe not such a good idea."

"He had a couple of chances to make a try for it, but here he is."

"It's a long way to Novorossiysk. Thirty hours, according to Levin." Viktor Levin was a contract skipper for the SVR. He, along with an executive officer, an engineer, a cook, and a steward—all of them, other than the skipper and the exec, trained intel officers—knew that they were carrying an asset that was not only of high value but also dangerous. Everyone was on their toes.

"Then we best get under way," Najjir said.

It was well after midnight and they had been under way at nearly top speed of twenty knots for a little more than an hour. Mac had been worrying about Pete nonstop, sorry now that his vanity had pushed him into not fighting back. He'd wanted to see how the Russians reacted to him.

He, Najjir, and Miriam were drinking champagne in the salon and having a light supper/early breakfast.

"I'm curious as to how you and Ms. Boylan just happened to be at the Jules Verne at that exact moment," Najjir said.

"Coincidence," McGarvey said. They were having smoked salmon with cream cheese, chopped onion, lemon wedges and, instead of capers, a good Iranian beluga caviar. It was all fine, but a poached egg and an english muffin would have been better. It seemed like forever since he and Pete had a decent meal.

"I don't believe in coincidences."

"You were the operational commander. What the hell were you doing there?"

"Taking care of business. The kids were dedicated, but they were amateurs."

"And you?" McGarvey said, turning to Miriam. "Where do you fit?"

"I was the diversion."

"Bullshit."

She smiled, but shrugged.

"Doesn't matter if you work it out in the end, which you're bound to, but it'll be too late."

"For what?"

It was Najjir's turn to smile. "Ask your Russian pals, if they show up."

It was seven in the evening in Washington and Otto was sitting at the kitchen counter drinking from a carton of half-and-half and eating the third package of Twinkies since he'd gotten home.

His tablet was powered up in front of him and he was connected with his darlings back on campus. Something wasn't adding up, and he was bothered.

Louise came from upstairs. "You'll be useless if you don't get some sleep," she said, giving him a hug. "You've been going nonstop for the past twenty hours." She took a drink from the half-and-half and ate one of his Twinkies.

"I'm missing something."

"Marty trash talking isn't worth the bother, though I would have liked to have been there when you beat the shit out of him. My hero."

Otto suddenly had it. "Pete," he said.

"She's at our consulate. Stable."

Otto looked up at his wife. "Mark Rowe; he's Marty's boy!"

FORTY-FIVE

□

Dr. Eduardo Iglesias and his team had flown down from Ankara to take care of Pete. They were still in the consulate's infirmary, which had been turned into a makeshift operating theater.

It was nearly three in the morning and Rowe had been waiting for two hours. He'd wanted to get it over with and disappear. Any operation that even remotely involved Kirk McGarvey was fraught with the possibility of some serious blowback, and he was becoming increasingly nervous.

But Marty's instructions had been crystal clear. "Boylan must never be in condition to answer questions. Finish that and you'll have a free ride, I can guarantee it."

"I'm going deep."

"No need. And in any event, that takes a lot of money, unless you want to live in some skid row shack."

"I'm listening."

"You won't get rich as a chief of station somewhere, but after a few years, if you want to retire early, you would be in a perfect position to take on some private contracting. Maybe as a security consultant."

"A COS where?" Rowe pressed.

"Don't push your luck, Mark. I won't put you in some shithole, I can promise you that. Maybe Athens, or Warsaw, something like that."

"London?"

Bambridge had laughed. "First things first."

. . .

Dr. Iglesias came out of the dispensary. He was a small, dark man who'd been born and educated in Cuba and had worked for the CIA since he'd entered medical school. Besides being a good operative, he'd been a damned fine surgeon and had been the doctor of choice for a lot of the Cuban government's elite.

Rowe jumped up from the chair he'd pulled out of one of the offices. "How is she?"

"She'll come out of everything with nothing more than lots of war wounds," the doctor said, his accent still Cuban. "The bullet wound in her side—which missed her liver by only a couple of millimeters—was the least of her problems. Someone used her damned hard. I hope McGarvey catches up with the son of a bitch who hurt her, and I'll sincerely pray for the man's soul."

"It'll happen," Rowe said, glad that his role would only seem to have been from the sidelines. And more than relieved that he had given Mac a working pistol. Insurance, he'd thought of it at the time, and the policy was marked "Payment due" if he could pull off the last task Marty had given him.

"She's still sleeping, and I'm going to keep her that way until she stabilizes. Another twelve hours and then we'll get her up to Ramstein, for at least twenty-four hours, then take her back to All Saints."

The state-of-the-art hospital that treated only badly wounded intel officers—most of them CIA operatives—was located in Georgetown. Pete had been there before, and McGarvey had been there so often, someone joked, that the hospital ought to be equipped with a revolving door.

"I thought you said that she'd be okay."

Iglesias gave him a sharp look. "She will be."

"That's good to hear, Doc," Rowe said. "Can I take a peek?"

Iglesias nodded. "Just for a minute, but don't disturb her."

It was a couple of minutes past eight in Washington, and Otto and Louise were sitting at the kitchen counter, working on a bottle of Beaujolais while staring at his laptop screen for word from Istanbul.

Erick Kraus, the overnight duty officer, had confirmed that Rowe had showed up at the consulate a couple of hours ago and that the medicos had finished tending to Pete's wounds.

According to the primary care doc who'd come down from Ankara, she would recover just fine. They were going to bypass Ramstein and fly her directly to Andrews no later than noon local.

Rowe stepped just inside the infirmary, which was not much larger than a couple of the average offices in the consulate. The portable operating lights had been switched off, leaving the room in semidarkness, the only light coming from the bathroom's partially open door.

For just a moment he had the feeling that this was somehow a setup, but Pete was hooked up to a number of IVs and monitors and she appeared to be unconscious, only a white blanket covering her from the neck down, her head turned slightly away.

It came to him that Bambridge was full of bullshit. There'd be no job as chief of any station. If he pulled the IVs, someone would come in and reconnect them. If he put a pillow over her face and smothered her, the heart monitor she was connected to would sound an alarm.

But security inside the building had always been minimal. This part of Turkey was not considered high risk. The two marine guards at the gate were frosty—it was a part of their training—but they were looking for trouble from the outside, not inside.

He was going deep, contrary to Marty's suggestion, but the DDCI did have a good idea in his head after all. And that was a job as a contractor or adviser—but not to the good guys.

Rowe had always considered himself a James Bond simply looking for a happening. Here and now was his prime opportunity, a place to make his chops. He had gone up against McGarvey and survived.

He was a made man.

The woman was not moving.

Rowe took out his Wilson carry and conceal pistol, which was modeled on the 1911 Colt .45 that had been the standard issue for the American military forever, until it was replaced by the Beretta. From his jacket pocket he pulled out a suppressor and screwed it onto the threaded muzzle.

The Wilson's claim to fame was that it was the most accurate handgun on the planet. But at close range it wasn't an issue.

Light on his feet, despite his bulk, Rowe stepped up to the gurney that had been used as an operating table and studied the side of Pete's head for a long ten seconds.

She was a good-looking woman. She and McGarvey had made a striking couple. In addition she was smart, well trained, and physically capable.

The errant thought crossed his mind that it would be a good deal to fuck her first and then kill her. But that was crazy.

He started to raise his pistol, when Pete suddenly turned toward him, a subcompact Glock 29 pistol in her hand.

"Your choice, Mark," she said.

He hesitated.

"Shit or get off the pot."

The thought of running, even with McGarvey after him, was a hell of a lot more appealing than the thought of spending his life rotting in some supermax prison.

He raised the pistol, but as he started to pull the trigger a thunderclap burst inside his head.

McGarvey had been pretending to sleep on top of the covers in his stateroom. He sat up, took off his shoes, and padded to the door. There was a lot of traffic, among them fishermen, this close to the Turkish shore. Najjir had assigned the two shooters to take four-hour shifts just outside in the companionway.

"I need some air," he said, loudly enough for the guard to hear but not so loud that his voice carried over the noise of the twin diesels. "I'm coming out."

The guard had stepped back, the room broom at the ready, when McGarvey emerged.

"I can't sleep. And I don't think that the Russians are going to let me do much wandering out in the open."

"Fuck you," the bulky guard said. He was dressed in black night fighters' camos, as the others had been, and his accent put him as an American.

"I'm going outside," McGarvey said. "You can either shoot me or come along."

Mac brushed past the man and at the end of the companionway went up the half dozen stairs to the aft deck. The running lights of at least a dozen ships dotted the still overcast night aft and to port and starboard. This was a busy waterway.

He stepped up to the rail, and the guard was right behind him.

"Care for a swim?" McGarvey asked.

He grabbed a handful of the man's blouse and rolled over the transom, the sharply cold water closing over him and the guard.

PART
THREE

Novorossiysk

FORTY-SIX

□

Otto was still at the kitchen counter, monitoring his darlings, while Louise was just taking the pizza she'd made out of the oven, when his rollover work number rang on his cell phone. It was Erick Kraus, the duty officer at the consulate in Istanbul.

"It was Mark, just like you thought it might be."

"Do you have him in custody?"

"He had his gun out, but before he could fire, Pete—Ms. Boylan—shot him between the eyes. He was dead before he hit the floor."

"How is she?"

"Fine, but she wants to know about Mr. McGarvey. I'll put her on."

"Where's Mac?" she said. She sounded out of breath, as if she had just run up a flight of stairs. But Mac had once told him that sometimes, when Pete got super excited, she tended to hyperventilate.

"How are you, really? Lou and I were worried."

"Goddamnit, Otto, I'm talking about Mac. Do you know where he is or don't you?"

Otto looked up. He'd switched to speaker mode when Erick had called, and Louise had heard everything. She shrugged.

"He's disappeared, but it may not be as bad as all that; could be he's on his way back to Istanbul."

"Back from where? What the hell are you talking about?"

"I think Najjir took him out of the city to a marina about ten miles from the Black Sea. Lou managed to get a series of good satellite passes from one of our Jupiter birds in geosync orbit, and we got a shot of four men getting out of a car and boarding a yacht. One of them was looking up, and my darlings have a fairly high confidence that it was Mac."

"Sounds like him, thinking maybe someone was overhead, so he looked up," Pete said. "What do you have on the yacht?"

"The *Farashatan*, registered to one of the distant royal cousins."

"Then let's nail that bastard."

"No need. The yacht's been in charter service for two years now. Oil revenues have been down, and distant cousins are at the low end of the feeding trough."

"So they're still docked there, or are they headed across to Russia?"

"They were on their way across, but a half hour ago they stopped and began to circle, like they were looking for something."

Pete actually laughed. "He was outgunned and he couldn't take over, so he decided to swim back to shore. Do you think they found him? Did they stop?"

"No. They're on their way back to Turkey."

"He's still in the water?"

"Mac's a damned good swimmer, and there's a lot of traffic where he went overboard—if that's what happened. Someone's bound to pick him up."

"Not unless Najjir sent a Mayday. Commercial ships don't maintain man-overboard watches," Pete said. "Was there any radio traffic from the yacht?"

"One short burst, via satellite. It was sent in what I think was one of the new quantum algorithms the Russians started playing around with a couple of months ago. My darlings are chewing on it, but it could take a bit of time."

"Christ," Pete said softly. "Any Russian warships on their way to where he might have gone overboard?"

"Not within a hundred miles. But as soon as Lou can snag some more satellite time, we'll take a look."

"Could be a couple of hours," Louise said, loudly enough that Pete could hear her.

"Nothing any sooner?"

"You know as well as I do that retasking any of our spy birds, especially a Jupiter, damned near takes an act of Congress. So I'm doing it the old-fashioned way."

"By stealing the time," Pete said. "We have to find him before the Russians do, because once they have him they'll kill him rather than admit he's there."

They could hear the desperation in her voice. "We'll find him," Otto said. "I've alerted Incirlik, and the CO promises he'll keep a chopper on standby."

The US Air Force base was located on Turkey's southeastern coast, not far from the border with Syria.

"He'd be sticking his neck out to send one of our resources into the Black Sea," Pete said. "Lots of Russians there."

"He's a good man," Otto said. "But what about you?"

"I want to stay here, but they ordered me out of the country. The doctor insists I get to All Saints ASAP. He's worried about my liver."

"Then do as he says," Louise said. "We'll pick you up at Andrews."

"Find Mac before the Russians do," Pete said.

"Will do," Otto told her.

"Promise?"

"Honest Injun."

Najjir came down from the bridge to the salon where Miriam was staring out the windows at the pitch-black predawn sea, waiting with a bottle of water. She looked almost as bad as he felt, and yet he kept assuring himself that they were going to come out of this situation just fine.

She turned to him. "What'd they say?"

"They have our position and they'll either find him alive or they'll find his body. Either way they'll fish him out of the water and get him to the base."

He'd radioed their situation to the maritime border guard's Stenka-class patrol boat, which had come out of Novorossiysk to meet them midsea, in what was essentially international waters. The 125-foot boat was originally designed for antisubmarine duty and could cruise at thirty-five knots. Armed with 12.7mm and 30mm machine guns, antisubmarine torpedoes, and a pair of depth charge racks, she was a formidable fighting vessel, with a crew of more than thirty officers and men.

"What about the Americans?" Miriam asked. "The man was the chief of the CIA. If they traced him this far—which is possible—mightn't they send someone to look for him?"

"They're not going to start a shooting war."

"Even if they think the Russians have him?"

"If they believe that, they'll send it to the diplomats," Najjir said. "Nothing to worry about now. He's off our hands, and we're well shed of him. We did our part and now it's time for the SVR to do its."

Miriam turned again to the dark windows. "You don't think they'll be waiting for us at the marina?"

"No reason for it."

Miriam shook her head. "He's out there. I can feel him. And even if the Russians find him alive and pull him out of water, he'll move heaven and earth to come for us. Especially when he finds out that his lover has been killed."

"The Russians will never admit they have him, and I guarantee that they'll never let him walk free. So stop worrying."

"Easier said than done."

"Fuck it, go ahead and worry. I'm going to get a drink, and when we get ashore I'm going back to the hotel for a few hours' sleep, and this afternoon sometime I'm flying out."

"To where?"

"A safe haven," Najjir said. "Something you might think of for yourself."

"Maybe I'll come with you."

"Not a chance in hell."

"Why?" Miriam asked. "I'm not such a bad lay."

"Business, nothing more."

"You enjoyed it."

"Playacting. And now that it's over I wouldn't fuck you for all the gold in Fort Knox."

"No?"

"I'm gay, sweetheart. And besides, you have a horseshit fashion sense."

"Pufta," Miriam said. "I almost hope McGarvey does come after you."

FORTY-SEVEN

□

McGarvey figured that he had been in the water for eight or ten hours, but aside from being cold, he was in pretty good shape. The dawn had broken cloudy, which made it more difficult to spot passing fishing boats—the ones he wanted to pick him up—but it would warm up soon.

Within minutes after he'd gone overboard the yacht had come back for him. But each time it got close, its spotlight sweeping toward him, he dove under the surface and swam in the opposite direction for thirty seconds or so before coming up for air.

The cat-and-mouse game had lasted for nearly thirty minutes, until the spotlight was turned off and the yacht headed southwest, back to the Bosphorus.

An hour ago the ferry to Yalta, on the Crimean peninsula, had steamed within thirty yards or so from him. A half dozen people were at the rails, but no one spotted him waving, and within a few minutes the ship was out of sight over the horizon.

He got tired just at dawn, so he took off his trousers, tied knots at the cuffs, and used the belt to tie the waist shut, trapping the air inside, in effect making a crude life jacket. It only held enough air to help keep him afloat for ten minutes or so at a time, but it allowed him to take catnaps.

Just now, the deflated trousers around his neck, he got a massive cramp in his left leg. Ignoring the pain, he began to swim, heading south, the hazy sun over his left shoulder.

All through the night large ships had passed him, some heading south, others north. But they traveled at such a fast pace that they were nothing but specks on the horizon for only a minute or so, before disappearing in the opposite direction.

At no time was he ever completely alone in the sea. At night he could see the lights of a lot of ships in every direction. When the dawn had come, most ships passed in the distance, except for the ferry.

Sooner or later, he suspected, the Russians would be coming for him, if Najjir had radioed or used a sat phone to report the situation. But if he had reported to someone, Otto might well have picked it up and called for help. Possibly from the US air base outside Adana.

And if the Russians actually did pick him up—which he thought was likely—and if Otto and Louise had managed to snag some satellite time, and knew where to look—which was a little less likely—the ball would be passed to State, who would put pressure on the Kremlin.

There were a lot of ifs in the equation, so for the near term, until he was picked up by whomever, he would work to not drown.

One good thought was that Pete was safe at the consulate, probably patched up by now, and starting to raise hell about his situation. She would move mountains to see that he was found and rescued, wherever he was.

He almost wished that he were a fly in the corner of the chief of Istanbul station's office at the consulate, watching the fireworks.

You will get off your fucking ass and find my fiancé or I'll rip your fucking heart out of your fucking chest with my bare hands. Now!

Someone behind him called his name on a bullhorn. "Mr. McGarvey."

He turned as an inflatable, with two armed men plus the driver, raced toward him from a patrol boat flying the white-blue-red Russian colors.

Pete was booked on a Delta/KLM flight direct to Dulles because, as Otto explained, it was the fastest way to get her home. Nothing was available from Incirlik, and by the time he could get something to her from Ramstein and then across the pond she'd already be touching down in the States.

She moved slowly, though she was ambulatory Irwin had personally escorted her to the airport, and he didn't leave until she was through security and on her way to the gate, a half hour ago. He'd managed a temporary passport for her, and one of the station's cell phones.

"Give it to tech support when you get home. They'll sanitize it and get it back to us."

"Will do, and thanks for everything," Pete had told him. "We won't forget."

"Get him back."

"Count on it."

At the gate, with twenty minutes before her flight was ready for boarding, she called Otto. "I'm at the airport. Is there any word about Mac?"

"The Russians picked him up a half hour ago."

"Is he okay?"

"Unknown at this point. But apparently he's aboard one of their patrol boats on the way to Novorossiysk."

"At least he's out of the water," Pete said. It wasn't the worst news. "What are the Russians saying?"

"The director called General Subotin last night, but that was before they had Mac."

"What are we doing about getting him home?"

"Marty and I are going over to the White House with Gibson, to see the president and his Russian adviser."

"Bill Rodak?"

"He's a friend of Marty's."

"You're bypassing State?"

"Gibson's call, and I agree with him. We need to make this personal right now."

"Before Mac has an unfortunate accident," Pete said, holding back tears of fear and frustration. She had walked away from the people already in line for the boarding call. "I want him back."

"We'll get him."

"Not in a body bag."

.   .   .

McGarvey had been given dry dungarees and a Russian naval officer's tunic without a name tag or insignia of rank, and had been brought up to the wardroom, where a young lieutenant brought him a cup of coffee laced with brandy.

"The captain will see you shortly, sir," the kid said. "Would you like something to eat?"

"I'll wait until I get back to Istanbul. I have friends waiting for me there."

"Yes, sir."

A slender man with blond hair and blue eyes came in. He was wearing the shoulder boards of a captain-lieutenant—two and a half stripes and four stars. His name tag read "Malikov." He didn't sit down.

"How are you feeling?" he asked. His English was heavily accented but passable.

"Happy that you rescued me. I was getting a little cold."

"I would imagine so. We'll be back at our base later tonight, or more likely very early tomorrow morning. Depends on the sea. We have some weather approaching. But they might send a helicopter for you. We'll have to wait and see."

"I would like to have the use of a sat phone to call my people and let them know that I'm safe."

"I'm sorry, but that is not in my orders."

"Exactly what are your orders, captain?"

"To rescue you and bring you back to the base."

"At Novorossiysk."

Malikov nodded.

"That's the new Spetsnaz base."

Malikov didn't respond.

"I'm sure that the SVR will inform my people that I wasn't found and that I'm presumed drowned."

"I must get back to my duties."

"You might be better served by tossing me overboard and reporting that you didn't find me."

"I've already radioed . . ."

"Too bad for you," McGarvey said.

FORTY–EIGHT

Gibson's limo, bearing the DCI plus Bambridge and Otto, was passed through the west gate. They were met under the portico by Bill Rodak's secretary, who escorted them to the Russian adviser's office in the West Wing, just steps from the Oval Office.

A news conference was scheduled in a half hour, and the press secretary's staff was busy putting finishing touches on the hot-button topics that were likely to come up.

"I'll take the lead," Gibson had told them on the way over from Langley. "But the fact is we're nearly certain that the Russians have McGarvey?"

"My darlings have the confidence level above ninety percent," Otto said, more than happy that the DCI was taking the situation seriously enough to bring it to the president's attention.

Marty had started to object, but Gibson held him off.

"We're here to see the president, who's expecting me, but first we'll get a few answers from Mr. Rodak."

"He'll verify what I've already told you," Bambridge said. He'd been in a conciliatory mood since the incident in the DCI's office. He'd even gone down to Otto's lair to apologize. He'd been under a lot of pressure over what he was calling Operation French Sting.

Rodak's office was next to the chief of staff's, and he got to his feet as they were shown in. Three chairs had been set up for them.

"Would you gentlemen care for coffee?" he asked.

"No," Gibson said. He sat down, Otto to his left, Bambridge to his right.

Rodak nodded for his secretary to leave, and he sat down. "How may I be of help, Mr. Director?"

"Marty has filled in some of the details on the French operation, which apparently he cooked up with advice from you. I'd like more details."

"I'm sure that Marty has covered all the bases for you in his usual thorough manner."

"I'd like your take before we see the president."

Rodak was surprised. "I didn't know that he was expecting you. He has a news conference in less than thirty minutes."

"We'll be finished by then," Gibson said.

Rodak shrugged. "Where should I begin?"

"Otto?" Gibson prompted. They had rehearsed the scenario before Marty joined them.

"The Eiffel Tower. The DGSE has a few questions they'd like answers to."

"The attack was only meant to seem real. Had Mr. McGarvey and Ms. Boylan—she's one of your people, I believe—not interfered, the contractor and the woman he was using as cover would have stepped in and made citizen's arrests of the would-be bombers."

"Who in reality were working for whom?"

"The Russians, of course. Who else?"

"And what were you guys trying to accomplish?"

Marty started to break in, but Gibson held him off, and Otto repeated the question.

"I'm sure that Marty has told you about the plausible deniability we thought was necessary to pull this off," Rodak said, directing his explanation to the DCI. "The situation between the president and Mr. Putin and our media shows no signs of letting up. We wanted this to be an arm's-length operation."

"Arm's length from whom?" Gibson asked.

"Why, the president and the agency, of course. I advised Marty to keep it totally independent. An operation that could be traced back to just us and no one else."

Otto wanted to call the man on the obviously stupid remarks, but he held off, and Gibson had warned him not to object to anything that seemed an outright lie. Of course, if the op had gone south and the tower had actually come down, the entire thing would have fallen on the agency's deputy director, and on the president's Russian adviser.

"The point of the operation?" Otto asked again.

"We believe—and wanted to prove—that the latest round of attacks against not only our internet but against a number of our communications satellites had been moved from Moscow to Paris. The Syrian bombers were working for the Russian cell right there."

"Why take down the tower?" Gibson asked. "It makes no sense."

"Because the French were oblivious to the Russian hacking operation," Bambridge said. "We wanted to hand the bombers over to them on a silver platter, with a street map direct to the four locations where the hackers were set up. An attempt on the Eiffel Tower would have woken them up."

"Did you try to explain what you believed was happening?" Gibson asked.

"Yes, sir. On numerous times."

"Did you keep an encounter log?" Otto asked.

"Of course not. This entire project was to be arm's length, as I've said all along."

"Until you handed over the bad guys to French intel."

"Exactly."

"But why such an elaborate ruse?" Gibson asked. "The entire thing could have blown up in your faces. Literally."

"I don't mean to be argumentative, Mr. Director, but when was the last time in memory that the fucking Frogs ever listened to us about anything?"

"You were sending them a wake-up call? Is that it?" Otto asked.

"Yes."

Rodak's secretary knocked once and opened the door. "The president will see you now, gentlemen."

.   .   .

President Thomas Weaver was just putting on his jacket when Martha Draper, his chief of staff, showed Gibson and the others into the Oval Office.

"You have ten minutes, Mr. President," she said.

"This'll be short, but have Dan ready to stall them if need be." Daniel Isherwood was the president's press secretary. "And no calls in the meantime."

"Yes, sir."

The president was a bulky man, with a square jaw and animated eyes, especially when he was angry. "The ball's in your court, Ed. You said that this has something to do with the Paris near miss?"

"It concerns Kirk McGarvey. I believe that you're familiar with him."

Weaver nodded, his expression tight. "Was he involved?"

"He and one of our employees who was with him happened to be at the Eiffel Tower when the situation began to unravel. They saw it for what it was and stopped the attack from happening."

"Casualties?"

"Less than one-tenth of one percent of what they could have been, had the tower come down."

"Then he's a hero again, just like New York," Weaver said, eyeing his Russian adviser. "But you told me that there was another issue, possibly involving one of my staff."

"Yes, Mr. President," Otto said.

"And you are?"

"Otto Rencke, our computer expert," Gibson said.

Weaver didn't smile, but he nodded again. "I've also heard of you."

"We're still investigating, but at this point it looks as if our deputy director and Mr. Rodak cooked up some sort of a scheme to bring down the Eiffel Tower, but in exchange for what, we don't know yet."

"I explained myself," Marty blustered. "We both did."

"Both of you are lying. And I will find out what you were really up to. Guaranteed," Otto said.

"And?" Weaver demanded.

"The Russians have taken McGarvey into custody and are bringing him to their Spetsnaz base at Novorossiysk, where they mean to debrief him before killing him and disposing of his body."

"That can't happen," Weaver said.

"No, Mr. President," Gibson said. "But they'll never admit they had him."

"Are you one hundred percent on this?"

"Yes, sir," Otto said.

Weaver picked up his phone. "I want to speak with Mr. Putin. Now."

FORTY-NINE

☐

Najjir telephoned Rowe's private number as he and Miriam rode back to Istanbul in the rear seat of a chauffeured Cadillac SUV the Ritz had sent for them.

The number was answered by a recording of a man whose voice was unfamiliar. "You have reached the office of Mark Rowe, who is away from his desk at this moment. If you would like to leave a message, press star. If you wish to speak with a representative of the consulate, stay on the line."

Najjir pressed the red Disconnect bar, but the connection remained intact.

The man who'd recorded the message came on. "Good morning, I'm Mr. Rowe's assistant. He said he was expecting a call. May I be of service?"

"Where is he at the moment?"

"I'm sorry, sir, I can't say. But if you would care to leave a message."

Najjir took the back off the throwaway phone, removed the battery and SIM card and, lowering the window, tossed all the pieces, one at a time, outside.

Miriam had been super nervous all the way back from where McGarvey had gone overboard. She'd expected that they would be met at the marina by the police. The deal with the Turkish army officer and his people was for a lot of money, and one time only. It had all the earmarks of a deal going south on them, and she had expressed her fears more than once.

When they had been met only by the hotel car and driver, she had relaxed, but only slightly.

"What was that all about?" she asked, when Najjir powered the window back up.

"I phoned a friend but he wasn't in."

"Mark?"

"Yes," Najjir said. He glanced at the rearview mirror in front, but the driver wasn't paying any attention to them. At least not outwardly.

"Shit," Miriam said softly. Worry was written all over her oval face.

"Nothing to be concerned about," Najjir said. He patted her hand, and she gave him an odd look, almost wistful, as if she'd rather be anywhere else but here.

At this point he almost felt sorry for her. She was a little girl who figured that she was in over her head. Either that or she was playacting, like she had been doing all along. Only, this role was a new one.

"Our flight to Paris isn't until first thing in the morning, so we'll just hang around the hotel and spend a pleasant day together doing absolutely nothing. Sounds good?"

She glanced at the back of the driver's head, then nodded. "We've had a couple of hectic days. Maybe I'll do a little shopping."

"Perfect."

Kenneth Endicott, the uniformed driver, opened the rear passenger side door for the lady and handed her out beneath the portico of the Ritz. The gentleman followed, and pressed a hundred-euro note into the driver's hand.

"Thanks for the lift," Najjir said, taking the woman's arm.

"Part of our service, sir," Endicott said.

When the couple disappeared into the lobby, Endicott drove around to the parking garage, where he shut off the engine and tossed his cap onto the passenger seat but remained behind the wheel.

In actuality he'd worked as a Ritz driver for the past two years and was nearing the end of his assignment. In reality he also worked for the CIA as an NOC—a deep cover agent who operated with no official cover. If he was outed, the CIA would deny knowing him.

His specialty was working up contacts among the well-heeled guests of the hotel—primarily those from the Middle East, mostly Iran but occasionally Saudi Arabia. In his first month he'd befriended a minor Saudi prince, for whom he supplied whores, especially the German girls who worked the Turkish bathhouses. His product for six months, until the prince was recalled home, had been close to gold seam. The prince had worked for Saudi intelligence, sent to Istanbul to spy on German spies—the girls who worked the Turkish baths.

The assignment this morning was a one-off and had been handed to him by Otto Rencke. And considering who Rencke was, the call had not come as a surprise, though only a very few people at Langley knew who Endicott was.

He phoned Otto's rollover number. It was only a little past four in the morning in Washington, but Rencke answered on the first ring. He'd been expecting the call.

"I just dropped them off at the hotel," Endicott said.

"How'd they seem to you?"

"He had it together but the woman looked and sounded as if she were standing on the edge of a cliff with no way back."

"Did they talk?"

"He told her they weren't flying out to Paris until first thing in the morning, so they were going to hang out here today and take it easy."

"His phone went off-line. What'd he do with it?"

"He took it apart and tossed the bits out the window. He called Mark Rowe, like you expected he might. I heard only his half of the conversation."

"I listened in," Otto said. "Stand by."

Of course Rencke had listened in. When he'd first heard of the guy, during advanced training, his handler told him that he'd probably never have contact, but if he did, not to be surprised at whatever went down.

"Don't ever cross the man, or try to blow smoke up his ass. If he gives you an assignment, no matter what it is, take care of it. If he asks you a question, or wants your opinion, answer him. But if you don't know, tell him so."

"Do I report it as an encounter?"

"As far as you're concerned he's even farther off the grid than you'll be. But treat the man with care. His closest friend is Kirk McGarvey, and you don't want to piss off either of them."

"Jesus," was all he'd been able to say. Rencke's rep was huge, but McGarvey's was interstellar.

Otto was back a minute later. "They're not booked under the Worley ID on any flight out of Istanbul, at least not for the next five days."

"How about by train, or perhaps a rental car?"

"Nothing."

"Another ID for both of them?"

"Anything's possible. But they used a leased yacht under the Worley name to take them into the Black Sea, so I think they'll probably use a charter air service to get them out of Turkey."

"To where?"

"I have a number of guesses, but none of them include Paris, London, or Moscow. Nor can I be one hundred percent they'll continue using the ID they came into the country with."

"What can I do?" Endicott asked. It was a no-brainer for him. If he did good for Rencke, and especially McGarvey, he would make some serious chops. Could lead to the one thing he'd wanted most from the beginning: to be in charge of the entire NOC program.

"If they leave the hotel and need a driver, can you make sure that it's you?"

"Yes."

"Then do it, but be careful. They're among the best I've seen. And right now they'll be suspicious of everyone. Say the wrong thing and they'll nail you."

"I have a couple of ideas."

"They've been using throwaway phones. Means I can't listen in unless they call someone I know."

"I'll be your eyes and ears here, sir."

"Good hunting," Otto said.

Endicott hung up his phone, grabbed his cap, and went into the hotel, taking the service elevator up to the fourteenth floor, where the Worleys had the east suite.

NOCs, by definition, thought of themselves as invisible in plain sight.

Worley and his broad might be as good as Rencke said they were, but almost no one ever really looked beyond the end of their nose.

FIFTY

□

McGarvey was in his cabin, staring out the porthole at the approaching Russian naval helicopter that was flaring just off the starboard side of the patrol ship, when two ratings, neither of them armed, came in. They'd brought an inflatable life jacket and a standard aviation crash helmet.

"My ride?" Mac asked.

"Captain's orders, please to put on life belt and helmet," one of the men said. He was very young and still had pimples on his chin.

McGarvey did as he was told, and they escorted him up to the foredeck, just forward of the AK-30 machine gun in its dome. The captain stood at the windows of the wheelhouse.

The ship came to dead idle speed as the helicopter took up position one hundred feet above the bow. The side hatch just behind the rear wheels was open, and a sailor in a flight suit and crash helmet held on to the winch cable, attached to which was a rescue sling, as it was lowered.

The rotor wash was very strong, knocking the sea flat but kicking up a lot of spray, which reached halfway up to the top of the wheelhouse so that McGarvey had to turn his head away.

One of the ratings grabbed the sling, and McGarvey held his arms out at his side as the sailor secured it across his chest and under his armpits, then stepped away.

The winch drew the cable up and McGarvey's body twisted around so that he was facing the wheelhouse as the helicopter pulled away to port, and he got a momentary glimpse of the troubled expression on the captain's face. He was the first man in the past twenty-four hours who seemed to realize the can of worms his country had opened by taking into custody a former director of the CIA.

Louise looked away from her computer screen and telephoned Otto. "They have him," she said.

"Are you sure it's him?"

"A Helix met the patrol ship and hoisted a man off the forward deck. I'm watching in real time, but I've already overstayed my welcome."

"Where are they headed?"

Louise gave him the coordinates, and the flight path the helicopter turned to once it was clear of the ship and even before Mac was aboard. "Bet you a month of Twinkies they're heading to Novorossiysk," she said, getting out of the satellite program and returning it to its previous routine.

"Just a mo," Otto said. He came back a second or two later. "Zero three eight degrees on the button. Novorossiysk. Good job, Lou."

Even before the hatch had been secured, the helicopter climbed at full power, the noise inside the cabin, as he was being strapped in, deafening.

An attractive woman, in her early thirties at the most, sleek black hair cropped fashionably short, the style framing her oval face, came aft and sat down next to him. She took a set of headphones from the bulkhead and gave them to McGarvey, then donned another pair for herself. She was dressed in Spetsnaz camos with bloused boots and the field insignia of a major, but no name tag.

"I'm very pleased to meet you, Mr. McGarvey," she said, her British-accented English cultured. "I did my doctoral thesis on your exploits." She held out her hand. "My name is Raya Kuzin."

McGarvey shook it. "I didn't know women served in the Spetsnaz."

"They don't."

"Who do you work for?"

"Actually I head a Kremlin special projects task force that answers directly to President Putin."

McGarvey had to smile. "I imagine that I've come as something of a surprise to him."

"You can't imagine," she said, returning his smile. "As a matter of fact I'm told that President Weaver called earlier today and asked about you."

"My people want me back."

"I wasn't privy to their conversation, but I imagine that was the substance."

"I'm sure that he denied knowing anything about it, but he promised to look into it personally and get back to Weaver."

The woman nodded. She was studying his face as if she were looking at a very famous painting that she'd only ever read about but had never seen in person. She seemed happy, enthused, even impressed.

"You're taking me to Novorossiysk, where you'll go straight to drugs. No use trying waterboarding; it doesn't work on everybody. But the psychotropic drugs you guys have been using for the past twenty-plus years sometimes fry the subject's brain. You'll never be able to send damaged goods back home. So you'll deny you have me."

"I imagine so."

"Won't work."

"No?"

"I have a friend who is looking for me."

The woman brightened. "Otto Rencke. I would like to meet him. The conversations would be fabulous."

"His wife will have already found out where I'm being taken."

"Louise, another fascinating character. Washington has always been filled with interesting people, but never so many as at this moment. I hope to go there soon. Perhaps after your debriefing is completed."

"That may be sooner than you think," McGarvey said. The woman was either a complete idiot or a damned fine actor. He thought the latter.

"Just to get the preliminary facts straight—we're all a little confused, frankly—what were you doing at the Eiffel Tower?"

"Having lunch."

"But why just at that moment? Did Langley know that an attack was imminent?"

"Najjir and the woman were working for you."

"You know this for a fact, or it's just what you believe? I mean to say that you and Ms. Boylan being there at that exact moment had to be much more than a simple coincidence. And from my studies I learned that you've always been a man who never believes in coincidences."

"Was there a question in there?"

"Yes. The couple were not working for us. Trust me on that fact. But what made you believe they were?"

"He told me so at one point."

She shook her head. "Misdirection. But I don't know why."

"Then why was he delivering me to you people?"

"You jumped overboard, Mr. McGarvey. We rescued you."

"That wasn't my question."

"I don't have the answer. But I expect that Mr. Najjir is an accomplished freelance—he's never spent a night in any jail cell I know of. But when you stumbled on his operation, he realized that he had picked up a valuable commodity, and he put you and Ms. Boylan up for auction. We won."

"You'll never be able to admit that you have me, so you'll have to kill me."

"Sadly true. But we'll have you for long enough to learn many interesting and useful things."

"You'll be personally involved?"

"I wouldn't miss the opportunity."

"Then I'll have to kill you before I escape."

□

FIFTY-ONE

Miriam got off the phone with the hotel's valet service desk and turned to Najjir, who was pouring another glass of champagne. "His name is Endicott and he's worked as a driver and guide for the hotel for two years."

"Was he vetted?"

"The chef d'valet assured me that he had been. The bloke sounded a little bit put out that I was questioning the bona fides of one of his staff. But he also told me that it wasn't at all unusual for a driver to ask a guest if any other service would be required."

Najjir shook his head. The situation didn't smell right to him. "He's more than just a driver. And I know damned well he listened to every word we said in the car."

"Do you think he works for the American consulate?"

"I think he works for the CIA."

"Christ, it would mean that he's on to us."

"It's a possibility we need to check out before we fly away tonight. Give him a call and tell him that we'll take him up on his offer. We'll meet downstairs in ten minutes."

As Miriam was making the call, Najjir used his last throwaway cell phone to contact the Skyjet service at the airport.

"Hello, this is Mark Morgan, just checking to confirm our flight to Berlin this evening."

.   .   .

Endicott was pretty well sure that the Worley character and the broad suspected him of something. He'd seen the look in the man's eyes at the door to the suite. Otto had warned that the guy was a pro, and it showed.

Stewart Blakely, the chief valet, was at his desk when Endicott came to the door. The man was ambitious. He'd worked his way up the Ritz chain, starting in a couple of Florida locations, before he was sent out here three years ago. He was bucking for the Ritz in London. And absolutely nothing would go wrong on his watch. He made no bones about it.

"The Worleys called. Want me to give them the grand tour, starting with lunch."

"I'm surprised, after the call about you that I got from the missus just three minutes ago."

"Checking to see if I was any good?" Endicott asked, his radar up.

"Something like that. Wanted to know if we'd done a thorough background check."

Endicott smiled. "Thanks for vouching for me."

"I do the same for any other employee here," Blakely said. "But I wonder why they thought it necessary to ask."

"Maybe I was a little too forward. A lot of Brits don't care for familiarity by the staff."

"But they've hired you."

"I'll be off then," Endicott said.

He went back to the garage, where he took his Glock 29 subcompact pistol from the locked leather bag he kept under the driver's seat. Checking to make sure the action worked properly, he stuffed the small 10mm pistol—a favorite of a number of other NOCs he knew—into his belt on his left side, beneath his uniform blazer.

He got behind the wheel and started the engine, but before he pulled out he debated whether he should call Rencke and let him know what was going on. But he decided to wait until he had something more definite to report.

.   .   .

Najjir and Miriam emerged from the hotel just as Endicott was approaching the portico.

They had changed into clean clothes, he with a linen blazer and slacks and she in a white, low-cut silk pantsuit and medium heels, a bright scarf around her neck tied in the French style, to one side.

"How are we going to work this?" Miriam asked.

"You're sure that you left nothing in the suite that could lead back to us?" Najjir asked.

"Of course."

She hadn't. He'd checked. "Then before we go to the airport, Mr. Endicott, or whoever he is, will meet with an unfortunate accident."

"The police will be notified and they'll come looking for us."

"Looking for the Worleys, who will no longer exist."

"I won't be able to return to London."

"Nor Moscow."

"No."

"Then we'll go home, and wait for the dust to settle. No one will follow us there."

"I thought we were going to Berlin."

"Jeddah will be safer."

Miriam nodded. "It'll be temporary for me, love. My idea of home is different than yours. But then you're a man, and you have money, and life is better for you there."

"Trust me, I don't plan on spending a minute longer in country than needs be," Najjir said. "And you're welcome to stay with me as long as necessary."

"Then what?"

"New faces, new names, new legends."

"All well and good, Karim, if that's your real name."

"It isn't."

"Well, whoever, what then?"

"New operations. I think delivering McGarvey to the Russians will stand us in good stead with the right people."

Miriam shivered a little. "I just hope to Christ that the son of a bitch doesn't take a runner, or God forbid the Russians actually release him."

"He won't and they can't," Najjir said.

Endicott got out of the car and opened the rear passenger side door for them.

They headed away from the hotel, and a block later Najjir pulled out his pistol but kept it out of sight, below the level of the driver's headrest, until they came around a busy corner.

"What do you folks have in mind first?" Endicott said. "If it's lunch, I know a perfect spot."

Najjir laid the muzzle of the pistol on the back of Endicott's skull. "Do you know Tarlabasi?"

Endicott stiffened, but kept his voice reasonable. "Sure, but why the hell anyone would want to go to a neighborhood like that is beyond comprehension."

"I suspect that you work for the Company and that you know, or think you know, who we are."

"Bullshit."

"Take the next left, and watch your speed. If a cop tries to stop us, I'll shoot you first, and then him. If you do exactly as I tell you to do, you might just walk away from this assignment."

"The odds aren't in my favor," Endicott said, looking in the rearview mirror.

"We are going to take your weapon—I'm sure that you're carrying—and your phone and steal your car By the time you get to a phone we'll have ditched the car and will be long gone."

Endicott made the corner. "Why should I believe you?"

"Do or don't, I couldn't care less."

"Anyway, I'm not carrying and I'm not a spy."

"I expect that you're an NOC, in a nice gig, chauffeuring your johns and listening to their private conversations."

Endicott said nothing.

"Two blocks, take the right."

"Fuck you."

"You either die now, or in the next minute or so, and we'll get out of the car and walk away," Najjir said. "Or you can take us to the factory in Tarablasi, where you might have a chance to take us down. McGarvey probably would have succeeded if he hadn't been dragging the broad around."

Endicott said nothing.

"Zero chance now, or a slightly better chance if you cooperate. Figure the odds."

Endicott wished he'd called Rencke, but he made the right. It was a shitty deal, but he was fast on his feet and a damned good shot. And this time it was the bastard in the backseat saddled with his own broad.

FIFTY–TWO

Pete got through customs and immigration, and Louise, long legs and bony shoulders, dressed in jeans and a white silk blouse, was right there, taking her in her arms.

They hugged for a longish moment, people still arriving parting around them.

"You look better than I thought you would," Louise said. "Did you manage to get any sleep on the flight?"

"It wasn't possible. What about Mac?"

"He should be in Novorossiysk by now."

"Then the Russians have him, no doubt?"

"Yeah. But Weaver phoned Putin, who promised to look into it, so nobody here is writing him off just yet. So don't you either."

Pete was bone tired, the wound in her side ached, as did pretty much the rest of her body, especially her breasts, where the son of a bitch had slammed his fists. But mostly she was worried and mad as hell. "Let's get to campus and see what Otto's coming up with."

"First, All Saints. They're waiting for you."

"Langley."

"Not yet. You need tending to, and when Otto's in his work mode we'd just be getting in his way. Besides, I have to tell you something about my hubby that'll knock your socks off."

Pete wanted to argue, but in her heart of hearts she knew that Louise was right. "What about him?"

"I'll tell you on the way into Georgetown. Where are your bags?"

"There's nothing," Pete said, despondent, again. "He'll try to escape and they'll shoot him."

"Like I said, Pete, nobody's writing him off. Anyway, he's been in worse jams."

Dr. Alan Franklin, the chief medico at All Saints, was waiting for them, and as soon as they came through the back entrance he had his nurse whisk Pete immediately down the corridor to the state-of-the-art emergency room.

"She'll want to get out of here ASAP," Louise said. "So unless she really needs to be admitted, just check her out and give her a pill or something."

It wasn't like Louise, and Franklin's left eyebrow rose. "This about McGarvey?"

"Yeah."

"There's been scuttlebutt."

"They got involved with something that started out in Paris, but moved to Istanbul. Pete got free in exchange for Mac, who they turned over to the Russians. We're pretty sure that he's at one of their Spetsnaz bases right now, but the Russians won't admit they have him."

"She knows?"

"Yes."

Franklin shook his head. "What's the prognosis?"

"We're working on it."

"You should get some rest, you and Otto, though I suppose that'd be futile medical advice."

"Mac's a friend," Louise said. "I'll be in the waiting room. Don't take too long, Doc.

"We'll see," Franklin said, and he left.

Otto didn't answer until the fourth ring, which was so unusual for him that Louise checked to make sure the number was right. When he came on he sounded dejected.

"How's Pete?" he asked.

"She's with Franklin right now. But she got through customs under her own steam, and she wants to come see you."

"I'm stuck."

It was the first time Louise had ever heard her husband say such a thing. "What's wrong, sweetheart?"

"Novorossiysk is coming up a complete blank, or just about. What encrypted satellite coms and even local en clair phone calls my darlings are monitoring make absolutely no mention of Mac, or of anything unusual happening. It's ordinary business, including training schedules and Ukraine operations. They're making no effort to hide anything."

"What about communications with the chopper that picked up Mac?"

"The man they picked up was identified as Anatoli Fedorov. He's an OR 8 michman, an engineering warrant officer. Broken leg."

"The man they picked up had no broken leg. It was Mac."

"Maybe so, but they're covering their asses pretty good. Fedorov is listed on the ship's company, and captain has asked for a replacement. The only screwy thing is that the chopper was towed into a hangar before the passenger was off-loaded."

"Bad weather? If it was the warrant officer, maybe they were protecting him from the elements."

"Blue skies."

"It was Mac."

"You're right. But it means that he's disappeared already."

Franklin had Pete's X-rays up on the computerized flat-panel screen. "Iglesias did a good job," he said turning to her.

"I'll live?" Pete asked.

"Now you sound like McGarvey."

"It's catchy. So, what's the verdict?"

"I'd like to keep you overnight for observation, but you'll live. Just try not to get into another fight in the next month or so."

"I'll try," Pete said, standing up.

"Where's Mac?" Franklin asked.

"He's in badland, and we're working to get him back."

Franklin shook his head. "You guys might give some thought to retiring. Settling down."

"Yeah," Pete said, and she left.

Louise looked up when Pete walked in. "So?"

"Lots of bruises, but the bullet missed my liver. Let's go talk to Otto."

They took the Roosevelt Bridge across the river and headed up the Parkway, traffic heavy as it usually was at this time of the morning.

"So what happened in Paris? Otto hasn't had time to give me all the details. He's been working around the clock and he's damned worried about Mac."

Pete was staring at the highway, but not seeing the traffic. She was right there with Mac.

"We'll get him back, guaranteed," Louise said. "Everyone's working on it, even the president. The Russians have him and they know that we know it. They're not going to do anything stupid."

"Accidents happen."

"What about Paris?" Louise repeated.

Pete had to smile. "He asked me to marry him."

"Wow," Louise said. "And you accepted?"

"Of course."

"He must have choked on it."

"Just about," Pete said. "You were going to tell me about something Otto did, that just about knocked your socks off . . ." One part of her couldn't believe that she was talking about shit that didn't really matter. Ordinary day-to-day shit.

Louise told her about the incident with Marty in the general's office, and Pete laughed out loud, and then she cried so hard that Louise pulled over to the side of the road and held her.

FIFTY-THREE

□

Raya Kuzin used the en clair phone in the base commander's office to call General Subotin at the SVR's director's dacha outside of Moscow. She knew that any phone calls—in the clear or encrypted—would be monitored by the Americans now.

"Who is calling, please," one of the general's house staff answered.

"Major Kuzin, I'm at Delta."

"He is expecting your call, Major. One moment please."

Delta was the unofficial designator for the Novorossiysk training base. General Subotin came on. "I hope that you have called with good news."

"I'm afraid not, sir. Anatoli died en route."

"He had only a broken leg."

"He'd been shot and bled out within minutes after we'd gotten him aboard."

The line was silent for several moments, and when Subotin came back he sounded resigned. "Then we'll never know what those bastards were trying to accomplish in Paris."

"It would seem not, sir."

"Too bad. But what about the other matter? I'm being pressed by General Gibson. He asked me to look into it as a personal favor."

"Nothing on that score, sir. The man who was fished out of the sea was our operator, there's no doubt about it."

"Not Mr. McGarvey?"

"No, sir. But I honestly wished it had been. I would have loved to interview him before we sent him home."

"I'm sure. When you get back to Moscow with your report, please copy me."

"Of course."

"Then thank you for your personal involvement. I'll pass it along to Mr. Putin."

"I'm truly sorry that the situation turned out as it did."

McGarvey, in shackles binding his ankles and wrists, was escorted by a pair of operators to a small concrete box of a room four stories beneath a hardened bunker, across the eleven-thousand-acre Spetsnaz base from the headquarters complex.

Coming in aboard the helicopter he'd gotten a good aerial view of the sprawling training facility, which in many respects was a near duplicate of the CIA's Farm. But nothing he'd seen from a couple of hundred feet above was any more detailed then the satellite pictures Louise had shown him and Pete a year and a half ago.

Spetsnaz special forces operators were trained just as rigorously here as the CIA's recruits were at Camp Perry.

A Spetsnaz captain, seated at a small metal table in the middle of the room, looked up. "Remove Mr. McGarvey's shackles. I don't think he means to cause us any trouble." The man's face was deeply scarred by childhood acne, but his eyes were warm and his expression was friendly.

"At least not for now," Raya said, coming in behind them.

The operators removed the shackles and left. Neither they nor the captain or the woman were armed.

Raya closed the door and invited Mac to have a seat in one of the two chairs facing the captain at the table. She had the same eager expression as she'd had on the helicopter ride to the base. She was genuinely glad to be at this place at this moment.

"You know of course that I won't cooperate," McGarvey said, sitting down. He was dressed in the same clothing he'd been given aboard the patrol vessel.

"Yes, we know this," Raya said. "But you must know that time is on our side, so we won't have to resort to drugs, at least not in the near term."

"Fair enough. But I will escape, and if needs be I'll kill you."

"Then we understand each other," Raya said.

"Shall we begin?" the captain asked. "Incidentally my name is Vadim Tarasov. I am the chief psyops officer here. Do you understand what this means?"

McGarvey nodded. "We have the same psychological warfare and counterwarfare division at the Farm."

"We know this, but our people are better," Tarasov said. "Let's start with your particulars—name, date, and place of birth, Social Security number, addresses. Data that we can easily verify with a soft credit check."

"You have that information."

"You never liked your positions at Langley—not as head of the Clandestine Service nor as DCI. You're a field man—always have been."

"True."

"So just out of curiosity, why did you take those jobs?" Tarasov asked.

"That's easy," Raya said. "Mr. McGarvey has always operated under the flag-waving comic book hero Superman's motto. Truth, justice, and the American way. A patriot and gentleman in the truest sense of those words."

"And a friend," Tarasov said.

"A loyal friend and lover," Raya agreed. "Who has lost every woman he's ever been involved with."

Raya stood to McGarvey's left. He looked at her, but said nothing. She and the captain were a good team. They were baiting him, and they knew that he knew it. But angry men made mistakes, especially at the beginning or near the end.

"Of course, you could not have heard about Ms. Boylan. She apparently died of her wounds at your consulate in Istanbul."

"A tragic love story," Tarasov said.

"One that he is all too familiar with," Raya said. "No one left to mourn him."

"Will you have anyone mourn your death?" McGarvey asked her.

. . .

Otto was in his inner office, looking up at an image of a woman on one of his large flat-screen monitors, when one of his darlings announced that Louise and Pete were at the door.

"Open sesame," Otto said, not taking his eyes off the screen. He was missing something. He could feel it around the edges, like the nagging start of a toothache.

"Who's that?" Pete asked.

"Raya Kuzin. She's one of Putin's chief advisers on things American—especially the CIA and especially Mac," Otto said, turning to her. "How are you?"

"I'll live," Pete said.

"Pretty girl," Louise said. "What's she doing up there?"

"Apparently she was aboard the helicopter that fished Mac out of the water."

"What was a Putin adviser doing in Novorossiysk at just that moment?" Pete asked. "That's gotta be more than a coincidence."

"They knew that he was coming to them, so Putin sent her out to conduct the initial interviews," Otto said. "Thing is, she called Subotin and told him that the guy they pulled out of the water was one of theirs. Supposedly a SVR ringer aboard the patrol vessel. She told the general that the man bled to death from a gunshot wound. And all that was on an unencrypted line."

"Why didn't she go through the Kremlin? Report it directly to her boss?"

"Because she knew that we would be listening," Otto said.

"So in effect she told us that they do have Mac. The SVR ringer story was just that."

"That's what I figured," Otto said. "The point is, why did she do it?"

"She wants something," Pete said.

"Yeah, but what?" Louise asked.

FIFTY-FOUR

□

The pretty blond Skyjet stewardess came aft to where Najjir and Miriam were finishing an early supper of eggs Benedict and mimosas in the well-appointed main cabin of the Gulfstream 350.

"Sir, the captain asks to tell you that our flight plan has been changed," she said.

"What the hell are you talking about?" Najjir demanded. He looked out the window, but nothing was visible except for desert to the horizon.

"We have been diverted to Riyadh."

"Not a chance in hell," Najjir said, something clutching at his chest.

Miriam's eyes were wide. "What's this about?"

"I don't know, but I'm damned well going to find out," Najjir said, un-doing his seat belt.

"The captain will speak with you, sir, but first there is a phone call for you."

"Who is it?"

"I don't know, sir, but they asked for you by a name that is not on our manifest, and the captain is most concerned."

Najjir snatched the phone next to his armrest. "This is Claude Degas. To whom am I speaking?" Degas was the name he'd used to book the flight to Jeddah, on the Saudi Red Sea coast.

The only immediate trouble that he could think of was that Endicott's body had been found in the old factory and the murder had been traced back to him and Miriam. But it had been a clean kill, with no witnesses.

Nor did he think that anyone had noticed them parking the car in a downtown garage and taking a taxi from there to the private aviation service.

"Ah, Mr. Najjir, this is Colonel Wasem. I'm calling on behalf of Prince Awadi bin Abdulaziz."

"You have the wrong person."

"Yes, sir, but the prince wants most urgently to speak with you and your companion, concerning Paris and, most recently, Istanbul."

"I don't know who you are or what the fuck you're talking about, but I chartered this flight to Jeddah and now I'm diverting to Cairo."

"I work for the GIP, as you once did, and if you will take a look out any window on the starboard side of your aircraft, I believe that you will reconsider."

Najjir looked to the right, as a pair of F-15C fighter jets with Saudi markings appeared, so close that he could see the pilots in each of the fighters.

"They have been asked to escort your aircraft, where once you have arrived the crew will be allowed to return to Istanbul."

Najjir exchanged a look with Miriam, who seemed about ready to jump out of her skin. If McGarvey had been found he would be in Novorossiysk by now, and even though the Russians had him, he would still provide some leverage with the Saudi intelligence agency, and whoever Prince Abdulaziz was.

"I understand," he said, and he put the phone down. "Bring us another mimosa, if you please, love," he told the stewardess, who nodded and went forward.

"What the hell is going on?" Miriam demanded, her voice low. She was frightened.

"That was a GIP colonel who says that some prince wants to talk to us."

"Fuck him."

"He mentioned Paris and Istanbul."

The captain came aft. His name was Webb and he was a Scot. "I don't know who the hell you people are, and I don't give a damn. But as soon as we drop you off in Riyadh we're gone."

"Be careful on your radios, or this aircraft and your crew might disappear somewhere out in the desert."

The captain started to say something, but he thought better of it, and went forward.

Colonel Yaser Wasem, who was in charge of the GIP's Special Projects North American Division, telephoned Prince Abulaziz's compound just outside the city. He got one of the prince's personal secretaries. "The couple who Prince Awadi wishes to see are en route."

"Were there any difficulties?"

"Nothing insurmountable."

"Hold, please."

"As you wish," Wasem said.

The secretary was back two minutes later. "We are sending a car for them. The aircraft will be refueled and allowed to fly anywhere, providing it is out of Saudi airspace. While on the ground the crew will be isolated. Is this clear?"

"Perfectly. Will I be required to escort the couple to the prince's compound?"

"No, and once they have left the airport and the aircraft and crew are gone, the GIP will withdraw its interest in the matter. Is this also clear?"

"Of course," Wasem said, but the secretary had already hung up.

The only troubling aspect was why he had been personally contacted to handle the situation that, so far as he knew, had nothing to do with North America. Although Prince Awadi was only a minor cousin, he was still a royal. And one of a particularly—some said—insane temperament.

He figured that realistically he had two options. Either he could ride it out and weather whatever shitstorm Prince Awadi was involved with. But the last time something the prince had cooked up ended in the execution by firing squad of a rising star within the GIP.

Or he could suddenly go to Washington to make an on-site personal inspection of his four networks—three in DC and the fourth in New York. Of course he would take his wife, Laila, and their two children, Izet and Rana, with him. He'd been approached by a couple of major US military equipment suppliers to work as a liaison. It could be a good life for them.

If he could get them out of the country without the prince finding out.

Prince Awadi was only one of more than one thousand Abdulaziz cousins, but his power as deputy minister of foreign finance and communications, as well as every other aspect of his existence, was nearly absolute. He was a royal.

But it was not enough for him. He wanted to be ambassador to the UN, where he could speak for the entire kingdom. His prestige in Washington as well as here in Riyadh, at the royal palace, would be beyond measure. And the wealth that he could accumulate because of his position would be equally uncountable.

But such a sudden rise entailed risks. Which he had willingly taken for the last two years, projecting his apparent insanity as a smoke screen. A misdirection.

He was on the fourth hole of the lush, green, par-three nine-hole golf course at his palatial compound north of the city. He was alone, so it gave him no pleasure cheating three pars in a row and just about to putt for a forty-foot birdy. But he was so close to bringing his big op, as he'd thought of his plan, to fruition, he wanted no one around him, in case he made a slip of the tongue.

But this thing now in Paris, which had blown up because of some stupidly improbable case of blind bad luck, needed to be resolved. And the son of a bitch and his whore flying from Istanbul were going to be the means of his success at last. And no one or nothing on earth, not Allah himself—God bless the Prophet and disciples—would get in the way.

Awadi's putt ended five feet to the left of the hole and easily twenty feet short. He wrote a three on his scorecard, then walked across the green and picked up his ball.

Back at his cart, he stuffed the gold-plated putter in the bag, sat behind the wheel, and called a number in Moscow.

A man answered on the first ring. "*Da?*"

"What is the current status of my shipment to Jeddah?"

"There has been a complication."

Awadi held his temper in check, avoiding screaming a thousand obscenities. "What complication?"

"Paris was not the distraction you promised it would be."

"The tower did not come down, but the police and French intelligence service are involved. They've asked help from the Americans."

"That's the problem. One of them has ended up here in our hands."

"One of who?" Awadi practically screamed. "What the fuck are you talking about?"

"A former director of the fucking CIA is here, and we can't admit we have him."

"It has nothing to do with our deal."

"It has everything to do with it. They're watching us so closely we can't fart without the bastards taking notice."

"How much more do you want, to make delivery as planned?"

"You're crazy."

"One hundred million euros?"

The Russian said nothing.

"Two hundred?" Awadi said. "Two hundred fifty?"

"Five hundred," the Russian said.

The figure—a half a billion euros—took Awadi's breath away. "Yes," he said. "Agreed. Give me a date."

"Forty-eight hours," the Russian said. "But not here."

"Where?"

"New York."

FIFTY-FIVE

It was two in the morning and Bambridge was sitting in his kitchen nursing a glass of red wine and smoking one of his wife's Marlboros. Filthy habit, he'd always thought, and he'd been an ever-present nag whenever she lit up, even though he'd smoked since he was fifteen and had not quit until three years ago.

But this morning the smoke, which made him slightly dizzy, was a comfort.

He'd tried one of the porn sites to contact Rodak, but the entire address was gone. The site had not just been shut down; it had been erased.

It was Rencke, of course. The son of a bitch was on the hunt, and the man wouldn't stop until he was eliminated. Wiped off the fucking face of the earth. Along with his geek of a wife. And McGarvey, and Pete Boylan.

Either that or he could run. Bury himself somewhere. He had accumulated enough money over the past several years, plus the mil and a half from this op, so that could afford to change his identity, including a little plastic surgery, and set himself up as a retiree. Someplace warm and anonymous. Somewhere in the Caribbean.

But Bill Rodak was the key. If the Russian thing went all to hell because of McGarvey none of them would be safe, but Bill had the connections to make problems disappear.

Marty's wife, Pamela, wearing pajama bottoms and an old T-shirt of his, padded into the kitchen. She got a wineglass from the cupboard and he poured her some wine.

"You're up late," he said.

"Did you know that the alarm system isn't working?" Pamela said. She was a shrew of a woman, with a narrow face and a beak of a nose. But she was sharp.

"Maintenance is coming over first thing to check it out."

She took the cigarette from him. "With everything going on lately, shouldn't they be here already?"

"What the hell are you talking about?"

She took a drag of the cigarette and gave it back to him. "You've been shittier than normal lately, more hours at work, nightmares about McGarvey damned near every night, and now smoking? What gives?"

"What nightmares?"

"You keep calling his name."

Marty turned away. If he had to take a runner, he'd figured to go it alone. But he and Pamela had been together for twenty-one years, too long a time to throw away. She'd told him more than once to dial it back. He was too uptight, too much of a prig sometimes. *Go with the flow,* she'd say. *Chill out.*

But such things were not in his nature. His job was the problem.

Quit, then, she'd say. *You're a bright man, lots of experience. You could set yourself up as a security consultant. A lot of those guys cash in on their Company experience. Why not you?*

Marty stubbed out the cigarette. "I may be in some trouble."

She nodded. "Tell me about it."

"I may have screwed up."

"Happens to everyone."

"This is the big time. McGarvey was taken by the Russians after his girlfriend was killed. I had a hand in it."

Pamela was silent for several seconds. She nodded. "Any chance they'll release him?"

"No."

"That's good," she said. "Any chance he could escape and make it back here?"

It was one of Marty's worst nightmares. "It's possible, but not very likely."

Again she was silent for a beat. "If he does get free, we wouldn't have much notice. Would that be a fair statement?"

"Yes," he said, the first faint glimmerings of hope rising at the back of his head.

"You have enough experience in the business, and you're a bright man, so I think you've probably already figured where we're going to go, how we're going to get there, and how we're going to survive—financially."

Marty nodded.

"Let's start with where?"

"The Caribbean."

Pamela smiled. "Good, I'm sick of snow," she said, and she poured them more wine as he lit two cigarettes.

Bill Rodak was summoned to the Oval Office at seven in the morning, and Weaver asked him to close the door. They were alone.

The president motioned Rodak to a chair and called his secretary. "I don't want to be disturbed. No phone calls."

Rodak had learned to judge Weaver's sometimes hair-trigger moods on the campaign trail. "Take no prisoners" was the mantra. But since then Weaver had grown into the job and had become a poker player, his moods almost always unreadable.

"Bring me up to speed on the situation with Mr. McGarvey."

"The French say that he has evidently disappeared."

"Last I heard he was in Russia, but Putin denies it."

"Yes, sir. But evidently he disappeared from there as well."

"And his fiancée?"

"She's back here in Washington."

"Was she badly hurt in the shoot-out at our consulate?" Weaver asked.

In Rodak's estimation, the biggest change in Weaver since he'd been elected was the depth of his knowledge and his understanding of it.

"I don't know all the details, but I'm told that she'll survive without any permanent disabilities."

"By whom?"

"Mr. President?"

"Who told you this, Bill? Who is your source at Langley? Is it still the deputy director?"

Rodak hesitated. "Yes, sir."

"He would know where McGarvey is?"

"Possibly. But I'm told that the man is unpredictable at best. A loose cannon."

"Ask."

"It could be that the CIA itself doesn't know where he's gotten himself to."

"Ask," the president said. "I would like an answer before noon."

Bambridge was in the garage, getting into his car, when Pamela came to the door.

She looked worried. "You have a call from the White House. Bill Rodak. Shall I tell him that you've already left?"

"No," Bambridge said.

"Trouble?" his wife asked.

"I don't know," he said, following his wife to the phone in the kitchen. "Good morning, Bill. I'm a little surprised to hear from you this early."

"The president would like to have a chat with us sometime before noon today."

"Concerning?"

"Kirk McGarvey. Anyone in your shop know what's become of him?"

"We're sure that the Russians have him, but at this point we don't know if he's dead or alive. If we come up with anything new I'll get back to you."

"He wants you here, Marty."

Bambridge's mind was going at nearly the speed of light. "Do we need to get Gibson involved?"

"I don't think that's necessary."

"I'll drop over first thing," Bambridge said, and he hung up.

"What's going on?" Pamela asked.

He smiled at her. "I think the president has just given us a way out."

FIFTY-SIX

McGarvey's cell door was opened a few minutes past eleven in the evening and two camo-clad Spetsnaz operators came in carrying shackles. He'd managed to get a few hours of sleep despite the bright overhead lights that had not been turned off and the noises that sounded like cement mixers, and sometimes jackhammers, just down the hall.

He sat up, swung his bare feet to the concrete floor, and held out his wrists so that he could be bound.

"There will be no troubles, Mr. McGarvey," a captain just outside the door said. Like the two with the shackles, he wasn't armed, nor was he wearing a name tag.

"Let's get this over with. I was on the Champs Élysées with my friend and we were sharing a bottle of Dom. I want to get back to it."

"That will depend on you."

"No, not me. Your drugs."

"You've been granted a reprieve. Only temporary, in the hope that you will begin to cooperate with us."

"'Tell you anything you want to know."

The guards placed a thick leather belt around his waist and secured it at the small of his back. The shackles on his wrists and ankles were secured by chains to the belt.

He easily could have overpowered the guards and the captain in the corridor, but he had no idea what he would be facing, except for the steel door with an electronic lock that he'd seen on the way in, beyond which was an elevated station, a guard seated behind thick glass and, around the corner, the elevator he'd come down in.

But in order to get out he needed two things: a weapon and a high-value hostage. Sooner or later he figured he would get both.

He shuffled out into the corridor.

The three Spetsnaz operators were tense, but not nervous. They were experts doing a job they'd been trained to do.

They were buzzed through the door, and past the guard station they took the elevator, but instead of going up—three floors, he figured, to ground level—they went down another three, to a featureless, well-lit corridor with white tile walls. Antiseptic looking, like a hospital ward, or a morgue.

Two doors down to the left Mac was taken into a brightly lit, clean room with a reclining chair equipped with restraints for the head, chest, wrists, and ankles. Two stainless steel rolling cabinets, along with two stools on wheels, of the sort used in doctors' examining rooms, were positioned against a wall.

His shackles and belt were removed and he was placed in the chair and the restraints were locked in place.

"Thank you, gentlemen," Raya said from the door. "You may leave us now."

The captain and two operators left, and Raya, still dressed in Spetsnaz camos, came in. She was followed by very slightly built man—almost a midget—in camos, over which he wore a white lab coat, a stethoscope draped around his neck. His glasses were so thick that his eyes seemed to bulge out of their sockets. But he had a warm smile.

"Good morning, Mr. Director," he said, in excellent English. "My name is Dimitri Nazarov. I'll be your attending physician for this morning's session. And I sincerely hope that my services will not be required."

"Probably not today," Raya said. "Depending, of course, on Mr. McGarvey."

"My offer still stands," Mac said.

"Which is?"

"Fly me back to Istanbul and I won't have to kill you or anyone else on base when I escape."

The doctor opened McGarvey's shirt and checked his heart and lungs, then hooked EKG pads to his chest, arms, and right leg, connecting them to a small machine on one of the rolling cabinets. "When did you lose your leg?"

"A while back," Mac said, not breaking eye contact with Raya. Something in her expression, in the way she held herself, was different than earlier. But he couldn't put a finger on it.

"It has been recently damaged. A gunshot?"

"Yes."

"You were lucky. Had it been your actual limb, you would have gone down."

Mac didn't bother answering.

Raya closed the door. "How do you feel?"

"I'll live."

She smiled. "One of your famous lines that has seemed to work to this point."

The doctor stepped away, and Raya brought one of the stools around to the foot of the chair and sat down so that she was looking up at McGarvey's face. "The proceedings here are being recorded, visually as well as audibly. For the record I am Raya Kuzin, special adviser to the Kremlin, here on the advice of President Vladimir Putin."

"Do you wish for medical assistance?" the doctor asked. His comment was also for the record.

"Not at this time," Raya said. "You served as director of the US Central Intelligence Agency for a period of less than two years. It was a position that you hated, and yet under your leadership the agency thrived like it hadn't since the former intelligence operatives from the Great Patriotic War were tasked by President Truman with forming it."

McGarvey said nothing.

"Can you explain to me how you could be so good doing something you disliked to do?"

"I listened to people."

"Yes, expand please."

"That, and I have a sensitive built-in detector."

"Of lies?"

"Of bullshit," McGarvey said. "Like now."

Raya smiled. "Could you explain?"

"Here I am, and you don't know what to do with me. If you let me go, you'll have to explain why the hell you got me and why. If not, you'll have to either kill me or stick me in some prison somewhere and hope to Christ my whereabouts never leaks. The blowback for your people, all the way to the top, would be nothing short of nuclear. In fact the best you can hope for is that I do try to escape, for which you would have a legitimate reason to shoot me."

"And in such a case how would we explain ourselves?"

"I fell into your laps—because of Paris—and before you could say no, I ended up here. And now you're screwed."

"Damned if we do, and damned if we don't."

"Something like that," Mac said.

"So what do we do?"

"You won't get anything useful under drugs, and you'll run the very real risk of damaging me permanently. Gets you back to the same corner that killing me and trying to hide the fact would put you in."

"Continue."

"Explain to me why you agreed to take me from the Saudi operative who we know as Karim Najjir, in exchange for what?"

"I personally don't know the answer to that question."

"What was the SVR's involvement with Paris?"

"I don't know."

"Has the SVR ever contracted with Najjir before?"

"I don't know."

"I suggest that you get answers to those questions before you start asking me about shit I did as a DCI years ago."

"I could, but I sincerely doubt I would get any answers that we could use to bargain in good faith for your life."

"Then try this one for size," McGarvey said. "What did the attack on the Eiffel Tower have to do with a tactical nuclear weapon that has gone missing from one of your Saratov sites?"

FIFTY-SEVEN

Almost immediately after the Gulfstream's forward hatch was opened, the heat of the Saudi Arabian desert slammed into the cabin.

"Son of a bitch," Miriam said half under her breath.

"Hold it together and we might just make it out of here alive," Najjir told her.

Neither the stew nor the captain and copilot even looked at them as they got their single bags and got off the aircraft, which was parked in a hangar across the field from the main terminal and equally far from the air force operations center.

A chauffeur in a Western-style suit got out of a deep-metallic-green Bentley convertible with white leather upholstery, its top down, and opened the door on the passenger side.

"Sir and madam, I've been instructed to take you to the prince."

"We'd like to check into a hotel and freshen up first," Najjir said.

"I'll just take your bags and place them in the boot, if you will get in the car."

"It's 'miss,'" Miriam practically shouted.

Najjir touched her hand. "May we have the top up?"

"No, sir," the chauffeur said.

He took care of their bags as they got in the car, and in moments they were out in the direct heat, the sun like a blast furnace.

Miriam wanted to say something, but Najjir held her off. The prince was punishing them for something, which he figured could only mean that this royal had been directly involved in the Paris operation. If that was true it could possibly mean that the Saudis were working with the Russians. But for what purpose he could not divine, except that he smelled a possible way out for them.

If the Russians were satisfied to make the trade—McGarvey for the Paris failure—perhaps the prince would be open to a bargain of some sort, though what that might be, Najjir hadn't the foggiest. Yet.

He gave Miriam a little smile and she shook her head in wonderment.

Leaning over, he brushed a kiss on her cheek and whispered in her ear. "Follow my lead."

On the other side of the city, traffic very heavy this morning, they took Highway 65 out into the desert to the north, toward Huraymila, about fifty miles away. The Saudi capital had become so large in the last twenty years or so that places that had been little more than outposts were now practically suburbs.

A pair of F-15 fighter/interceptor jets, with the same markings as the ones that had escorted the Gulfstream, flashed a few hundred feet overhead, screaming to the northwest in the general direction of Kuwait. Along with the increase in traffic, foreign workers, and new construction everywhere, the Saudi military, especially its air force, supported by the US, had grown almost exponentially ever since the sharp rise of ISIS and the other troubles in the region, with Iraq and Syria.

The country had become, for all practical purposes, a heavily armed American frontline base. The royal family hated the arrangement, but in practical terms bowing to Washington's will was the only way the country could remain safe.

Its only other choices were either to sever its ties with the US and ask Russia for help or to develop its own nuclear capabilities, as Iran had tried to do.

Neither was a palatable solution.

But worst of all, the royals had come to the point where they simply did not know what to do, and the entire country had been on a diplomatic slow simmer for a half dozen years, and recently the heat was rising.

Prince Awadi's walled compound was five miles outside Huraymila, the main entrance secured by tall iron gates. A pair of uniformed guards in desert camos, armed with M16s, came out of the main post as the gates swung open and the chauffeur pulled through and stopped.

"The prince expected you sooner," one of the guards said. He was narrow shouldered and dark complected with deep-set black eyes.

Najjir thought the man looked like a ferret. Dangerous and unpredictable.

"Then let's delay no further," the driver said.

"Have they been checked for arms?"

"At the airport."

The guard received a message in his earbud and he stepped back. "You may proceed."

The main house was a sprawling whitewashed structure, some portions of it two stories, with turrets, minarets, and gold leaf scrollwork around the windows and roofs. *Gaudy* was the first thought that came to Najjir's mind.

The prince's private secretary met them at the front door. "The prince will speak with you on the south patio," he told Najjir. "Madam will be attended to."

This time Miriam held her tongue, for which Najjir was grateful. Prince Awadi had the reputation of being a dangerous nutcase, only indulged by the family because of his American connections, which flowed from his wife, who had been sent out of Saudi Arabia to New York, where she got her degree in US history at Columbia. She was of royal blood and had money of her own, from her father, and she had attracted a lot of admirers in New York and Washington during her four years in the States.

Awadi, dressed in a bright orange golfing outfit of matching trousers, tight-fitting Spandex shirt, and baseball cap, complete with orange golf shoes, was seated at a glass table, drinking champagne, the Krug in a gold ice bucket next to him. His nose was prominent, his eyes hooded, and his complexion dark. But the expression in his eyes was neutral as Najjir was escorted in and the secretary withdrew.

"Good morning, sir," Najjir said, taking a seat across from Awadi, without being asked. "May I have a glass of wine? The drive up was parching."

Awadi said nothing for several beats, but then nodded.

A servant instantly appeared with a glass, filled it and set it in front of Najjir, then left.

Najjir drank it down and offered his glass for more.

The instant he'd seen the prince sitting at the table in his silly costume, he understood that subservience would be exactly the wrong tack. Awadi wanted something, it was written all over his face. And he was frightened.

Najjir held his glass steady, and after another beat Awadi got the champagne and filled it.

"You want to know about Paris, about Kirk McGarvey, and about the Russians."

"Yes, but before you begin, consider this: I may have an assignment for you. But if you lie to me, or if you leave anything out, including your opinions, I will have you and your woman executed this very day."

"I was hired to bring down the Eiffel Tower, using three ISIS kids, by what amounts to a double-blind control officer. Someone in the GIP, I suspected. Perhaps even directed by yourself."

Awadi said nothing, nor did his expression change.

"Kirk McGarvey and a woman by the name of Boylan, who is an officer with the CIA, happened to be at the Jules Verne and interfered in the operation. I do not believe they were there by chance, though I can't say who might have directed them, or how they came by their knowledge."

Najjir sipped his wine.

"I had a backup team standing by in case of trouble, and with their help we managed to capture the woman, which drew McGarvey to us in Istanbul. She was killed in a shoot-out, but we managed to capture McGarvey and turn him over to the Russians."

"Why?"

Najjir shrugged. "Money, of course. I knew that since Paris was a failure I wouldn't be paid, and I had expenses. McGarvey was too valuable an asset to walk away from."

"What is your price?"

"What was my price for the tower?"

"No. I want you to go to New York and kill two men. But the timing will have to be perfect."

"Who are these men?" Najjir asked.

"Americans, but interestingly enough they work for the Russians," Awadi said. "Will you take the assignment?"

"At what price?"

"One million euros."

"Two million."

Awadi nodded.

"Do I have a contact in New York?"

"Yes, a Russian SVR colonel who works under cover at the UN."

"Then consider it done, my prince," Najjir said, and he laughed. Once again he had escaped the hangman's noose.

FIFTY-EIGHT

As soon as he got to the CIA, Bambridge went next door to Gibson's office, but the general wasn't in, and his secretary didn't expect the director until later this afternoon.

"He didn't mention to me that he would be gone this morning," Marty said.

"No, sir."

Bambridge held back from asking the smug bastard, whom Gibson had brought over from his old Pentagon staff, where the director had gotten himself to. He was pretty sure that he wouldn't have been given an answer, in any event.

Back at his desk he considered phoning Rodak, but held off on that too. A DCI being out of the office for the better part of the day didn't mean a thing in itself. Very often they met with people on the Senate's Subcommittee on National and Central Intelligence or with other congresspeople who wanted individual briefings.

And from time to time he went over to the Pentagon for an exchange of information. The new director of national intelligence had never served in the military and wasn't close to any of the Joint Chiefs, so briefings were never as extensive as they had been since the previous administration. The task had fallen back to the CIA.

Next he phoned Rencke to see if they'd been able to nail McGarvey's exact whereabouts, but the geek's machine, speaking in a woman's voice that sounded faintly familiar, answered.

"I'm sorry, Mr. Bambridge, but Mr. Rencke is out of the office at the moment."

"Can I reach him at home?"

"No, sir."

Bambridge hung up and dialed Rencke's rollover number, but it did not ring, so he called Rencke's computer again.

"May I be of assistance, Mr. Bambridge?"

"I'm trying to reach Otto, but the rollover number I have for him does not answer."

"I'm sorry, sir."

"Please dial his new rollover number."

"I'm sorry, sir, I do not currently have that number."

"Bullshit," Marty shouted.

"May I be of any other assistance?"

"Fuck you," Bambridge said, and he slammed down the phone.

His secretary knocked once on the door and came in. "Is there a problem, sir?" he asked.

Bambridge looked up. He was annoyed, and frightened now. "If I'd needed you I would have fucking called you. Get out."

"Yes, sir."

He sat for several moments staring at his wife's photograph. She was very often a total pain in the ass, and sometimes he wondered why he had put up with her for so long. But very often she gave good advice, and in his heart of hearts he understood that she was smarter than him.

She was ready to go to ground, and that was good enough for him.

He called her at home. "Pack a few things; we're going away soon."

"Do we need our passports?"

"No, the ones in the dresser are expired."

"I understand," Pamela said. "Are we going by car or should I call our travel agency and book tickets?"

"I'll take care of that too," Bambridge said. "But let's have lunch at the old place, say one o'clock?"

"I'll be there," Pamela said, and she hung up.

Their old place was Clancy's, an Irish bar not too far from Union

Station. He'd never mentioned it to anyone other than Pamela, whose suggestion several years ago had been to have a private go-to place. Just for the two of them.

Next he telephoned Rodak's private number. "Yes."

"I'm just leaving Langley now."

"He's expecting you."

Hanging up, Bambridge opened his safe and took out his go-to-hell kit of passports, IDs, and photographs under the names James and Betty Flannery, at an address in New York City. They both wore glasses. Her hair was pinned back in a bun, and his was streaked with gray. The changes were minor, but enough to match the passport and other photos.

He held the packet in his hand for a long moment or two. He'd had these things for a number of years now, changing the photos from time to time to more closely match their actual ages. The kit in a clear plastic baggy had been nothing more than an exercise in spycraft. An exercise, until now.

A subcompact Glock pistol with two magazines, a silencer, and a cleaning kit were contained in a small zippered leather case, and for a moment he stayed his hand from reaching for it. If he needed to shoot his way out of a situation, it would already be too late to disappear.

But he had no intention of being arrested, put on trial like Ames and Hanssen, and spend the remainder of his life in prison.

He locked the safe, wrapped the gun case in a folded *Washington Post*, and left his office, not bothering to say a word to his secretary.

The security guard at the White House gate notified Rodak, who showed up at the entrance to the West Wing just as Bambridge pulled up in his Chevy Bolt EV.

"You just may have a chance to get out of this shit with your ass intact," Rodak said.

"My ass? You're just as deep into the shit as I am."

"But it was your idea."

"One that you wholeheartedly agreed with," Bambridge said. "I'd become the new DCI and you would hand an almost certain reelection to your boss. We're both stakeholders here, Bill, and don't forget it."

They entered the West Wing, passed the Cabinet Room, and walked directly down to the Oval Office, where the president's secretary announced them and they went in.

"Close the door," President Weaver said. "And no interruptions for the next five minutes."

When the secretary had withdrawn, the president typed something on his computer keyboard, and after a moment looked up. "The recording devices in this room have been turned off, and neither of you is wearing a wire. Do you understand that this conversation never took place?"

Bambridge had no earthly idea what to say. He nodded.

"Bill tells me that you and your wife are probably going to disappear. I assume that you have a place in mind, and the means to get there in secret, so that issue is not on the table."

Bambridge started to deny it, but Rodak cut him off.

"No one will try to trace you," Weaver said. "You simply decided to retire early, and where you went is no one's business."

"What can I do for you, Mr. President?" Bambridge asked. He could think of nothing else, except that he was being given an opportunity here, though not the one he'd hoped for.

"Bill will give you the details, but for now I can tell you that Kirk McGarvey is definitely being held by the Russians at their Spetsnaz base at Novorossiysk. At the moment they have no other choice but to execute him, destroy his body, and deny they'd ever had him. And if it were strictly up to me, I wouldn't say a word."

There was a *but* there, Bambridge was sure of it.

"But I'm going to give them a way out, and you're going to provide it," Weaver said. "Do you understand?"

"No, sir," Bambridge said. He felt as if he were standing at the edge of a very deep gorge and only the slightest misstep would send him to his death.

"The Russians have a bigger problem on their hands, and we have the means to help them. In exchange, we'll get Mr. McGarvey and solve their problem."

"I'm not sure that I follow you, sir," Bambridge said.

"Oh, but you do. It was you and Bill who cooked up the scheme to begin with. I'm only sending you to undo it."

"Paris was a distraction," Rodak said.

"Except for McGarvey," Weaver said. "Now get to it. I expect the entire thing to be cleared up within the next seventy-two to ninety-six hours."

Rodak walked Bambridge back outside, where he handed him a file folder. "Your instructions."

"For what?"

"You're to go to New York, find this man, and kill him."

Bambridge stepped back. "Are you out of your fucking mind? I'm an administrator, not a trained operative."

"Then why do you have a pistol and fake passports in your car?"

"I'm going to ground."

"Yes, and we won't get in your way," Rodak said. "The dossier and photograph were printed on a paper that will disintegrate within the hour. They can't be copied, so I suggest that you pull over somewhere and memorize the contents."

"Christ."

FIFTY-NINE

It was very early in the morning, McGarvey figured around five or so, when Raya got up from where she'd been seated across the table from him and yawned. She had merely chatted with him for the past several hours, sending the doctor away almost immediately.

"Breakfast, I think, and then a few hours' sleep, before we start again this afternoon," she said.

"It's a waste of time," Mac said.

"On the contrary, your mentioning a missing nuclear weapon has any number of people in Moscow excited. They want to know more, as in how you came by such knowledge."

"Then it's true?"

She managed a smile. "Well, if it is, Mr. Director, we're all in what your people might call a world of shit."

"My source is usually accurate. The confidence level was high, the last time I checked."

"Rencke?"

Mac shrugged.

"Are we being hacked?"

"You guys started it."

"Cyber warfare has a lot of people in the Kremlin worried."

"In Washington and Langley too."

Raya shook her head. "What the hell are we supposed to do with you?"

"Subotin shouldn't have agreed to take me."

"In that, we agree one hundred percent."

She went to the door and it opened. The same two guards who'd brought him were there with the shackles. But she waved them back.

"I'll escort Mr. McGarvey back to his cell."

"But we have our orders, Major," one of them said.

"Yes, you do, now get the fuck out of my way, *pizda*."

The guards stepped aside, and Raya motioned for McGarvey to come with her, and she marched down the corridor to the elevator.

Something had changed in her attitude toward him. Earlier she had been confident and even friendly, but she was troubled now. Maybe even a little frightened. The missing nuclear weapon, if Otto's sources had been correct, had to have shaken up the Kremlin all the way to the top. To Putin himself.

His people had to be scrambling now, trying to figure out not only what to do with a former DCI but also how to find the missing nuke, and who took it, and how, and why.

They got on the elevator, and when the doors had closed, Raya produced a key and shut the car off.

"You will escape now, and I would like it very much if you didn't kill me," she said. "I've been instructed to help you."

If it was a setup to get him outside, where he would be shot to death, he wasn't seeing it in her eyes. "What do you have in mind?"

"What did *you* have in mind? You said that you would escape from here, and kill me doing so."

"The border with Ukraine is only a couple of hundred miles north. I thought that you could drive me up and I'd get across on my own."

Raya managed a slight smile. "I'm sure that once they realized not only who you were, but who I was, they would have been more than delighted to have us both. A reversal of our present situation, except that they would have hailed your rescue from us, and the capture of a key aide to President Putin, as a coup."

"I'm sure that they would. But Moscow would have to retaliate. Me showing up with you in tow would have been over the top."

"But if you came across alone, it would be better. So just before the border you would have killed me and disposed of my body." She reached for the elevator key. "Something like that?"

McGarvey had to shrug. "I would have changed my mind. You're not the bad guy here."

"Chivalry?" she asked. "Don Quixote tilting at windmills to save his Dulcinea?"

"Not quite."

She turned the key and they started up. "In fact I have the same helicopter that fished you out of the sea, waiting to fly us to the Black Sea Fleet base next door, where a transport jet will take us to Moscow. Mr. Putin would very much like to talk to you before he sends you home."

"I'm sure that General Subotin isn't happy."

"He hasn't been told."

There had been just the faintest glimmerings of a possible coup in the making. Putin was very unpopular in some circles, among them the SVR. Otto had mentioned it a year or so ago, but only as something highly speculative that only one of his darlings had picked up.

"Less than ten percent confidence, kemo sabe," Otto had said. "But interesting nevertheless."

"Have you shared this with Walt?" Walter Page had been the DCI at that time, and Bambridge his DDO.

"Of course."

Which meant, the errant thought struck Mac on the way up in the elevator, that Marty could have known about it for that long as well. The possibilities just now were tantalizing.

The corridor on the ground floor, leading to the front of the administration building, was empty of people at this hour. But in the operations center at the rear of the long, low building, people came and went with some apparent urgency. This was a Spetsnaz base, so if ops was humming, it meant one or more field missions were in full swing, or at least ready for launch.

No one paid them any attention as Raya went past the CO's office and outside, where a Gazik was parked.

No one was anywhere in sight, though the parking lot was well lit, as were the guard towers along the security fence in the distance. The evening was overcast and warm, the air still, but all of Mac's senses were on high alert. Trouble was very near.

"Do you have a pistol for me?" he asked.

"No need," she said, getting behind the wheel, as Mac got in on the passenger side.

She drove them a quarter mile to the hangars along the main runway, where a Hind helicopter was warming up. The crew was expecting them, and before they got aboard they were given life vests and helmets.

McGarvey looked over his shoulder, but no one was behind them. They had merely walked away. It made no sense.

The helicopter trundled out onto the apron and in moments they were airborne for the short flight to the navy base. The Black Sea, off to their left, was dotted with the lights of outgoing and incoming ships. This was Russia's main port and it was busy 24/7, every day of the year, sunshine or sleet. Plus the city was a vacation spot of sorts, the weather usually Mediterranean. Yet the Spetsnaz base had been built because of the proximity to Ukraine, which was in effect surrounded by Russian forces.

A bright flash bloomed in the woods to the east and was gone in a second or two.

"Spetsnaz night ops?" Mac asked.

"They're training for something big," Raya said.

"Big?"

"I have no idea. But when they do night training ops, I'm told, something important is on the table. Same as your SEAL Team Six operators."

The navy base sprawled along the coast and inland, well toward the side of the bay nearest the Crimean Peninsula less than one hundred miles away. Lights were everywhere, though there didn't seem to be much activity visible as they came in for a landing just fifty yards from a Tupolev TU-154M, which was a narrow-body three-engine jet that was sometimes used as a military VIP transport.

They jumped down onto the tarmac and surrendered their vests and helmets. As they walked toward the jet, the chopper took off.

It was barely airborne and away when a half dozen military troop transports came from the other side of the Tupolev, lights on, sirens blaring. Almost immediately at least one hundred heavily armed men in black camos leaped from the vehicles and formed a cordon.

"SVR?" Mac asked, raising his hands at the same time Raya did.

"Da."

"Evidently Subotin knows more than you thought he did."

SIXTY

☐

Otto had sent Louise back to Pete's apartment to get a few things, and then to their safe house in McLean. Pete had objected; she wanted to stay until they found Mac. But she was dead on her feet, and in the end Otto won out.

"The surveillance systems are up and running, but I don't want you guys to go anywhere unarmed, and that includes inside the house."

Staring at the display one of his darlings had put up on the main monitor, he phoned the house. It was just past nine in the evening, and Louise answered on the first ring.

"What's up?" she demanded.

"Everything okay there?"

"Just peachy. Like I said, what's up?"

The screen showed the image from one of the newer Aurora surveillance satellites that was in geosync orbit covering a swath of Russian territory from the border with Ukraine all the way down to the Spetsnaz and Black Sea bases.

It was mostly dark on the tarmac of the fleet's main airstrip, on which a Tupolev transport aircraft was parked, boarding stairs pulled up to the open hatch.

His program had picked up the anomaly just a minute ago, because he'd asked for anything that could be characterized as an unusual happening. The images he was looking at were in infrared and showed what was more than a hundred bodies formed in a circle around two others. The troop trucks in the background, emitting strong signatures from their engines, were almost certainly military vehicles.

Otto told her what he was looking at.

"Is it Mac?" Louise asked.

"I think so," Otto said. "Give me probable identifications on the two figures in the middle," he told his darling.

"I have ninety percent confidence that the one on the left is a female, and ninety-two percent that the one to her right is male."

Pete was on the line with Louise. "Is it Mac and that broad from the Kremlin?"

"I don't know. Darling, probability?"

"Unable to assign."

"Your best estimate."

"Based on a loose data set, there is a possibility that Ms. Boylan's query may be accurate."

"Can you get a lock on the Tupolev's tail number?"

"It is RA-85572, the Russian Defense Ministry aircraft that crashed on takeoff from Sochi into the Black Sea on May 2016, no survivors from ninety-two passengers and crew."

"A plane that doesn't exist," Pete said.

"Assuming it is Mac and Putin's adviser, who sent the plane and who's holding them at gunpoint?" Louise asked.

"My guess would be that Putin sent the plane and General Subotin sent his people to stop it," Otto said. "Your best guess, darling?" he asked his program.

"No estimate above eight percent from the available data, but extrapolating from previous queries about tension between the SVR and Kremlin, I can assign a very loose possibility of forty-five percent that the troops on the tarmac are SVR," the computer program replied. "But, Otto darling, that is just a WAG."

"A Wild-Ass Guess," Louise said.

"That's good enough for me, goddamnit," Pete said. She sounded strung out. "How the hell do we get him out of there?"

"We don't, but Weaver will, because the president's going to owe me a favor," Otto said. "Stay put. I'll get back to you, soon as."

Otto caught General Gibson at home in the middle of a dinner party. A violin concerto was playing in the background, and a woman laughed softly.

"There is a new development that will require a possible immediate action order from the president."

"Just a moment, I'll take it in my study," the DCI said.

On the screen, Raya Kuzin, if it was her, stepped away from Mac and held her right arm over her head as she was holding up something. It was impossible to make out what it was, but Otto thought that she had taken out her identification booklet.

Gibson came on the line. "I assume this is about McGarvey."

"Yes, sir," Otto said, not taking his eyes off the monitor. A figure stepped away from the other soldiers and came forward. "Is your computer up?"

"It is now."

Otto sent the images from his main monitor. "This is the end of the main runway at the Black Sea Fleet HQ in Novorossiysk. I think that the two figures in the middle are Mac and Raya Kuzin, a Putin adviser. The troops surrounding them are most likely SVR sent by General Subotin."

"What's your confidence level?"

"Low to medium."

"Is it good enough for you?"

"Yes."

Gibson was silent for a moment. "Seems as if they're having a conference."

"Figuring out what to do with them. Going up against someone as highly placed inside the Kremlin would be dicey at best, even for the director of the SVR."

"There've been internal differences. What do you want to tell the president?"

"Let him see these images and ask that he call Putin immediately before the situation escalates out of hand."

"And the favor Weaver will owe you for?"

"The Russians are missing a nuclear weapon, and I think that if we can get Mac back home, Weaver can promise Putin that we'll find it for him."

At that moment the figure that had broken away from the cordon suddenly stepped back, raised his right hand, and pointed what could only be a pistol at Mac and Raya.

McGarvey spun on his heel inward toward Raya, shielding her with his body as he bulled her to the pavement at the same time the officer in black camos fired one shot that missed high and wide—but not by much.

Raya screamed something in Russian at the officer, who had stepped closer and held the pistol directly at her head from a distance of less than two feet.

He started to shout something, when McGarvey swung his prosthetic leg in a sharp, powerful arc that knocked the man off his feet.

Before the SVR officer could react Mac was on him, snatching the pistol out of his hand and jamming the muzzle in his face.

The other troops immediately stepped forward, training their automatic weapons on McGarvey alone, ignoring Raya as she scrambled away on her butt.

"Do you speak English?" Mac asked the officer.

"Yes," the man said.

"Your people fire and I fire," Mac said.

One of the troops shouted something, but the officer raised a hand, gesturing him back, and looked up at McGarvey. "You will not get off this base alive, Mr. Director."

"Then neither will you, and your boss will be in trouble. You understand this?"

"I'm following my orders, sir, my very specific orders," the officer said. "Even if you somehow managed to kill all of my men here and try to get off this base, more would come. You can't fight the entire Russian Army."

"I could try," McGarvey said.

The officer hesitated. "I will have to call for further orders."

"Captain," Raya said. She was sitting up and holding out a cell phone. "Our president would like to have a word with you."

SIXTY-ONE

McGarvey sat next to a window on the starboard side of the Tupolev and watched as the rising sun reddened the sky to the east. They'd been airborne, flying toward Moscow, for less than an hour, and Raya had spent most of that time in the aircraft's communications center, forward, giving him space to work out what the hell had happened on the tarmac.

The aircraft had been sent by Putin, and the troops holding them at gunpoint had been ordered there by General Subotin. It had been another move of nearly outright rebellion, the SVR against the current Kremlin hierarchy. The delicate and extremely dangerous chess match had been going on for nearly eighteen months, and Mac had a fairly strong suspicion that the missing nuke had something to do with the power struggle.

But Pete was home safely and at least that worry was off his plate. For the moment.

Raya came back and sat down across from him. "We'll have something better for both of us to change into once we reach Moscow." She had taken a hit to the side of her face when she'd fallen to the pavement, and her cheek was already swelling.

"Thanks. I don't think I look very good in a Russian naval uniform."

She smiled. "You'll do," she said. "And thank you for what you did back there. You risked your life to save mine. But then you're a romantic, willing to give his life for a cause."

"You're not the bad guy here."

"You've already said that."

"But I'm still a problem. So what next?"

She shrugged. "The president wants to talk to you. From what I could gather, your president knows that we have you, he wants you back unharmed, and he was willing to strike a bargain. My question is, how did your people know what was happening to us at that exact moment? Unless your spy birds are better than ours."

"I don't know."

She smiled again. "Rencke would know, and so would his wife."

McGarvey glanced out the window again. The nearly cloud-free morning promised a beautiful day. "You guys are still facing a bigger internal problem, and I have a feeling a missing nuke might be a part of it, or maybe even a catalyst."

"Or a counterpoise. One thing balancing another. And a little revolution now and then is good for the soul, don't you think?"

"When that happens, people get killed in big city squares."

"In front of the Kremlin?" Raya said. "I don't think so this time. But a few officers will most likely be shot."

"General Subotin?"

Raya spread her hands. "That one, I don't know."

"But you'll never be able to let him out of the country."

"Just like you, too many secrets? Which actually is why I think you'll be sent home."

McGarvey turned away again. But there was more. He could feel it gathering on the horizon. But then, there was always more.

They touched down at Kubinka Air Base, about forty miles west of Moscow, a little after nine in the morning local, where they were met by a lieutenant driving a Gazik, who took them over to separate rooms in the base officers' quarters.

Neatly pressed jeans, a white shirt, a dark blue blazer, and well-shined loafers had been laid out for Mac on the bed, along with shaving things in the bathroom. After he'd cleaned up and gotten dressed he went downstairs to the day lounge, where Raya, freshly showered and dressed in a skirt and stylish silk blouse, was waiting for him.

"You look better," she said.

"So do you."

The same lieutenant drove them over to where a Mil Mi-8 helicopter with 9th Fighter Aviation Division markings was warming up.

"We have a helipad inside the Kremlin, just like your president does on the White House grounds," Raya explained.

"I know," McGarvey said. "Do you have a cell phone I could use? I think my people might want some answers."

"I'm sure they do, but that'll have to wait until you meet with the president, and then it will depend on him. But I think it is very likely that you'll be on a plane back to Washington this morning."

"Aren't his security people worried that I'll try to kill him?" McGarvey asked.

Raya smiled faintly. "No."

It took them fifteen minutes to get over the Kremlin Wall, where they set down on a helipad not far from the president's office in a blunt three-story building made of mustard-yellow bricks with white trim. The flag flew from the roof, indicating that the president was in residence.

Raya accompanied Mac over to where a man in a Western-cut business suit was waiting for them.

"Welcome to the Kremlin, Mr. Director. The president is expecting you. But he will be brief; you are expected to leave for Washington on the Aeroflot Air France flight at quarter before noon."

"Will the president see me?" Raya asked.

"Remain here."

She nodded.

McGarvey turned and shook her hand. "Take care of yourself," he said.

"I'm very glad to have met you," she said, and she gave him a brief hug.

"If you will just come with me, Mr. Director," the secretary said.

. . .

Putin was sitting behind his desk, talking on the phone, when McGarvey was shown in. He said something Mac did not quite catch, and hung up. The secretary withdrew, closing the door, leaving them alone.

The president of Russia exuded raw power, of the charismatic sort as well physical. He was a much smaller man in person than Mac had imagined him to be, but the expression in his eyes and the set of his chin and the way he held himself, outwardly at ease but ready at an instant's notice to strike, were the marks of a man well versed in hand-to-hand combat. He had the same look of total confidence as most of the SEAL Team 6 guys Mac had met.

"We're pressed for time, so I will be brief, Mr. McGarvey. I need your help."

Mac hadn't been offered a seat. He stood in front of Putin's desk like a schoolboy facing his principal. "That comes as something of a surprise, Mr. President, considering the circumstances."

"Beyond my control, until this moment. But you and I are kindred spirits in many respects. In fact we had a close connection some years ago."

"I'm sorry, sir, I'm not following you."

"I was an officer in the KGB as you were in the CIA. We were adversaries."

"Still are."

Putin smiled faintly. "Your intelligence information is correct. We are missing a small tactical nuclear warhead. In the wrong hands such a thing could tip the balance of power on just about every continent. You understand this."

It was an extraordinary admission that simply didn't ring true in Mac's head. Too many strings attached. Too many questions on the table. He nodded.

Putin wrote a name on a slip of notepaper and held it out. "This is the name of a man at our embassy in Washington who might be able to help you."

McGarvey took the slip, but the name meant nothing to him. "Help me do what?"

"Find the weapon and return it to us before it gets into the wrong hands."

"If it already hasn't," McGarvey said. "And what about Paris, the Eiffel Tower? And bringing me here?"

"I have absolutely no idea," Putin said. "Will you help?"

"Yes, of course."

PART

FOUR

Washington and New York

SIXTY-TWO

Pete, Otto, and Louise were all waiting for McGarvey as he emerged from the international terminal at Dulles, weary from the trip, and a little frightened about what would happen next if Pete insisted she had to be involved. Which he figured she would.

She came to him, limping a little and favoring her left side, and he took her in his arms and held her very close but without pressure. "You feel good," he said.

"You too."

When they parted, Mac looked into her eyes, to make sure that she had come through in one piece, and he had to smile. Nothing had changed with her.

"You had us pretty worried," Louise said, giving him a hug and a peck on the cheek. "Maybe the two of you should consider retiring. Be a lot easier on my heart if you did."

"Not quite yet."

Otto, who had stood back, gave him a look. "More?"

"Putin asked me to give him a hand."

Pete looked up at him. "It's not over?"

"I'll tell you in the car on the way to my apartment. I need a shower and a change of clothes."

"And then?" she asked, as they headed outside to where Otto had parked across from the cab queue, an FBI placard on the dash.

"Something to do here in town, and then we'll see."

"Putin admitted they had a nuke missing?" Otto asked.

"Yes, and he wants it back before it gets into the wrong hands."

"Could be it's already too late," Pete said.

Pete packed a few of Mac's things in a small bag as he was showering. Louise had suggested that they all circle the wagons at their house in McLean until this business was done and over with. She and Otto were missing Audie, who was in safe hands down at the Farm, where she always stayed when there was trouble of one sort or another.

"Maybe we should all retire when this is over with," Pete said on the way over.

"You will, starting right this minute," Mac told her.

She laughed.

"Good luck with that," Louise said.

"I'm serious, goddamnit. I almost lost you in Paris and again in Istanbul. I'm not going to let it happen again."

"We can talk about it later. But there's not one chance in hell that I'm going to let you out of my sight again."

"You can brief us all at the house," Louise said. "I'm making spaghetti and meatballs, and Otto's making the 1905 salad from Sarasota that you guys like."

"A homecoming," Pete said. "I like that."

They sat at the kitchen counter drinking Chianti while Louise cooked and McGarvey took them through everything that had happened, from the time he'd been picked up in Istanbul until his face-to-face with Putin.

Otto brought up a photo of Raya Kuzin on his laptop. "This the girl?"

"Yes."

"Well, she wasn't lying. She does work for Putin and she made her doctoral chops on studying you."

"Pretty lady," Pete said, raising an eyebrow.

McGarvey had to grin. "She told me that I was fascinating," he said, and everyone laughed a little. It was one light moment in the midst of a complicated operation that had almost cost his and Pete's lives. An op that wasn't over.

"He gave me the name of a Russian—Aleksandr Fomin—who works at their embassy here in DC. Said he might be able to help."

Otto brought up the name on his laptop. "Fomin is a special adviser to their ambassador."

"What's his topic?" Pete asked.

"Military affairs."

"He'd be a man who could know something about the missing nuke," McGarvey said. "Send him a message with my name. Tell him I'd like to talk to him about a mutual friend in Moscow."

"When?"

"This evening. Eight, on the steps of the Lincoln Memorial."

"I'll drive," Pete said.

"No."

"We're covering each other's back ever since you popped the question in Paris. So you might as well get used to it."

Fomin answered Otto's email almost immediately, as if Putin had told him to expect the call. And he showed up at the Lincoln Memorial precisely on time.

Pete sat on a bench just a short way from the Reflecting Pool, within sight of the steps where Mac was seated.

Fomin was fairly tall with blond hair and a round, pleasant face. According to his profile he was a well-respected man at the Pentagon who, according to a couple of generals, had the same ambitions as nearly everyone did: to keep Russia and America from going to war with each other. He was dressed in a light sport coat and white shirt but no tie.

He came up the half dozen steps and sat next to McGarvey. "A pleasant place, this," he said. His English was good, slightly British. Among other things he was a linguist and had studied for two years at Oxford.

"Thanks for agreeing to talk to me."

The Russian smiled faintly. "I had no choice, Mr. Director."

"So the White House and the Kremlin have a problem."

"It would seem so."

"Which is what, in addition to your missing nuke?" McGarvey said.

"Turn the tables, wouldn't it be enough for your government?"

"I guess. But I agreed to help, for all the obvious reasons. Our governments aren't involved to this point, only you and I. What can you tell me?"

"The answers may be in New York, with one of our people. Trouble is we can't do anything about it, because your FBI is on the case. His cover name is Viktor Kaplin. Works at the UN for our representative, though exactly what his function is no one seems to know."

"SVR?"

"Yes. Colonel Vladimir Kazov. He was under investigation by us, until the FBI got involved and we had to back off. Actually we hoped your people would solve the problem for us by arresting him as a spy and either put him prison or send him home."

"What do you think he was involved with?"

"Money. He was stealing your secrets—mostly IT and some industrial stuff—and selling them to the highest bidder."

"Do you think he was involved with your missing nuke?"

"There's no direct evidence."

"There never is."

Fomin shrugged. "But there it is. And unfortunately it is all the help that I can give you." He looked toward Pete. "Pretty woman."

Mac had to smile. "What do you suggest?"

"Just between you and me? Go up to New York, find the bastard, and give him his nine ounces. Save us all a lot of grief."

"I'll need proof."

Fomin got up. "That's up to you, Mr. Director. But I can give you one other tidbit. Important, I think, but puzzling. Two highly placed Washington insiders are already up there. Looking into the same matter, I suspect."

"Names?"

The Russian smiled. "That's one direction in which I'm definitely not going. Good luck."

SIXTY-THREE

□

Bambridge had delayed leaving Washington for two days, on Pamela's suggestion that they both think everything out. And carefully. He'd even gone into Langley and worked at his desk until the director informed him that McGarvey was on his way home.

Sitting now in his room at the Mandarin Oriental Hotel, looking out the window at the traffic below on Columbus Circle, he could not believe what had been brought up to him from the front desk.

He had debated calling his wife, but it was possible that their home phone was bugged, though he had a lot of sophisticated security measures in place. And at this point he had no earthly idea what to do next, except that he had been backed into an incredibly tight corner, with no way out that he could see.

The dossier and photograph Bill Rodak had given him was of a Russian spy working at the UN, under the name Viktor Kaplin. He lived in an apartment off Riverside Drive on the Upper West Side.

He was one of the men involved with the theft of the Russian nuclear weapon, and he was the bagman for the money coming out of Moscow. But the second man, whose dossier had just been delivered, was supposedly Kaplin's partner.

Bambridge held up the photograph of Bill Rodak, along with his dossier and the address of an apartment he kept here in New York, just a couple of blocks from the UN. Both had been printed on the same type of paper as the material Rodak had given him at the White House and were already beginning to fade.

But the message was clear, and there wasn't one chance in hell that he was going through with either hit. It was time now to bail out.

He telephoned the front desk. "This is eight oh two. Could you tell me who delivered the envelope that was just brought to my room?"

"No, sir. It was just dropped off at the valet station with your room number. Is there a problem, sir?"

"No," Bambridge said.

He tore up the photo and dossier, flushed them down the toilet, then got his jacket, took the elevator down to the lobby, and walked across the street into Central Park. He was going to ground, before even more shit came his way, and if it meant leaving Pamela behind, so be it. But first he had to cover his own ass.

McGarvey and Pete checked into the Grand Hyatt just before noon. The hotel was a few blocks from the UN, which was their starting point, but what Fomin had said about two Washington insiders already up here had bugged him on the plane all the way up.

They went downstairs to have lunch in the Lounge, overlooking Forty-Second Street, Pete still walking with a slight limp. When they were settled at a table and had ordered drinks, she cocked her head to one side. She did that when she wanted something.

"You hardly said a word since last night," she said. "What gives?"

"I want you to go back and stay with Otto and Lou."

"We've already covered that. I mean what else did Fomin tell you that you haven't shared with me?"

"Nothing that makes any sense."

"Come on, Kirk, this is me you're talking to. I'm not going back to DC, and I can't work in the dark up here. So what's it going to be?"

McGarvey had known better than to underestimate her, and yet he wanted to protect her—put her in the safest haven he could think of, which right now was with Otto and Louise.

Pete reached across the table and touched the back of his hand. "Maybe I'll say no. Get you off the hook."

McGarvey had to laugh a little, despite himself. "This is me you're talking to, remember?"

She nodded. "Okay, we've got that over with. Now, what did your Russian pal tell you?"

"He said that a couple of what he called 'highly placed Washington insiders' were up here, and probably looking into Kazov."

Pete got it almost immediately. McGarvey could see it in the sudden dawning on her face.

"Impossible," she said.

"Yeah," McGarvey said. He phoned Otto, who was in his office.

"You guys okay?"

"Everything is fine so far. But I need a couple of answers. It was something else that Fomin told me, that got me wondering."

"I'm listening," Otto said.

"Is Marty at his desk?"

"No. His secretary said that he was taking a few days off. When I called his house his wife said that he'd gone fishing, down around the Farm somewhere."

"Is he there?"

"If he is, he's off the grid."

"One more. I want you to check on Bill Rodak," McGarvey said. "Find out if he's taking a couple of days off."

"Okay, now I'm really listening. What bug did Fomin put in your ear?"

"He said that a couple of Washington insiders were up here doing the same thing we were. He apparently knew who they were but he wouldn't give me their names. Said it was a direction he wasn't going. Wished me luck."

"Stand by a mo," Otto said.

"Mark Rowe was working for Marty, and the son of a bitch tried to kill me," Pete said.

"And he and Rodak are pals."

"The deputy director of the CIA and the president's chief adviser on Russian affairs. Plus a missing nuke that Putin wants you to find. What the hell did we stumble onto in Paris?"

Otto was back a minute later. "His secretary says that he's on a fact-finding mission for the president."

"Where?" McGarvey asked.

"The UN. So what are these guys up to—assuming that Marty is up there too?"

"I don't know, but I'm going to find out."

"If it has something to do with the Russian nuclear weapon, I think that we could be in some serious shit. You better nail these bastards ASAP. And in the meantime do you want me to take this upstairs?"

"Not yet."

"Keep in touch, kemo sabe. Because I think it's a real possibility that more shit could be coming your way in the form of Karim Najjir and the woman he's working with. Though how the hell that all fits together is beyond me right now."

"Work on it."

"Yup," Otto said, and he was gone.

Bambridge sat on the low concrete wall across from the wading ponds in Heckscher State Park, watching the mothers watching their kids play in the water. It was a little cool today but no one seemed to mind. Nor did anyone notice him. He was anonymous here.

Using one of the throwaway phones he'd brought with him, he called Rodak's private line in the West Wing. It was answered on the second ring by Bill's aide, Steve Tavel.

"May I help you?"

"Let me talk to Bill, if he's not tied up."

"He's out of the office just now, Mr. Bambridge. Should be back in a couple of days. Anything I can help you with?"

"Nothing important, I just wanted a quick word. Is he reachable?"

"Yes, sir. He's in New York at the UN. You might try Ambassador Rigby's office. She'd know where he was."

All the air seemed to go out of the park.

"Would you like me to give her a call and pass the word for Mr. Rodak to call you?"

"No, it can wait until he gets back to town," Bambridge said. "What's he doing at the UN?"

"He said something about a fact-finding mission for the president."

SIXTY-FOUR

☐

Najjir and Miriam, traveling under the last of the several work names they'd brought with them, were in a cab from LaGuardia into Manhattan at 12:30—just twenty minutes after their British Airways flight from Riyadh had touched down and they had been passed through customs and immigration with no problems.

She'd been morose and mostly silent on the long flight, which was a blessing to Najjir, who thought that she was too noisy at the best of times. And most of what she talked about was drivel in any event. But she was damned good cover.

"So what's the drill?" she asked, keeping her voice low and conversational for the cabbie's benefit.

"Soon as we settle in and have a little lunch we're going to ask the good colonel to meet us at the UN. It's neutral ground."

"Where are we staying?"

"The Grand Hyatt. A man I used to know recommended the place, and it's just up Forty-Second Street from the UN."

Miriam gave him an amused look. "I didn't know that you had friends. What happened to him?"

"I'll tell you one of these days."

Colonel Vladimir Kazov was an anonymous mouse of a man whose cover job was as a minor secretary to Mikhail Borisov, who was a second deputy assistant to the Russian ambassador to the UN. Kazov's job was fact checker for the Russian mission. The American media was so loosely controlled that ten different versions of an important story were often reported in as many television, newspaper, and internet outlets.

His specific job over the past months was to separate the wheat from the chaff in stories concerning President Weaver, one of the most hated presidents in recent American history. The job was not an easy one, in a large part because Kazov was under nearly constant surveillance by the FBI.

But it was almost always an interesting game of cat and mouse, which he enjoyed.

It was already late for lunch and he was about ready to leave his office when his encrypted cell phone buzzed. The caller did not identify herself, because it was unnecessary.

"An interesting development may be coming your way from Washington, but if you play it right you may come out in a better position than you're in at the moment."

"I'm listening."

"Two men who you've been working with are already there in New York, wanting to talk to you about the contract they negotiated six months ago."

"Yes?"

"But the former director of the CIA and presumably his partner are also on their way to see you."

"How did the CIA get my name?"

"A mutual friend gave it to him last night when they met at the Lincoln Memorial."

Kazov nearly hung up, on the instinct of self-preservation alone, but he stayed his hand. "Why, exactly?"

"Because his primary goal—or at least one of them—is to find the two men from Washington. They want to unravel the attempt on the Eiffel Tower and try to learn what connection that event might have with your nuclear warhead."

"And the rest of the op? Do you think that they have a glimmering?"

"I don't get that impression," the caller said. "But listen very carefully to me now, Vladi. This game that you're playing with the Americans could backfire very badly. Our president is himself very concerned. Do you understand?"

"Perfectly," Kazov said, his voice calm, though he was seething with anger. Several millions of euros were at stake. A considerable fortune that would allow him to go to ground permanently.

"Can you take care of it?"

"Who is this former CIA director?"

"Kirk McGarvey."

Kazov was standing behind his desk, but he sat down, his stomach suddenly sour. "Who is his new partner?"

"The woman CIA interrogator. The same as the past couple of years."

"But I was told that she was shot to death in Istanbul."

"Apparently not. She was also there at the Lincoln Memorial."

"I got the impression that Mr. McGarvey was in Novorossiysk."

"He was, but Mr. Putin sent him home."

"Why? It makes no sense."

"Oddly enough, our president thinks that McGarvey could well be the key to reaching CKCHIMERA." The code name was the operational designator that had been developed when it became obvious to everyone—except Americans at home—that Weaver would win the presidency. It was Russia's most dangerous gamble in the past half century or more. Mr. Putin's presidency was at stake, as was his complete control of the military, and especially of the SVR.

"What am I to do?"

"Mr. Bambridge and Mr. Rodak have come to New York to kill you."

The news wasn't terribly surprising.

"But they're amateurs. So it should not be impossible for you to eliminate them instead. Perhaps staged to look as if they had a falling out and killed each other."

"No one will believe such a thing. My God, Bambridge is the CIA's deputy director."

"Yes, with the mission of protecting the United States from all enemies foreign and domestic. And of course Rodak has worked for us for the past twenty years. But his scheme to cause Weaver to lose the election and then force him into an impeachable situation because he could not handle a serious crisis—a nuclear crisis—with us is on the verge of failure. Rodak is a traitor, and Bambridge, in an effort to arrest him, was involved in a shootout in which both men died."

"No one will believe it."

"No one will be able to disprove it."

"What about McGarvey?" Kazov asked.

"I suspect that he'll lose interest when Bambridge and Rodak are eliminated."

"What about the nuclear warhead?"

"It never existed," Raya Kuzin said, and she hung up.

Najjir and Miriam had only one bag each, and they didn't bother with the services of a bellman. They were staying in New York only long enough to carry out their mission from the prince and then disappear, and he didn't want to leave a big impression on the hotel staff.

The clerk at the desk only checked his passport, under the name of Charles Sampson, which matched the Amex Gold Card. "Will you and Mrs. Sampson be needing the services of our concierge? Dinner reservations perhaps?"

"No," Najjir said.

"Yes, sir."

They were given a room on the twelfth floor, facing Forty-Second Street and, crossing the lobby to the bank of elevators, Miriam happened to glance over her shoulder just as one of the doors opened.

"Bleeding Christ," she said half under her breath, and she nudged Najjir into the elevator.

"What?"

"Don't fucking turn around," Miriam said, reaching over to push the button for eleven.

SIXTY-FIVE

McGarvey and Pete left their handguns in the hotel room safe and took a cab over to the Russian Mission to the UN on East Sixty-Seventh Street, a few blocks from the southeast corner of Central Park.

The well-kept twelve-story building was set back fifteen or twenty feet from the sidewalk, protected by an iron fence and guards in blue shirts just inside. It was directly across the street from the Park East Synagogue.

Pete pointed it out. "Odd," she said.

"Actually the Soviet Union was the first country—even before us—to recognize Israeli independence."

"That's even odder yet."

"Gave the Russians a place to get rid of their Jewish problem without killing them."

They presented their IDs at the gate. "We're here to speak with Deputy Mikhail Borisov," McGarvey said.

"Does he know that you are coming?" the security officer asked.

"No, but President Putin suggested that we come to discuss a matter of some importance."

The guard stiffened for an instant, but then called someone. A half minute later they were allowed through security and inside to the lobby area, where their driver's licenses were checked again by another security officer.

A young man in a business suit, white shirt, and tie stepped off the elevator and came across the lobby to them and held out his hand. "Mr. Director, Ms. Boylan, welcome to the delegation."

They shook hands.

"I'm Mr. Borisov's personal secretary. If you'll just follow me, he's most anxious to speak with you."

"And surprised we're here?" Pete said.

The secretary smiled. "Yes."

They followed the secretary to the elevator, which went up to the tenth floor, busy with the undertone hum of conversations from offices with open doors and clerks scurrying back and forth.

"We're busier than normal just now. The Security Council votes in two days."

"Ukraine just won't go away, will it?" Pete said.

The secretary ignored the comment and took them to an outer office near the end of the corridor. He knocked once on the door and then let them in. "I'll just leave you now."

A tall, heavyset man with thick black hair combed straight back got up from behind his desk, buttoned his suit coat, and nodded. "Mr. Director, Ms. Boylan, yours is an unexpected visit."

"Thank you for agreeing to see us without notice, especially today," McGarvey said.

"When you mentioned the president's name, you attracted our attention," Borisov said. He motioned for them to sit down.

When they were settled, his pleasant smiled faded. "Let's come directly to the point, shall we? As you said, we are busy at the moment."

"We'd like to have a word with Viktor Kaplin," McGarvey said.

"He's one of my assistants. May I know why you didn't telephone him directly, instead of coming to me first?"

"Kaplin is just his work name. In reality he is SVR Colonel Vladimir Kazov, who at this point is under investigation by the FBI."

Borisov shrugged. "You did not get this from Mr. Putin."

"No, but your president asked me to help unravel what is turning out to be a serious problem for all of us."

"Which is?"

"One of your nuclear warheads is apparently missing from a depot at Saratov, and it could be on its way here to the United States."

Borisov held himself very still for a longish moment, only his gaze switching from McGarvey to Pete and back.

"We suspect that Colonel Kazov might be able to help us find it."

"Preposterous."

"Maybe not," Pete said.

"If you have proof, turn it over to the FBI, let them arrest him."

"No proof yet," McGarvey said.

"You mean to put pressure on him to see how he reacts?" Borisov asked. "If he is actually a high-ranking officer in the SVR, do you think that he would make such a mistake. If you believe that, Mr. Director, you are a naive man."

"And are you aware that there is a serious problem between the SVR and the Kremlin?"

Borisov got to his feet. "Get out of here immediately or I will have security escort you out of the building. And I'll personally see to it that the FBI is informed that you are meddling in their investigation, if indeed such an investigation actually exists."

"Ask the colonel to come here," McGarvey said.

"I'm calling security," Borisov said, picking up the phone.

"I'm betting that a man in his position would know that we're here, and has already left."

"Not today," Borisov blurted. "He's needed."

"Call him."

Borisov hesitated, but then dialed a number. "Have Viktor come up, I'd like to have a word on the Fox News outlets."

He hung up and waited a moment before he sat down. "It'll prove nothing if he's gone."

"Everyone is needed here," Pete said.

"He's doing his job."

"Which job is that?" Pete asked.

The phone buzzed. Borisov let it ring a second time before he picked it up. "*Da.*"

Whoever had called was not telling Borisov what he wanted to hear.

"Who telephoned him?"

Borisov gave McGarvey a sharp look.

"Get him on his mobile and tell him to return immediately."

Borisov put the phone down. "You were correct. Mr. Kaplin left the building just minutes ago, after he received a telephone call."

"Who phoned him?" Pete asked, but McGarvey had a feeling he knew the answer.

"Your deputy director, Mr. Bambridge."

"We're staying at the Grand Hyatt. Have Mr. Kazov call me."

Bambridge and Kazov entered Central Park's East Green, off Fifth Avenue between East Sixty-Ninth and Seventy-Second. Only a few people were seated on blankets, having picnic lunches, the city noises of traffic and even sirens in the distance muted here.

"I'm going to ground, but I had to come here to tell you that trouble is definitely coming your way," Bambridge said.

"We've known the possibilities all along, Martin," Kazov said, seemingly unconcerned.

"This is in the form of Kirk McGarvey."

"I know this. He and his woman showed up at the delegation just minutes after you phoned."

Bambridge was stopped in his tracks. "Jesus Christ."

"No, he has nothing to do with it. But I think for both of our sakes that you get out of New York as quickly as possible."

Bambridge shook his head. None of this made any sense to him. Weaver was supposed to go down, but now it seemed as if everyone else except for the president was going to disappear. "McGarvey," he muttered.

"An inventive man. He actually met with Putin."

"There's more," Bambridge said, regaining a little of his composure. McGarvey was already his enemy, but whatever else happened, he didn't want Kazov on his trail as well.

"Yes?"

"I was sent here to assassinate you."

"On whose orders?"

"Bill's. But I got another kill order delivered to me at my hotel."

"Yes, I know, because I sent it to you," Kazov said. "There's no doubt he'll be coming up here to make sure that you do your job. And we're going to make it easy for him, because I'm going to disappear in twenty-four hours."

"To where?"

Kazov smiled. "Tell Bill that you killed me and disposed of my body."

"He'll want to know where."

"In the Hudson, and you'll show him."

"What now?"

"I'm going back to the delegation to take care of some unfinished business."

SIXTY-SIX

☐

Najjir and Miriam were in their hotel room, trying to figure out what was going on. But the fact that McGarvey and his woman were here was completely unexpected and nothing short of stunning.

"You're absolutely sure that it was them?" he asked.

"For the thousandth time, yes I'm bloody well sure. I damned near pissed myself."

"It's a long way across the lobby—"

"I can bloody well see, can't I? The broad was limping, but she wasn't holding on to his arm as they were coming down the stairs. Independent bitch."

"Question is, how'd he get out of Russia?" Najjir had to ask. He was deeply shaken.

"Question is, what the hell is he doing in New York, and at this fucking hotel? Can't be a coincidence."

"No."

"Your call, luv. But I say let's cut and run for the hills."

"I'm not going to walk away from the money the prince has offered."

"Won't do either of us any good if we're dead," Miriam said. "And if the prince actually pays us."

"He would become my next project if he didn't. And he damned well knows it."

Najjir stood at the window, looking down on Forty-Second Street, half expecting to see McGarvey and the woman getting out of a taxi. He could imagine them waiting in the lobby.

"What do we do now?" Miriam asked.

"Our jobs."

"Assassinate the deputy director of the fucking CIA, and the Russian spy he's been working with?"

"That's why we came here. You bought into it."

"I thought it was a bleedin' joke."

"No."

Miriam hesitated for a moment. "The question still stands: How?"

Najjir took out his cell phone, pulled up the number of the Russian UN delegation, and called it.

"You have reached the Russian Federation Delegation to the United Nations, how may I direct your call?"

"I wish to speak with Mr. Kaplin."

"Who shall I say is calling?"

"Giles Worley."

"One moment please."

"Are you nuts?" Miriam asked.

"He can't know why I'm here," Najjir said.

The operator came back. "I'm sorry, sir, but Mr. Kaplin has left the building. Is there a message?"

"Tell him that I'm in town and would like to have a drink. We're old friends."

"Shall I say where?"

"That'll be up to him. But he can reach me at this number."

"Yes, sir."

Najjir broke the connection. "Now we're going downstairs for a drink and a late lunch."

Najjir got them a seat in the Lounge, from where they could see a part of the lobby, including the elevators. They were both armed.

Their drinks came—a Heineken for her and pinot grigio for him—when his phone rang. The caller ID came up blank, but he knew who it was.

"Yes."

"Giles, I haven't heard from you in forever," Kazov said. "You're here in New York?"

"At the Grand Hyatt."

"Nice place. Would you like me to come over for a drink?"

"If you have the time. From what I've read, your people have a vote in the Security Council on Wednesday."

"I'll make the time. Say in the next twenty minutes?"

"Yes. And Prince Awadi sends his greetings."

"I see," Kazov said, after a slight hesitation. "I'll be bringing a friend."

"Who's that?"

"Marty Bambridge. The other man the prince sent you to assassinate. Should be interesting."

Kazov rang off, and Najjir pocketed his phone. "There has to be a leak somewhere," he said.

"What are you talking about?" Miriam asked. She was concerned.

"Vlad told me that he's bringing Bambridge with him."

"That can't be a coincidence either."

"He said Bambridge was the other man the prince sent us to assassinate. The advantage will be ours."

"What the hell are you talking about? We have to get the fuck out of here right now. Or do you actually think that McGarvey's being here was just another coincidence?"

"No. But we're going to eliminate that problem as well. I'm not going to have that bastard and his woman coming after me. All four of them are going to die tonight. And you're going to help."

"You're nuts."

After Kazov left, Bambridge took his time walking back to his hotel, trying to get it clear in his mind what the hell he was going to do next. Sitting in a booth in the bar, he took out his phone to call Pamela, when it rang. The number was Bill Rodak's.

"I met with him but what you wanted me to do was impossible," Bambridge said.

"Not to worry, Marty, I'm going to help out. Where are you staying?"

"The Mandarin Oriental," Bambridge said without thinking. "It's on Columbus Circle."

"I know where it is. I'll meet you there when I'm finished here. Say sometime after seven at the bar? There's been a new development that you need to know about."

"Yes, and I'll have something for you. Give me a call when you're on your way."

"Of course."

When Rodak was off, Bambridge telephoned his wife, who answered on the first ring, as if she was expecting his call.

"Is it time?" she asked.

"Nearly so, but something has come up that I have to take care of first."

"Can you tell me about it?"

"It's why I called," Bambridge said.

The room was mostly deserted at the moment, only a couple at the bar and four men in a booth well out of earshot. Nevertheless he lowered his voice.

"A file was delivered to me here at the hotel. It was an order to take out a second man. And you'll never guess who."

"Bill," Pamela said.

Bambridge was stunned. "How the hell do you know that?"

"Simple logic, darling. Your Russian knows why you're there, and he knows that Bill could be there for the same purpose. He wants you to take him out. There can't be any doubt that Bill was ordered to take you out, and by the same guy. A shoot-out at the OK Corral in which the both of you end up in the morgue. A falling-out of thieves."

"So what the hell am I supposed to do?"

"I'll tell you exactly what," Pamela said.

□

SIXTY-SEVEN

McGarvey and Pete took a cab back to the Grand Hyatt, but as they came up Forty-Second Street Mac sat forward and asked the driver to let them off next door, at the entrance to Grand Central Station.

"What gives?" Pete asked as they went inside.

"Just a feeling. We're not here under cover, and I left word for Kazov to call us. Could be that Najjir is here as well."

"It's a convention."

"Yeah, and right in the middle of a lot of innocent people."

They nodded at the policewoman at her stand just before the entrance to the busy main concourse. On instinct McGarvey glanced up at the Italian restaurant on the second level. He had been here not so long ago, when a man he'd been chasing dropped a baby in its carriage, which was wired with explosives, over the railing.

It'd been a very close call, but Mac had managed to break the baby's fall and disarm the several bricks of Semtex before they detonated in the midst of an extremely busy rush hour.

"He was up there, wasn't he?" Pete said, catching his thought.

McGarvey nodded. "Maybe Otto and Lou are right. Time to get out of the business."

"If that's what you want, I'm game," Pete said. "But I don't think retirement would suit you. Unless you play golf."

"I never learned."

McGarvey's phone buzzed. It was Otto.

"Can you talk?"

"Just a minute," McGarvey said, and he and Pete went over to a position near the stairs down to the marketplace. No one was in earshot. He put the phone on speaker mode, but lowered the volume. "Go ahead."

"Marty's using a throwaway phone that I haven't been able to trace, until just a little while ago. But he called his wife at home, and I've had their phones bugged forever. Anyway, there's a shitstorm of troubles coming your way."

"That's why we're here."

"Marty had a chat with Kazov, who said that Bill Rodak had orders to kill Marty. In the meantime Kazov ordered Marty to take Rodak down. The common cause was that Rodak was supposedly working for the Russians through Kazov. But Marty's wife told her hubby that Kazov's plan was for Marty and Rodak to duke it out and kill each other. She called it 'the gunfight at the OK Corral.'"

"Too much could go wrong with that scenario. No guarantees that they'd both die, unless Kazov or someone else was waiting in the wings to make sure it went down that way."

"His wife is almost certain that there never was a missing Russian nuke. That was just misdirection. The real intent was to discredit Weaver to a point where he would be impeached. From the start, Putin directed Bill to make a Russian connection stick, even before the election. But obviously it didn't work. So the missing nuke story was put there, and all of a sudden Weaver was supposed be sucked into ordering the assassination of at least Kazov, and Marty—our deputy director—was supposed to be the triggerman."

"Still way too much could go wrong," Pete said.

"Which is why I'm betting that your friends from Paris are back in the mix. Probably right there in New York to make sure all the pieces fit— everyone who's supposed to get killed actually dies. That's Rodak, Marty, and Kazov himself."

"Peachy."

"Plus you and Pete," Otto said. "You're not under cover, so it's almost a given that at least Kazov knows where you guys are."

"We know that for a fact," Mac said. "Because I left him a message at their delegation for him to call me."

"Makes you guys ground zero," Otto said. "But I have a feeling that's exactly what you wanted."

"Digging them out one by one would take forever, and it'd be even tougher to simplify the entire mess to the point that the media couldn't get it wrong."

"All to save Weaver?"

"Not the man, just the presidency," McGarvey said.

"What do you want me to do, kemo sabe?" Otto asked.

"I think the next move is going to be Marty's."

"His wife thinks that same thing. She told him to phone the general and tell him the truth, only upside down. Marty's unraveled the plan to discredit the president, and he thinks he can stop it by eliminating Rodak and Kazov."

"Gibson would pull Marty out of there immediately," Pete said. "Then he'd call Cohen and lay it all out." Sam Cohen was the FBI director.

"No proof. Anyway, if the Bureau has Kazov under surveillance, they already know that Marty met with the man in Central Park."

"Proof or not, our hotel is definitely ground zero," McGarvey said. "If Kazov is pulling the strings, he'll have everyone here, this afternoon, maybe this evening."

"The Bureau will be all over him."

"I'm sure that he'll have no problem ditching his minders."

"Whatever. It'll be messy," Otto warned.

"This kind of stuff always is. But I'll see if I can't throw some of them a little off balance."

The phone was silent for several long beats, until Louise came on.

"I've been following all of this," she said. "After this shit is done and gone, you two need to either retire or at least take a long vacation. Otto and I will stand up for you guys at your wedding, and Audie can be the flower girl."

McGarvey looked at Pete. "What wedding?" he asked, and she hit him.

. . .

They took the stairs up one level, above the main concourse, then outside across the avenue where cabs pulled up, and then crossed to the lobby entrance of the Grand Hyatt.

"Are you expecting someone to be here already, watching for us?" Pete asked.

"I hope so," McGarvey said.

"The point being?" she asked. She was nervous.

"I'd like to get them all here and then lead them out of the hotel. I don't want any collateral damage."

"We're not armed."

"If someone is there, they'll be in the lobby somewhere, or maybe up in the Lounge, where they'd have a good view."

"They'll be carrying."

"Most likely," McGarvey said. "I'll provide the diversion while you go up and get our pistols. But I don't think whoever shows up—especially if it's Marty—will have much stomach to start a gunfight. Not here."

"You'll bet our lives on it?"

"No, just mine."

"Goddamnit. I knew you'd say something like that."

Inside, they passed the area where the bellmen dropped the bags of guests checking in and those leaving. Out from under the overhang, Pete went left toward the elevators and McGarvey walked into the lobby, just to the left of the escalators from Forty-Second Street.

He scanned the couple of dozen or more people in the broad lobby, some of them seated, others coming or going, for a familiar face or faces. He knew all of the players from in-person contacts, except for Kazov. But Otto had sent him several photos of the Russian.

Pete got on one of the elevators and the doors closed.

SIXTY-EIGHT

□

Bambridge had gone back up to his room to try to think out what Pamela had told him to do. First he was to shoot Kazov to death right there in the lobby, the moment he showed up this evening. Then he was to call the FBI and get them over to the hotel. And finally he was to call the media to let them know that the deputy director of the CIA had personally bagged the bad guy behind a recent string of events.

"Even McGarvey will have to be impressed," Pamela had promised him.

"It'll take more than that."

"You're going to hand him Bill's head on a platter. The Paris thing, the nuclear weapon, the whole works. You've been chasing down this issue for several months, only supposedly going along with Bill so that you could find out what his real intentions were."

"And?"

"He's working for the Russians, and Kazov was his operational officer here in the States. The whole point was to bring Weaver down. But single-handedly you will have saved the presidency. And Weaver is big on returning favors. Might just fire Gibson and put you in charge."

"I don't know."

"Dream big, sweetheart. And if you pull this off, we won't have to go to ground."

"And if I don't?"

"The weather in the Caribbean is nice all year long."

Bambridge's cell phone rang. But the caller ID was blocked.

"You need to come over to the Grand Hyatt right now," Kazov said. He sounded pumped up.

"I thought we weren't meeting until tonight."

"Something's come up."

"What something?"

"An opportunity."

"I'm not going anywhere unless you start making fucking sense. I'm tired of this shit, Vlad, and I want out."

"Are you familiar with the name Karim Najjir?"

"He's the Saudi operator you hired for the Paris thing."

"And the guy who got the drop on McGarvey and handed him over to the SVR."

"Who turned him loose on Putin's orders. This whole goddamned thing is going south. And I'm going to ground right now."

"You have a job to finish. We both do."

"Fuck it, I'm no assassin."

"Well, I'm pretty sure that Awadi sent Najjir and the broad he's with here to kill us both. He's at the Hyatt, and together we ought to be able to take him down and come out of this as heroes."

"Goddamnit."

"Rich heroes. Going to ground takes a lot of money."

"Who the hell is Awadi?"

"The Saudi prince I used to come up with Najjir, and who, by the way, has offered to buy our nuclear weapon from me."

Bambridge was silent for several beats. His instinct was to put down the phone and disappear right now. He had no qualms about leaving Pamela behind. But Kazov was right. Going to ground in style did take a lot of money.

"What do you want me to do?"

"Meet me at the viaduct entrance across from the train station as soon as you can get there."

"Armed?"

"Of course," Kazov said. "And call Bill, tell him to meet us there."

"Jesus."

"It all ends this afternoon, Martin. And you'll be able to call your own shots: You either come up rich, or as today's hero, or both. And you won't have to shoot anyone, unless it's to defend yourself."

Bambridge telephoned Rodak, who answered on the second ring. It sounded as if he were standing on busy street corner somewhere.

"What do you want, Marty?" Rodak asked.

"Vladimir wants to meet us at the Grand Hyatt. The entrance on the viaduct across from Grand Central."

"What the hell are you talking about? The son of a bitch wants you to kill me, and now we're all supposed to meet somewhere? Kiss and make up?"

"Prince Awadi has sent the guy and his woman, who did the Paris thing for us, here to kill us both. He's evidently trying to cover his tracks. He's also offered to buy the missing bomb."

"There is no bomb."

"But apparently there's money on the table."

"So what does he want us to do?" Rodak demanded.

"I'm not sure, but Vlad and I will be armed, and I assume you will be too. The three of us should be able to take him down."

"And hand him over to the FBI."

"You'd be the hero."

"And you'd be the man who saved Weaver's ass."

"What about Vladimir?"

"I'm sure that, between us, we could get him sent back to Moscow instead of to jail," Bambridge said. "We might just come out of this whole shit case in one piece."

"And there's always tomorrow," Rodak said. "I'll be there."

Bambridge checked his pistol and holstered it under his left arm, then put on his jacket. Before he left the room he phoned Pamela and told her everything that had just happened.

"This could go bad for any number of reasons," she said.

"Better than going to ground and having to look over our shoulders for the rest of our lives."

"First you have to bag this Saudi assassin and his woman."

"Three against one."

"Three against two. By all accounts she's an accomplished killer too. So just don't get into this without putting your male pig attitude on a back burner."

"I'll let you know soon as."

"Good luck, sweetheart."

SIXTY-NINE

□

McGarvey had taken a seat in the expansive lobby, which at this time in the afternoon was not terribly busy, so that if it came to a gunfight—which he didn't think was going to happen here—the risk to innocent bystanders would be minimal.

From where he sat he could not see Najjir or Miriam, but he had a direct sight line to the stairs. No matter what, though, he didn't think that Najjir would try to run. The man had come to finish the job he and the woman had started in Paris.

Mac's phone buzzed. It was Otto.

"Bambridge just got off the phone with his wife. He and Kazov are on their way to you."

"What about Rodak?"

"They're not together, but he's coming too, and you're the target. What do you want to do?"

"I don't want to spark a hostage situation, so we'll keep the NYPD out of it for the time being. We get SWAT teams guys charging in, Najjir will not going down willingly."

"What about the Bureau?"

"Call the Bureau's New York SAC and find out if someone is on Kazov, but I think they probably lost him, or at least he'll ditch them before he comes over here."

"They'll want to know why we're interested."

"Tell them that you might have something in the next fifteen minutes or so."

Otto was silent for a long moment. "This could go south in a New York minute, you do know that."

"I don't think anyone is going to start a shooting war in the lobby. They're going to want to make a deal or deals to save their own skins."

"Everyone has their own agenda, and I think taking you and Pete out of the picture is on the top of everyone's list."

"Except for Marty. He wants to come out of this a hero."

"Which makes him a loose cannon—the most dangerous one in the bunch."

"And my ally," McGarvey said.

Najjir and Miriam appeared at the head of the stairs and paused.

"Showtime," McGarvey said. "Call the SAC now."

"Will do, and I'm going to give the NYPD the heads-up, no matter what you say. They can cordon off the hotel. No sirens."

"Not until everyone shows up."

"Leave your phone on."

"This ends here and now," McGarvey said. He pocketed his phone but did not shut it off.

Pete got off the elevator, came down the two stairs to the lobby floor, walked over to McGarvey, and sat down beside him on the couch, placing her open shoulder bag between them. She looked up.

"Everyone is heading this way," McGarvey said. "Marty, Bill Rodak, and Kazov."

"Is Otto on top of it? We might need some backup."

"He's giving the Bureau the heads-up, and as soon as the others get here he'll have NYPD closing down every way out of the hotel."

"We could defuse the situation by getting up and walking out the door."

"No," McGarvey said, and Najjir spotted him.

"Is this about me?" Pete asked.

"I nearly lost you," McGarvey said, and he left it at that.

"Let's grab a cab and get the fuck out of here," Miriam said, as she and Najjir started down. "It's the safe play."

"It ends here," Najjir said, his eyes never leaving McGarvey's.

"Goddamnit, he'll have backup."

"Not him."

"I'm not playing into this shit. I'm walking away from this right now."

"Understand that if I come out of this alive, you'll be my next target."

Miriam shook her head in disbelief. "You macho motherfucker, if we both come out of this in one piece, you'll be my next target."

"Then we understand each other."

"Perfectly."

No one in the lobby was looking at them as Najjir and Miriam came across. McGarvey took his Walther out of Pete's purse and, keeping his finger on the trigger, lowered the pistol out of sight beside his right leg.

"May we join you?" Najjir asked.

"Of course," McGarvey said. "But if either of you reaches for a weapon I will shoot you."

"We're here to talk, not to fight," Najjir said, and he and Miriam sat down across the low coffee table strewn with sections of *USA Today*.

Pete reached into her purse, but left her hand there. "I told you that we'd be back."

Najjir shrugged nonchalantly. "The business in Paris and Istanbul was just that. Unfortunate timing all around but, given the circumstances, we had no other option."

"Nor do we have a lot of options," Pete said directly to Miriam. "Either kill both of you here and now, before this shit gets out of hand, or call the FBI and have them take care of you. And I think you can guess my first choice."

"Nobody's going to start a war this afternoon. We're here to work out a compromise."

Bambridge got out of the cab at the viaduct entrance to the Grand Hyatt. As soon as he'd paid the driver and the cab left, Rodak came out of the hotel and they shook hands.

"Is Vlad here yet?" Bambridge asked. He was jumpy.

"I haven't seen him, but we have another, bigger problem, and I think we ought to make a one eighty and get the hell out of here."

"What's that?"

At that moment another cab pulled up and Kazov got out. When he'd paid the driver he came over. "The Three Musketeers, together at last."

"Bill thinks that we should walk away from the entire situation," Bambridge said. "And I'm just about ready to agree with him."

"You're both armed, I assume, as I am. And we're facing one man and his woman. Both of them criminals. I think the French would give us medals if we took them out. So let's get it over with and go our separate ways."

"It's more complicated than that," Rodak said.

"No one here in New York or, especially, in Washington will be happy about you guys participating in a shoot-out in a hotel lobby. But your president will come out on top, as he usually does."

"You'd have to return to Moscow, and there would be questions," Bambridge said.

"Nothing I can't handle."

"Goddamnit, neither of you is listening," Rodak said.

"What?" Bambridge demanded.

"I took a look. Najjir and his broad are down in the lobby seated across from McGarvey and Boylan. And it looks as if they're having a quiet little chat."

"Christ," Bambridge said softly.

"Then we end it here and now," Kazov said. "McGarvey and his woman were unfortunately killed in a gunfight. The important thing is the terrorists were taken down as well. God bless America. *Vive la France.*"

"You're talking about McGarvey, for Christ's sake."

"We take them from behind," Kazov said. "In it all or lose it all."

SEVENTY

□

"For the sake of argument, let's say that what you did to my fiancée and me was just part of an operation that went bad," McGarvey said. "We happened to be in wrong place at the wrong time."

"A bit more complicated than that, but for the sake of argument, continue," Najjir said.

"What do we do about the innocent people on the ground near the Eiffel Tower who lost their lives because of you?"

"Or the people you killed in Paris and Istanbul?"

McGarvey shrugged, his grip tightening on the pistol at his side. "They were in the wrong place at the wrong time."

"Yes."

"You said that you wanted a compromise. What are you proposing?"

"That we walk away from here, of course," Najjir said. "My lady and I will disappear, and you and your lady will return to Washington the heroes for having saved the day."

"What about the plot to bring down President Weaver?"

"I know nothing about it," Najjir said. "My brief was to attack the Eiffel Tower, which would ultimately end up in the French cooperating with you to bring down a group of Russian cyber attackers operating in Paris, who were aiming at damaging or even bringing down the power grid and therefore most of the internet in the U.S."

"How about the nuclear weapon missing from Russian depot outside Moscow?"

Najjir shook his head. "As I've already said, our operational orders were very specific. Bring down the tower and get out."

"But you had backup teams and fallbacks. You must have expected trouble."

"Of course. Doesn't every operation come with risks of failure? You of all people should understand this."

"You arrogant prick," Pete said, and she started to bring her pistol out of her purse, but McGarvey reached over and stayed her hand.

"We're not getting into a gun battle here in public. So if we do let Mr. Najjir run—maybe back to his bosses in Saudi Arabia, or should I say, to Prince Awadi—we can always find him."

Two women in designer jeans, one with a light silk blouse, the other wearing a blue blazer, packages in hand, came up the escalator, to the left, and started across the lobby.

"At one time I was a paid field officer for the GIP, but I went freelance, as you say, some years ago. And I think that I have heard of the prince, though he's only a minor cousin. One of a thousand. So even if he is involved, I seriously doubt if he would have the money to pull off an op as complicated as the Paris one."

"Who do you work for?"

"That, I can't say," Najjir said, spreading his hands. "But you can understand that one has to be careful with his sources, especially the ones with the money."

"There's the rub then," McGarvey said. "The Paris deal was a failure. We saw to that. So your need for money to recoup your losses had to have been greater than your common sense. So you delivered me to the Russians. To someone most likely working in or for the SVR. The mistake, of course, was that the SVR and the Kremlin are at odds with each other just now. So Putin sent me home to help him solve a problem of a missing Russian nuclear weapon."

"As I have said, I know nothing about such a weapon."

"Perhaps not, but I think the people who do would be very interested in you."

"Good heavens, why?"

"Because you gave me to the Russians. They'll want to know why, and they probably won't believe anything that you tell them."

Najjir smiled. "Then we've reached another impasse."

"Not at all. Because talking to me you've become a magnet. A counterpoise, actually, for another counterpoise—for the missing nuclear weapon that doesn't exist, for the chance to take down President Weaver, and for taking me out of the picture."

"I'm not following you," Najjir said, but he was clearly rattled.

"I'm sure that you're familiar with the names Vladimir Kazov, Bill Rodak, and Marty Bambridge."

"Bleedin' hell," Miriam shouted.

McGarvey looked in the direction she was staring in time to see the three men passing the reception desk and heading directly toward the lobby.

Najjir jumped up just as the two women with the packages, coming from the dining room, walked past, and he drew his pistol with one hand and clamped his free arm around the neck of the woman in the blazer. The other one dropped her bags and scrambled away.

McGarvey jumped up, pointing his pistol directly at Najjir's head as the Saudi dragged the struggling woman a few feet back, then stopped. "Otto, we have a situation. Pull the pin."

"I'm on it," Otto's voice came from the cell phone in Mac's jacket pocket.

"But with velvet gloves. We have a hostage situation here, Marty and the other two are heading our way."

Pete was pointing her pistol at Miriam, who was sitting back, her hands in plain sight.

"You're either going to die here in the next few seconds or you're going to come with me," McGarvey said.

"You shoot and the woman dies."

"Do you think Kazov gives a shit about one hostage?"

"Of course not, but they're here to take you down. And if they can do that I'll suddenly be worth something. I'm holding the winning hand."

Marty, Rodak, and the Russian were less than fifty feet away. Everyone else in the lobby, realizing that something was going on, had either scattered or dropped to the deck. People in every big city in the world had become attuned to developing terrorist situations. Five men and one woman all holding pistols was not a good sign.

Without a word McGarvey walked directly toward Najjir and the woman, who was so frightened she couldn't scream.

"We can deal," Najjir said.

The woman, almost as if it had been rehearsed, moved her head sharply to right, just out of line with the muzzle of the pistol at her temple, and Mac fired one shot, hitting Najjir in the middle of the forehead.

The Saudi's pistol discharged, the bullet ricocheting off the tiled floor, and he collapsed, dragging the now hysterical woman with him.

McGarvey turned as Kazov began shooting, his first rounds going wide. Marty had stopped, the pistol in his hand lowered, but Rodak began firing, one of his shots just grazing Mac's left arm, above the shoulder.

Pete had turned and begun firing at the three men, momentarily drawing their attention, as McGarvey sprinted to the left, away from her, at the same time directing his fire at Rodak, who went down.

An instant later one of Pete's rounds hit Kazov in the side, staggering him back, and McGarvey switched aim to the Russian and began firing at the same time as Pete.

The man was hit at least three times and he dropped to the floor beside Rodak.

SWAT team police rushed in from the viaduct entrance as well as up the escalators from Forty-Second Street.

Marty laid his pistol on the floor and raised his hands high above his head. "I'm Martin Bambridge, deputy director of the CIA," he shouted at the top of his lungs.

Miriam had taken out her pistol and was pointing it toward Pete. "Bitch," she swore

Mac caught the action out of the side of his eye and turned on his heel. "Incoming."

On instinct Pete ducked left as Miriam fired, the round going wide.

Mac fired two shots, one catching Miriam in the shoulder, the other in the side of her head, and she went down.

"Put your weapons down, now!" one of the cops shouted.

McGarvey and Pete both made a show of placing the guns on the floor and raising their hands.

"All clear?" Otto asked.

"All clear. But Marty's come out of it," McGarvey said.

Otto laughed. "Not for long, kemo sabe, not for long."

SEVENTY-ONE

McGarvey, Pete, and a belligerent Marty Bambridge were driven by the FBI to the Teterboro Airport private jet terminal across the river. On General Gibson's orders Otto had sent a CIA Gulfstream VIP jet up to fetch them, and once the confusion at the Hyatt had been brought under control by the FBI, working with NYPD, McGarvey and Pete were released into the custody of Bambridge, to be returned to Langley.

Their weapons had been taken from them, but not their cell phones or any other personal belongings, nor had they been placed in restraints, though a pair of special agents had been sent along as escorts.

The jet was warming up on the tarmac outside one of the hangars when they arrived and got out of the car.

"Quite an afternoon, sir," one of the FBI agents said to Bambridge.

"Yes, and thanks for your help," Marty said. "Couldn't have done it without you."

The other agent turned to McGarvey. "Hope this all gets straightened out, Mr. Director," he said.

McGarvey nodded.

Bambridge broke in. "It sure the hell will, and I promise that heads will definitely roll," he said, but his words held no real conviction.

Their Bureau minders left, and they boarded the aircraft, where the pilot and copilot were already at the controls.

"Good afternoon," the steward, a young man from the Company's housekeeping division, greeted them warmly. "Your hotel rooms were cleared out and your bags just now arrived. I put them in back, not in the hold, in case there was anything you needed."

"No weapons?" Bambridge demanded.

"No, sir," the steward said, and he led them back to their seats. "We have immediate permission to take off as soon as you're settled."

"I have something to get out of my bag first," Bambridge said, and he went aft to where the few pieces of luggage had been jammed on the floor between a pair of facing seats.

"Drinks?" the steward asked. "A cognac, Mr. Director?"

"Champagne," Pete said. "For two."

"Yes, ma'am," the steward said, and he went to the galley.

"Well?" Pete said when he was gone. "You haven't said a word in last hour."

"Because I've been trying to work it out."

"It's over. The principals have been bagged and Marty's feet will be put to the fire as soon as we get back. What's left?"

"This is something between Putin and Weaver that's been brewing since before the election, and as crazy as it sounds, Marty's the only one left with the keys to the kingdom."

"Are you talking about some kind of a deal between Putin and Weaver?" Pete asked, shocked.

"I don't know, except that it seems important to the Russians to bring down the president. Even to the point that there's an ongoing rift between the SVR and the Kremlin."

"The reason being?"

McGarvey had been thinking of nothing but, since Putin had secured his release from Novorossiysk. "I don't know, but it was something Putin said to me in his office before he sent me back. He said that he and I were kindred spirits in many respects."

"With a translator?"

"No, just us."

"Could you have mistaken his English?"

"I don't think so. And he said that he and I had a close connection some years ago. Said that we were adversaries."

"Do you have any idea what he was talking about?" Pete asked.

"Not a clue. But Marty knows something that might help."

"Mac," Otto's voice came from the cell phone, still in speaker mode.

McGarvey took it out of his pocket. "We're about to get airborne."

"Don't," Otto practically shouted. "He made another call to his wife just a minute ago. Told her that everything had fallen apart. The center would no longer hold. She told him that it was too bad, but he knew what had to be done and he had the means to do it at his disposal."

McGarvey jumped up and turned around, almost knocking into the steward coming back with their wine. Marty was seated in the rear, his back to them.

"I think the crazy bastard is going to try to hijack the plane and bring it down," Otto shouted.

The steward heard that, and he dropped the wine and raced to the cockpit to alert the flight crew.

Mac went to Marty, but the deputy director wasn't moving. He was slumped slightly to the right side, his eyes half open, a little foam at the corners of his lips. He was not breathing.

Pete was at this side. "Christ, the son of a bitch committed suicide."

The captain came back. "What the hell is going on?" he said, but then he stopped when he understood the situation.

"Now we'll never know," Pete said.

"Don't be so sure," McGarvey said, and he looked up at her. "My past has always had a way of catching up with me."

"How do you want to handle this, Mr. Director?" the pilot asked.

"Take us home. I'll strap him in."

AUTHOR'S NOTE

I always like hearing from my readers, even from the occasional disgruntled soul who wants to pick a bone with me, or point out a mistake I've made.

You may contact me, McGarvey, Pete, and Otto, by sending a message to kirkcolloughmcgarvey@gmail.com. Please understand that because I'm extremely busy, quite often I won't be able to get back to you as soon as I'd like. But I will make every effort to answer your queries.

For a complete list of my books and reviews please visit Barnes & Noble, Amazon, or any other fine bookseller.

If you would like me to do a book signing at your favorite store, something I have absolutely no control over, or if you would like me to attend an event as a guest speaker or panelist, please contact:

Tor/Forge Publicity
175 Fifth Avenue
New York, N.Y. 10010
Email: torpublicity@tor.com

If you wish to discuss contracts, movie or reprint rights, or e-business concerning my writing, contact my literary agent:

Susan Gleason Literary Agency
Email: sgleasonliteraryagent@gmail.com